Readers love
AMY LANE

I0525104

Candy Man

"Oh God…. I friggin LOVE Amy Lane!!! This book broke my heart wide open, and then filled it with kittens, puppies, candy, and most importantly love! It was so perfect!!!!"

—Love Bytes

"…this book was nothing short of amazing… if you haven't read it yet, go do it RIGHT NOW."

—MM Good Book Reviews

"Thank you, Amy, for keeping your promise. *Candy Man* is sweet, without being syrupy, and the gentleness of Adam and Finn's love story was heartwarming."

—Rainbow Book Reviews

Beneath the Stain

"Amy Lane at her best…"

—Prism Book Alliance

"…be prepared to fall in love in this book. Be prepared get crushed a little. It's Amy Lane. You know it's coming."

—It's About the Book

Shiny!

"Once again, Amy Lane has written a wonderful, humorous, romantic story, which both tugged at my heart and made me laugh."

—Live Your Life, Buy the Book

By AMY LANE

Behind the Curtain
Beneath the Stain
Bewitched by Bella's Brother
Bolt-hole
Candy Man
Christmas with Danny Fit
Clear Water
Do-over
Food for Thought
Gambling Men: The Novel
Going Up!
Grand Adventures (Dreamspinner Anthology)
Hammer & Air
If I Must
Immortal
It's Not Shakespeare
Left on St. Truth-be-Well
The Locker Room
Mourning Heaven
Phonebook
Puppy, Car, and Snow
Racing for the Sun
Raising the Stakes
Shiny!
Sidecar
A Solid Core of Alpha
Super Sock Man
Tales of the Curious Cookbook
Three Fates (Multiple Author Anthology)
Truth in the Dark
Turkey in the Snow
Under the Rushes
Wishing on a Blue Star (Dreamspinner Anthology)

GREEN'S HILL
Guarding the Vampire's Ghost • I love you, asshole! • Litha's Constant Whim

Published by DREAMSPINNER PRESS
http://www.dreamspinnerpress.com

IMMORTAL

AMY LANE

Published by
DREAMSPINNER PRESS

5032 Capital Circle SW, Suite 2, PMB# 279, Tallahassee, FL 32305-7886 USA
http://www.dreamspinnerpress.com/

This is a work of fiction. Names, characters, places, and incidents either are the product of author imagination or are used fictitiously, and any resemblance to actual persons, living or dead, business establishments, events, or locales is entirely coincidental.

Immortal
© 2015 Amy Lane.

Cover Art
© 2015 Anne Cain.
annecain.art@gmail.com
Cover content is for illustrative purposes only and any person depicted on the cover is a model.

All rights reserved. This book is licensed to the original purchaser only. Duplication or distribution via any means is illegal and a violation of international copyright law, subject to criminal prosecution and upon conviction, fines, and/or imprisonment. Any eBook format cannot be legally loaned or given to others. No part of this book may be reproduced or transmitted in any form or by any means, electronic or mechanical, including photocopying, recording, or by any information storage and retrieval system, without the written permission of the Publisher, except where permitted by law. To request permission and all other inquiries, contact Dreamspinner Press, 5032 Capital Circle SW, Suite 2, PMB# 279, Tallahassee, FL 32305-7886, USA, or http://www.dreamspinnerpress.com/.

ISBN: 978-1-63216-920-4
Digital ISBN: 978-1-63216-921-1
Library of Congress Control Number: 2014921689
First Edition May 2015
Printed in the United States of America
∞
This paper meets the requirements of
ANSI/NISO Z39.48-1992 (Permanence of Paper).

To my husband, Mate; and my kids, Chicken, Big T, Zoomboy, and Squish; and to my workwife, Mary. Because I am seized by the madness far too often and you are the people who suffer the most—and the people who love me for my madness at the same time.

AUTHOR'S NOTE

This is set in a fairy-tale kingdom a long, long time ago. This is also set in our backyards, yesterday. Fantasy is always a little more cutting than our real life. Let it be so.

BLADES IN THE NIGHT

THE WORLD is so much bigger now. I see the things that spawned my destruction.

Once upon a time there were a prince, the third son o' a young and powerful king. He spent his years being spoiled—and deprived. Spoiled by anything that met his whim, and deprived o' a greater purpose. When he were old enough, he took his portion o' his father's kingdom in guardsmen and set out to find a kingdom o' his own. He found a village—a nameless village—and named it, and announced himself king.

The people were not impressed.

They asked him to move on, and he refused. So the farmers and tradesmen banded together and met his troops on a barren wheat field in late fall.

Very few o' them lived to the next day.

The prince took over and brought in his father's tradesmen to attach a tower to the plain village wall. Unlike the stone wall, the tower were built o' polished granite, and it rose high above the little town itself. A little courtyard were built behind the tower, and the prince established his kingdom. He had no thought for the great forest just a length away from the village, but the villagers and surrounding farmers did. That forest were their monarch, and he could not bother to see.

Mostly, he left us alone.

But sometimes he rode out and remembered he were our monarch.

For the first ten years o' my life, I cared not. My life had other concerns.

When I were but ten, my stepfather sold me to the smith with my mother's blessing. My stepfather were a filthy bugger—and I were getting old for his taste then, old enough to threaten to cry bloody murder if he visited my pallet again while my mother worked or slept.

That were when he would threaten me, make me touch *it*, taste it, hold it in my mouth.

He'd threatened to stuff it up my bunghole the week before he sold me, and I laughed at him. It were too big, I said, thinking he were joking and trying to frighten me into doing all the other things.

But his sneer—always ugly—now twisted his face to the likeness of the copper demons on the Prince's castle, and I cringed away from him on my little pallet of rushes.

"Yer a noisy fuckin' li'l puke," he snarled. "Silence is yer name, silence ye should be!"

My mother were gone, doing laundry for the fine folk in the castle, and she took my little brother, Aubrey, with her. It were just me and Kump, and Kump liked it that way.

"Ye wanna hear how noisy I get? Ye try shovin' that thing up me arse!" I hollered, and he smacked me across the face and into the wall. My head rang and my nose throbbed, but didn't none of that compare to the pain that followed next.

I don't remember much o' it—screaming into the stuffed wool pillow, mostly, thinking my body would split in two.

When he were done he collapsed on top of me and licked the blood from my cheek.

"Don't worry none," he growled. "We'll sell ya off to the smithy. Ye think *my* cock hurts, he's been reamin' his apprentice fer years!"

I'd seen the smith's apprentice, Diarmuid, who were older than me, but not all grown—not old enow to be heard in council yet. Sandy brown hair, blackened by the soot and pulled from a rectangular face grown ruddy from the heat of the forge. I had an impression o' almond-shaped eyes, a full mouth, wide shoulders, stoic silences, and a way of taking his time with the little'uns. He spoke to the crowd o' children at the village in a way that were both kind and slow.

Any man who'd do to Diarmuid what this piece o' shite had just done to me were a misery indeed.

My mother returned that day, shoulders bowed, eyes searching out anything but the bruises on my face and the blood on my pillow.

Her one word, as her gaze glanced off me like a sword from stone, were, "If you did what he asked, Teyth, he wouldna be so free with his hand."

I glared at her, a core of me bleeding, and not just what were in my breeches.

And then I turned away.

My name means silence. It's what I became.

But two nights later, my stepfather returned to my pallet while my mother snored next to him, pacified by the wine, and Aubrey huddled in the corner next to me, doing what he always did—pretending to be asleep.

The filthy fucker reached for my hand in the dark so I could touch him, and his own great hock of ham closed around the knife I'd lashed to my wrist, blade out. He swore, tripped backwards and fell on his arse, leaving a big bloody handprint on the dirt floor.

My mother leapt up in her nightshirt, coming to fawn over him, bind his hand, and warn him to be careful when going outside at night to take a piss.

The whole time, Kump glared at me impotently. Yeah, I knew retribution were coming, but I didn't give a ripe royal shite.

Still, when Kump told me gleefully, showing his rotten teeth, that I truly *were* to be sold, I quailed.

The smith would use me the same way? That were what he threatened, weren't it?

I made plans then, to ply my blade and escape—but Kump saw through that. Swear, that man could sniff out fear like a coyote sniffs out a corpse to feed on.

"Ye do it, rat, and I'll shift me attentions to yer brother." He leered at Aubrey, who sat at our mother's feet as she mended rich people's clothes. Aubrey played quietly with sticks, pretending they were horses, and every so often made a comment or cast a smile up at Mum. She'd smile down distractedly and pat him on the head, tousling his dark hair.

He were a gentle, placid boy, not brooding or close like me.

I looked back at Kump with flat eyes. "Everybody dies," I said, quiet. "Dogs. Horses. Men. Just depends when, and how awful. Remember *that* when ye look a' me brother. Remember tha' everybody dies."

Kump glanced away from me furtively, under his eyebrows, like maybe the specter of death loomed over his shoulder threatening him with a scythe even as he stood there. He touched his face with his bandaged hand, and I smiled a little, but it were not a child's expression—I knew that even then.

"I'll remember it," he muttered. "I'll remember it every minute I look at *you!*"

I maintained my look—flat, level, friendly as a sword blade—until he scuttled off like the vermin he were. I kept my inner black quakings to myself.

He were right. I would die. My da had died in the brief, bright battle that forged our village. We'd been but a dirt spot along a river, or so the heralds proclaimed, but then the prince had come along and made us a *town*.

And for our gratitude we were supposed to give him tribute—sheep, cattle, daughters.

Sons.

My da, so my mother said, went to battle with the other men of the village, and they all lost their lives in defense of what we called our spot of earth.

So she said.

But I don't remember her washing other people's clothes when I were small, and I don't remember her sewing late into the night. Perhaps it were because my da were gone, but if that's so, what in the name of the seven sweet hells were Kump for?

But Kump or no Kump, the fact remained that Da had gone off one misty morning before the winter and had never come back, leaving Mum to bear Aubrey all on her own. The fact remained that it would be just as easy for me to disappear.

Kump had threatened me with that, in the black o' the night, the first time he'd shown me his thing.

I found my fear o' the real dark, the dark of the misty morning, the dark o' where you didn't return—that were the real enemy. Kump could be survived. Mum's dealings with the people who worked for the white prince—that could be endured.

But the darkness of the misty morning… it were plain. The thing that terrified Kump could terrify me, as sure as breathing.

MUM CRIED, the morning Kump grabbed me by the wrist and dragged me from the cottage. I weren't allowed no keepsakes, which were fine—I had none. Before Kump I'd had a small poppet to clutch, but I'd given that to Aubrey. I'd had a wee wooden horse too, but Kump'd thrown that in the fire the first time it got in his way.

Mum knit me jumpers for the winter, but I didn't get one of those either, although it were autumn, and my arms and legs were blue as we journeyed from our small cottage at the edge of the river. The village were upstream, which meant our water weren't as pure as the other direction. I remember this weren't much problem before the great castle were built, but now, part o' me chores were to venture up and around the great wall of the town, to where the water were still pristine.

As Kump dragged me away from the cottage that were my only home, Mum held Aubrey and comforted his tears. I had one last moment to kiss his mop o' dark hair, and then I were trotting to keep up.

I didn't mind being spiteful then. "Ye'll have to fetch the water from now on, Kump—ye might even work *yer* arse off for once."

His muttered oaths—surprised and dismayed—were worth the bruise I sported as he half-dragged, half-threw me through the wooden gate in the man-high stone wall and then through the muddy streets.

The village itself bustled with people, activity, shouts from neighbors, bigger shouts from merchants. Aye, the streets were muddy, but the waste and such were carried away by pipes and not open—at least not until the river. It weren't a bad place, not really. Kump hauled me past the bakers' with their morning rolls displayed. I looked yearningly after those, since Kump'd grabbed me before my porridge. The girl at the booth looked after me sympathetically, but she eyed Kump with distrust, and I understood. Yeah, sure, she'd feel bad for a scrawny kid, but she didn't want to feed the barrel-bellied, black-toothed whore's cock hauling me behind him.

I made note of her, though. She could be an ally, maybe, if the smith were as bad as I feared.

We neared the smith's, one of the few brick stalls along the marketplace. The smoke from a chimney, pumping from the great blast furnace, were hard to miss, but there were more. The back of the stall extended and spread. I recognized that the storefront were only part of the building. There were living quarters—in fact, a snug little brick house—behind that brooding exterior, and for some reason that reassured me.

Not a cottage, not a dank alleyway corner between the wooden buildings and canvas slats o' the rest of the town, but a house. Almost a grand one, seeing that the stall were nearly as big as Mum's cottage.

I liked this, coveting it on sight. It had room for a small boy to hide, and room for him to be alone.

Not that there would be much time to do either, I wagered, given that the smith and his boy were both working already this morning, sweat pouring down their faces, backs, and bare arms as they took turns heating metal at the blast furnace and pounding it into shape on each their own separate anvils.

Both o' them wore leather aprons that left their backs bare but covered their chests to the throat and part o' their shoulders as well. The aprons themselves were scarred and scorched, and the men themselves bore various burn scars—but both o' them, laboring away in the early morn before the sun began to heat the land, had looks of fierce joy o'er their faces. For a moment I forgot my fear and my sadness at leaving Mum and Aubrey, and I stared at the two o' them, doing this thing they loved.

How could they love it so?

Then the younger one lifted the thing he were laboring over up in the air with his tongs, and I saw it were a sword hilt, but one crafted… oh, ever so beautifully. It were not pure steel, I reckoned, but steel gilt with gold, and the strength and delicacy of the filigree tore at my heart. Oh! But to make something like *that,* something o' beauty, something that would last and not rot in the ground like me da—or me, if Kump ever had his way.

I yearned to hold hammer and tongs then. I could do it. I could *make* that thing o' beauty.

"Who's this, now?" the smith asked, turning toward me with a broad grin across his black-and-gray bearded, burn-marked face. His bare pate shone under his sweat and the wakening sun, and there were a gap between his teeth. His thick lips were pink under that great scorched thatch of hair on his chin, and his chest and stomach were as wide as three men.

He were bloody terrifying.

I heard a woman's sound from me own throat and were horrified to find I'd gripped Kump's hand—*Kump's*—like a beggar, and I were nearly in tears.

The smith flinched back, and his next expression were dark as the seven thunders and barbed like lightning.

Thank the gods he aimed that thunder fury at Kump.

"Yer 'ere to give him as an apprentice?" he growled, and Kump took a step back, jerking on my arm as he did so.

"Aye," he stuttered, staring down at the boots on his feet. There were holes in them, and the blackened nail of his big toe kept making an appearance like a diseased worm. "Ye told me ye'd pay—ten silvers, ye said."

"I told ye I'd pay *the boy,* ye filthy bugger!" the smith roared.

Kump glared at him. "Well, I had me hand at the raisin', didn't I? I were the one who labored to get the boy food, I were the one who put up with his puling and his little brother's puking, and I were the one who kept a roof over his head—don't I get some recompense?"

Mum did all that!

I wanted to scream it, but Mum said I did not hardly cry as an infant. Hence my name.

The smith shook his head and cast a look at the boy, Diarmuid. I knew Diarmuid's name 'cause I'd seen him before on my few trips to town hanging at the edge of my mother's skirts, and something about his long face, like a rectangle with a chin, settled me a bit. I'd never heard *this* one yell.

Diarmuid nodded in some sort of agreement.

"Boy?" he said, and his voice weren't a rough growl yet. Perhaps he didn't speak over the clatter of the forge the way the big man did.

I managed to look at him without dropping me water, and he nodded like we'd had a real conversation.

"We'll treat ya right," he said soberly. "Ye hungry?"

I remembered the baker's daughter and nodded, my vision suddenly dark with it. "Aye."

"C'mon, then. I'll get ye summat."

He set the sword in an oaken barrel of water, and it hissed as it quenched. Then he hung the tongs from a great board on the side of the stall that held hooks, hammers, tongs, and other implements of a dozen different sizes before taking off his massive, triple-thick leather gloves.

Those he set down in a wooden crate, where he retrieved a loose green tunic. He swapped out the apron for the tunic, which clung damply to his sweaty skin, and turned to gather me with a look. "Follow me. Cairsten'll make sure ye get the coin coming to ye."

I turned to Kump, who seemed to be having some sort o' battle with the smith, but it were all in their glares. With a growl and a jerk, I yanked my hand from his grasp and turned to trot after Diarmuid.

He walked a path through the back of the stall toward the dark, bricked-in cave beyond. For a moment I heard the blood roaring in my ears from the prodigious dark, but I also heard Diarmuid's grunt ahead o' me and were comforted. The corridor shrank to an oaken door, and this Diarmuid opened into a room, brightly lit on the other side by windows—true windows, with panes o' glass and all.

I looked around the room, delighted. The floor were sanded wooden boards, and there were thick furs rolled up above each window as though to drop when the weather turned, to seal the hearth and the kitchen with the big raw wood table in a comforting cocoon. There were a cold box in one corner, with a drain that I assumed went out to a garden in the back, and a wood stove in another corner that weren't lit as of yet. A pot o' something hung over the embers of the fire at the hearth in the middle of one wall, and Diarmuid grabbed a wooden bowl from one of the cabinets over the stove and dished some up for me.

He pulled honey from another cupboard and a plate o' butter from the cold box, dressed up what were in the bowl, and set it down in front o' me at the battered square table while I sat on one of the chairs and stretched my toes to touch the ground.

I stared at the bowl with wide eyes and then back up at him. His face were coated with soot, and his hair escaped its queue in stiff quills, but he smiled slightly and the hellish visage melted into an ordinary boy of about fifteen or sixteen.

Suddenly the porridge didn't seem like a magic trap, a poisoned potion ready to render me senseless. I don't even remember the conscious choice to take a bite, but it filled my mouth, grainy and warm, sweet and butterfat, and I closed my eyes and shivered. I swallowed reluctantly, and only because another bite waited for me.

I opened my eyes again and saw that Diarmuid's thoughtful gaze hadn't left my face.

"Wha'?" I asked through another mouthful of porridge.

"No breakfast?" he asked.

I shook my head no. "No time. 'E couldna wait to be rid o' me, tha' one." I shoved another bite in my mouth and licked the bit o' sweet that gathered at the corner.

"We'll feed ye every day," Diarmuid said honestly. "We'll work ye, yeah-yeah, no lie, but we'll feed ye. Cairsten'll make ye learn yer letters, an' we take turns readin' in the evenings. Don't worry none—is not as hard as it seems. We willna...." He swallowed grimly. "We willna strike ye, willna touch ye—we'll just work ye. Cairsten'll take an apprentice if I ask him—but ye need to wish it."

I took a bite o' porridge, and then another, and closed my eyes with each morsel. Ah, gods.

"Could I eat this every morning?" I asked, thinking on the gruel Mum cooked every other day.

Diarmuid frowned. "No," he said, sounding surprised. "Sometimes we have eggs."

I shuddered, the ecstasy of eggs for breakfast apparently being the price o' my soul.

"Aye, then," I agreed, and then stopped in the middle o' my next mouthful. "But Aubrey...."

"Aubrey?"

"Me little brother." Gods, but I would miss him.

Diarmuid grimaced. "Does tha' one beat on him?" he asked, and until that moment, I hadn't thought about my swollen nose, or the bruises I must have had under my eyes, or my split cheek.

"Only me," I said. "'E ignores Aubrey, mostly." I swallowed the last bite in my bowl, when suddenly, instead of sunshiny butterfat and sugar, it sat like the steel they'd been forging outside. "Do ye think he'll start on Aubrey now?" I looked around sadly, thinking that, for a bright, shining moment, I'd almost had this place as me own home.

"I dinna know," Diarmuid said, his voice coarsening. He must have come from the outlying villages beyond the trees. I'd heard those people as they traveled the marketplace, and they spoke like that. "But I know nothing good will come o' sending ye back with him."

"But... me little brother!" Suddenly the bright wood and sturdy brick seemed like that trap I'd feared, the one sprung on me with porridge and the promise of eggs.

"We'll check on him for ye," Diarmuid promised fervently. "If tha' one starts in on him, we'll do summat. Cairsten, 'e dinna stand for no beating, not on children, ye ken?"

He sounded upset—his accent were thicker and his words tilted so hard into song I almost couldn't fathom him. But he were promising me a safe place to sleep, good food, and that I didn't need to forsake the one person I'd known whom I would miss.

"Aye, I ken. Is a promise, then?" I asked.

Diarmuid nodded, spat in his palm, and held it out to me. I spat too and took it, and we shook.

"Stay 'ere," he commanded, his voice losing its thickness now that I weren't threatening to leave. "I'll go deal with tha' one. Ye got no need to see him again."

Well, I *did* see him again more than once coming through the village, Mum following a few steps behind, dragging Aubrey by the hand, but Diarmuid kept that promise. "Tha' one" was all he and Cairsten the smith ever called him, and he never touched me again.

I stayed put in my chair as Diarmuid left, having no crystal ball nor deck o' cards into the future. Instead I had boredom, and the exhaustion o' not sleeping fast in me own bed for far too long a time. Diarmuid opened the great oaken door to the roaring of the forge, and when it shut behind him, the quiet o' the house soothed me to do a thing I would not have thought of back in Mum's wee cottage.

I laid my head on the table, looking around me. That quickly, with a full belly, I fell asleep.

I do not know how long I stayed, but I awakened to voices and the thumps of boots on the floorboards.

"'Ere 'e is," boomed the smith, Cairsten. "Paid all tha' money for the scamp, and he's sleeping on our kitchen table!"

I dragged myself awake by the eyelids, as it were, and tried a sleepy scowl in the direction o' that great, booming voice.

"Sorry," I mumbled. "Were I to start?"

"Not much to start, lad," Cairsten said kindly, throwing his barrel-built, muscular body into a wooden chair that *looked* like it were built o' four-by-fours and halves o' trees, but that creaked with the fierce weight o' *his* body. "We were closing down for the day. Any jobs that come in can be waiting for the early morning and don't need doing now."

"Do ye always work so early, then?" I asked hesitantly, because it seemed a strange way to do business.

"It grows too hot in the forge in the summertime," Diarmuid supplied. He rooted through the cabinets as he spoke, assembling, I figured, the contents o' our evening meal. "We get used to the early hours so we can run the forge before the full heat o' day. But in the winter, when the sun comes later, we get up later, and the forge keeps us warm after last night's embers die."

I smiled a little, liking the simplicity of it. "Aye," I acknowledged. I remembering finger-aching cold and being rousted from me bed to fetch water, and this seemed a better way.

"Yer not asking about today, then?" Cairsten asked, a slight smile under his dark hair.

"Yer gonna show me my chores," I said knowledgeably. Funny how I thought I knew so much when in fact I knew nothing, not even the shape o' the darkness.

Cairsten laughed, a great booming noise that shook the paned windows in their frames. "Nay, boy—not on yer first day. We'll tame ye all right, but first we gots to bathe ye."

I wrinkled my nose at him. "A *bath*? But there's no holy day tomorrow!"

Diarmuid grunted. "I told ye," he said, disgusted, and Cairsten shook his head in response.

"Tha' ye did, but I were thinking good on the—"

"Don't," Diarmuid snapped. "Don't ever ye think good on him." Diarmuid cast me a veiled glance. "Not tha' one. He dinna deserve nobbut!"

"Aye, aye," Cairsten acknowledged, holding his hand up to forestall what looked like a flash of Diarmuid's temper. "I hear ye." He turned his attention back to me. "We'll start with a bath, boy, and move on to putting sheets on yer bed, showing ye letters, finding ye clothes. I think Diarmuid's old things might fit ye fine, and we'll need a good suit o' yer own. Did ye not have that at yer cottage?"

I shook my head and looked at the brown-and-gray stained jerkin and breeches I were wearing. "Is all I have," I said, embarrassed.

"Well, now ye have more," Diarmuid said with decision. "Bath first."

They worked as a team, as they did out at the forge. The smith went and fetched the tub while Diarmuid pumped water, first into a pot to boil, and then into bucket after bucket that he dumped into the tub. There were steam rising from the surface before they had me strip naked and step into the tub itself.

Cairsten picked up my clothes using a pair of forge tongs. "I'll just… just see to these," he said grimly, and I watched him go, feeling dismal and half-drowned and sorry for myself.

"Me knife," I said, thinking of the blade in my pocket. It weren't really a knife, but it had kept me safe from Kump that one night, and all the kindness in the world couldn't set my mind at ease regarding the bald, barrel-chested, black-bearded smith.

"Ye need a knife?" Diarmuid asked, pressing a piece o' lye soap and cloth in my hands.

"I…. It were handy," I said, trying for dignity. "What's this for?"

"Rub the soap on the cloth, and rub the cloth…." Diarmuid grimaced. "*Every*where."

I gazed at him blankly. "Everywhere?"

"In yer hair 'til it's soaked, then under yer arms, between yer legs, behind yer knees, on yer manhood—*everywhere.*"

The water were already making me flush, or I might've flushed all on my own. "Are ye watching to make sure I do?"

Diarmuid grimaced. "I'll turn me back if ye wash the crease o' yer arse and everything in there."

"Why?" I asked boldly, but I were already doing it. His back were broad and stoic. He didn't seem interested in touching me, and, well, he'd fed me. Small boys are animal, feral—feed them, give them safety, they'll curl at yer feet and never sniff another soul. I were no exception.

"Ye smell," he said frankly. "We have to live with ye. Would be good not to smell ye, day in, day out."

"Excuse me—"

"And ye get sores if ye dinna wash!" He must have felt uncomfortable, because his voice were thickening with that forest accent again.

I looked at my arms and realized he were right. I already had them from the stiff edges of the coarse, chafing fabric.

"They sting in the water," I told him, as though this had just occurred to me. Well, maybe it had.

He turned and caught my eyes. "Next bath, after living in clean clothes, they willna sting so much. The next one, they'll be near to gone."

"How do ye know?" I asked. Aye, I were but a child—but it were occurring to me, looking at me thin limbs, me shins covered in sores from me ragged trousers, that I weren't much good to these two great, brawny men who could make good porridge and hammer metal and bend it to their will. How could I earn my keep here, where I might have eggs for breakfast one day?

"I were the same when Cairsten found me, only covered in blood to boot. He were taking a fixed wagon to a thatcher's cottage in the woods. He found me there. I were nobbut four or five."

"How'd ye get there?" I asked, intrigued in spite o' myself.

"I dinna know," Diarmuid said, shivering. "I knew me name, and I kept pointing deeper into the forest. Cairsten said… well, he said he felt summat wrong that direction. He took me with him, cared for me. Were father to me. 'E's a good man, Teyth. Ye'll see."

I scrubbed myself, careful o' me sores, and thought on it. "I willna be no trouble," I said after a moment. "I don't need no raising. I can make porridge fine, haul water, herd chickens and pigs, sweep hearth…." I looked around me uncertainly. There were no chickens or pigs as far as I could see, and Diarmuid had made a better porridge than ever I could. "I…." I bit my lip. Now that some of the grime had been stripped away, I could smell the *lack* of the smell I'd worn on my skin. "I… would rather not go back," I said baldly, thinking sadly on Mum. I were an evil boy—Kump had always said so. Mum had begun to agree with him at the end there. And now I'd just gone and proved them both right by turning my back on them.

"Well, we'll find things for ye ter do," Diarmuid said, and again I were reassured. It were wise o' him, I thought later. He didn't say I could stay right off, although that were what he and Cairsten probably planned the minute they looked at me. He said they'd find things for me to do. Right there, he'd known about me, about the heart o' me. He'd known I'd want to make a place, want to grasp a thing that were mine between my fingers and never let go.

When I were clean, he brought out some clothes. They were patched some, and had been worn, but were also soft and clean, and finer than anything I'd had before. I put on the cream-colored jerkin and the fawn-colored pants and petted them almost sorrowfully.

"Pretty," I grunted. "How long'll they be clean?"

"About three days—then we'll wash them and ye'll wear another set. We pay a woman ter wash our dirties."

"Like me mum," I said knowledgeably.

"Aye, but we pay more than the prince," Diarmuid said, as though that were a matter o' course.

I gazed at him, mouth open, and then he showed me to my room.

Well, it were more *our* room, but it had two beds in it, one on either side, with a great space between. He talked as he walked me down the long hallway, shadowed now in the late afternoon, and spoke o' having guests sometimes who needed to stay while Cairsten worked on their wagon wheels or harvest implements. They usually took the spare bed, as long as they behaved themselves, and if they didn't, he kicked them out on the street.

"What'll they do now?" I asked, thinking that a bed—a *whole bed*—were far too grand for me.

"They come with bedrolls," Diarmuid said with a shrug. "Probably sleep in the front room."

There'd been a space between the kitchen and the hall with a couch, chairs, and another hearth, as well as oil lamps suspended from sturdy brass stands.

"A bed," I repeated, feeling lost. "Tha's...." I could not think of the word. Generous? Special? Appreciated? *Coveted*? All of the above. But Silence I were named and silence I would continue to be.

Diarmuid pulled out several old sets of clothes from a chest o' drawers that sat at the end of the room under another great window with furs bunched above it. "Here," he said, undismayed at being put out o' his place. "This drawer on the bottom is yers. Mine are on the top. Ye have two nightshirts now, so remember to change at night, yeah?"

I nodded, unfamiliar with this custom as well. Abruptly I were grateful for Diarmuid, for his story o' being a naked, bloody child wandering the woods. It made the four o' us in our squalid hut somehow less horrible, less poor.

I wanted to tell him it hadn't used to be that way. Kump had sold Mum's bed the same way he'd sold me—for food, for grain liquor, for something, anything but to till the land my father had died to keep. My own wee bed, he'd chopped up for kindling. The ropes suspended on the bottom had stunk o' creosote as they'd burned.

"I'm clean now," I said, feeling small. "Clothed. What now?"

"Now we should make dinner, yeah?"

"Aye."

He took me to the kitchen and pulled some salt pork from the cold box. He cut up a big quarter o' it and, using the big-bladed knife that looked honed to split a hair, cubed that before throwing it into a pot o' water. He hung the pot on the hearth above the embers, taking a boiling pot o' water off the trivet to make room. When he were done, he pulled out fresh squash, fresh corn, and potatoes. He chopped them all up and threw them in with the rendering pork, and added a red vegetable I'd never seen, with some spices I'd never imagined would go into food.

The pot o' boiling water he dumped into the tub, which still sat large in the kitchen. While the stew cooked, he added another tub o' cooler water, and then looked at me as though trying to figure a puzzle.

"Go sit on the couch, Teyth," he said after a moment. "Here." He disappeared back into the room and came back with what I knew to be a book only because the preacher used to read from one when we went to the church on holy days.

For a moment I felt betrayed. A holy book? An endless list of rules I must not violate or I'd be spending all the days after I were dead in a boiling pit o' fire?

Then I looked at it more closely and realized it were different—flatter, taller, wider. The leather cover were embossed with pictures—livestock, cottages, castles—and I fingered each picture with curiosity. How had these been made? I would learn later of tooling, of taking the picture and embossing a shape in the softness of something, then heating it to make it harder. I would learn of painting and dyeing, not because it were something I would do, but because from that day, from the day o' seeing Diarmuid's work with the sword, o' touching a book made to be seen, I felt a hunger for the fruit o' the artisan, the thing, the bare thing, made for beauty.

It would addict me one day, gnaw at the heart o' me, but this day it merely caught my fancy as I touched the forms o' sheep, chickens, a farmhouse, a plow, all etched into the cover o' the book.

I opened the book and saw pictures, with symbols below. I ran my newly cleaned fingers along the edges, making the natural connection between word and picture, and the idea entranced me. I pored over the book, oblivious to what Diarmuid were doing while I looked, and it weren't until I heard him grunt to push his way out of the tub that I realized he'd been there, naked and washing, while I lost myself in the book.

I startled, frightened. Kump had... well. Yes.

Diarmuid kept his back to me, though, and he'd laid out his clothes and a bathing sheet on the counter. He weren't naked for long. When he'd pulled up his breeches and pulled the tunic over his head, I promptly lost interest. He were clothed. There were no danger there when he were clothed. He glanced at me as he straightened himself, and although I saw the movement, I didn't return the look. I were squinting at the book in the encroaching darkness, and I didn't want to lose any light.

That first night—I would remember it.

Diarmuid didn't call me to help set the table until the stew were done, and when I looked up from that book, I saw that the oil lamps had been lit. Cairsten's hair and beard were dripping water, and his clothes were fresh too—he'd come in and bathed, and I'd never looked up. Diarmuid used a hose to siphon the water from the tub into the garden behind the cottage, and when that were done, he and Cairsten moved the great wooden tub—which were big enough for a grown man—back into the garden as well.

I'd put a bowl and silverware at each place, and, at Diarmuid's urging, a mat under each bowl. There were wooden cups as well, and to my delight, milk from the cold box.

Two bowls o' food in one day, and this delicious feeling o' being clean, with no grime, and no fear, stuck to my back.

I simply ate, silent, listening to Diarmuid and Cairsten talk shop.

"The new steel—" Diarmuid began.

"Substandard," Cairsten replied on a swig o' milk.

"Thought so. No give."

"Needs an alloy."

"What ye think?"

"Tungsten?"

"Expensive."

"For this commission, we need it."

"Aye—but I dinna like the master."

"Me neither, but I do like to eat."

"Where do we draw the line?"

"The one who won't pay," Cairsten said, and they both laughed.

I watched them talk as they ate. Sometime while I'd been reading, Diarmuid had changed the stew for some pot bread on the fire, and the whole cottage smelled o' it now. They'd intersperse their terse words with hearty bites o' stew or bread and gesture with their spoons. It were animated and cozy, a language I did not yet speak, but I wished to.

I finished me stew as their conversation continued, and sat quietly. Cairsten looked at me carefully as he spoke and tipped his head at Diarmuid.

"Eh?"

"Middlin'," Diarmuid replied. "Wary o' us."

"Don't blame him. He said anything?"

Diarmuid winked at me. "Ask him?"

Cairsten regarded me patiently from those almost merry blue eyes. "Diarmuid been treating ye right, little man?"

"He took me knife," I said, surprised when that were the first thing out of my mouth. I hadn't *felt* ungrateful, but I sounded it. I flushed. "But he let me look at the book. I liked the book."

Cairsten met eyes with his apprentice, and he nodded.

"If we get yer blade back, boy, where will ye keep it?"

"Under me pillow," I replied promptly. This would be good. Cairsten would know, so if he *were* evil like Kump, he'd have warning.

Again that speaking look. "Aye, then. I'll get yer knife. Maybe after some time here ye'll keep it in yer drawer or on yer belt. Aye?"

I eyeballed him distrustfully. "If ye think so," I said, because "No!" sounded abrupt.

He grimaced. Cairsten were a wise man, I would learn. There were no right answer in that moment, so he had no answer. Usually, this were when wise men failed.

After dinner he sat me down and had me tell him what I'd learned while looking at the book. I told him what word I thought were for cat, and which for horse, and he had me pick them out o' another book.

Diarmuid cleaned up from dinner, but occasionally he'd help me out with a mime or a mouthed word, and I smiled shyly at him. He were funny when he weren't asked to speak.

At one point in the quizzing, I found my attention drawn to the fire on the hearth and the warm, sleepy glow in my gut. Cairsten shook my shoulder gently. I leapt, surprised, half-asleep, smacking him in the face with my hand as I flailed. He grunted and held up his hands, but although he were shocked by the smack in the face, he seemed unsurprised by the wild flailing.

"Easy, Teyth—it's bedtime, is all. Ye need to go lay down."

"Oh," I murmured, vaguely stunned. Suddenly I were flooded with shame. They'd been nothing but kind. Even if they asked the same price as Kump, they'd more than given their share, and I'd paid them back with a smack to the face. "I'm sorry," I whispered. Awkwardly, like Mum soothed Aubrey, I patted his cheek. "I didn't mean...."

"No worries, boy. Go sleep, eh?"

"Don't forget to change into yer night shift," Diarmuid said mildly. He knelt in front of me and pressed the knife into my hand. "And be careful with this, Teyth. I dinna like it under yer pillow."

"It keeps me safe," I said shortly. I remembered Aubrey hugging Mum, hanging from her when he were tired. I would have done that to Diarmuid, but I didn't need to. I could walk perfectly fine.

The hallway were dark and long, and away from the fire the little house became cooler, bordering on cold in the chill winter. The edge of the knife were cool to the touch as I carefully set it under me pillow.

Then, using the faint light from the living room, I did as Diarmuid said and changed into a night shift before snuggling under blankets of soft wool and sheets that were finer than the coarse serge on top of my pallet o' straw.

I were tired in spite o' my nap, and confused. But comfort is hard to resist, and I didn't as the feather-ticked mattress sucked me down into the dark.

The comfort did nothing to allay the shaft o' ice in my bowels when I felt a hand on me arm in what seemed to be the darker than dark. I didn't cry out, but my fingers found the haft of the knife under my pillow and I lashed out with it in panic.

Diarmuid's startled moan brought me full to waking.

"Sorry, Teyth!" he muttered, holding his hand over his forearm. "It were time to get up. I dinna mean ter fettle ye none!"

I gasped, and focused, and realized the black welling and dripping under his fingers were blood.

Like an anvil to the head, all of the kindnesses of the day before flooded back, and I felt tears start for the first time since me da disappeared in the dawn.

"Cairsten!" I hollered. "Cairsten! Come quick! I killed Diarmuid! I'm sorry—I'm sorry—I doona mean ter, but e's bleedin' and e's dyin' and I killed 'im and—"

The thunder of the man's feet rumbled the floorboards as he came flying from his own room down to ours. In two steps he hefted the furs from the windows—I didn't know they'd been let down—and the room were flooded with the pregray light o' almost dawn.

"I'm *fine!*" Diarmuid insisted, holding his hand over the wound, and Cairsten—who wore a nightshirt that near to covered the hairy tops o' his toes over his breeches, which he were probably in the middle o' pulling up—scowled at him.

"Go get the bandages, D'—no mucking about with a knife wound, eh?"

"'E dinna mean ter," Diarmuid said, almost desperately. "Cairsten, ye canna—"

Even in the half-light, I could see Cairsten's grimace. "I ken, Diarmuid—now go bandage yerself."

I were crumpled on the bed by now, wiping my face on my nightshirt, staring in horror at the blood on the blade. I'd painfully sharpened it on our hearthstones when Kump weren't in the cottage—and look what it got me.

Cairsten's weight next to me didn't frighten me now. Anything he wanted to do to me, I'd earned.

"Can I see, boy?" he asked gently.

I handed him my weapon without looking.

"Is good work," he pronounced after a moment. "Ye sharpen this yerself?"

"Aye." I didn't know why he were asking me these questions, but he were.

"I'm thinking ye've had cause to use this?"

I glanced at him and figured that when he turned me out, this would neither help nor hurt my case. "Aye."

"That'un, the one who sold ye here—did ye use it on him? He had a bandage I saw around his hand."

I shrugged. The wound had been dirty and infected. I had that to thank, more than Kump's dirty conscience, for being left alone this last week. "Aye."

"Were...."

I glanced at him, because he didn't seem the type to hesitate—even I knew that.

He swallowed and tried again. "Were ye in bed then as well?"

I looked toward the window, where the sky were lightening by degrees. The back window faced the garden here, too, and a fruit tree with gold and scarlet leaves overarched the corner of the window. Pretty, it were. I'd never see it green, now.

"Aye," I told him, my eyes on that stark silhouette.

"No one will do tha' here," Cairsten said. "Can we put the knife under the mattress instead? Between the ropes?"

I glanced at him, and the gush o' tears surprised even me. "Will I be staying?" I asked, begging with my heart if not my tongue. I could see that tree turn green. I could sleep in clean clothes and learn to read that book and eat honey in my porridge and learn to make beautiful things—it were as though I'd just learned words, so many o' them stopped up in my throat.

"Aye," he said softly.

I started to cry in earnest then, and his great, brawny arm wrapped around my shoulders. "I'm sorry I hurt Diarmuid," I whispered. "I'm so sorry. He's been nothing but kind." I sobbed harder, and he just stayed, rock steady, an arm to shore me up until I were done.

"Ye ready ter work today?" he asked when my body had stopped shaking.

I hiccupped. "Aye," I said, willing something, anything but the sudden adult knowledge of the thing you could not take back.

"Good. Let me put the knife under the mattress, and I'll leave ye to dress."

That were their habit for the next bit o' time. They left me alone to dress. And as Diarmuid had the night before, they cloaked their own nudity from me. They knew. What Kump had done, what I had done to Kump, they knew.

And they took me in anyway.

There are debts you cannot repay, and debts you can repay in the worst of ways. And debts you incur just by living.

The scale has yet to be forged that would measure what I owe.

THE IRON FROM WHICH
WE'RE FORGED

THE THING about being born is that you wake up and the world is strange, and you cling to the familiar—your mum's face, the sight of the sky, the taste o' milk. And as you grow, you take in a few new things every day, and they become familiar too. By the time you have words, your world has the things you know, and they are so natural that when you are asked to speak o' them, you cannot. These things are not spoken, they simply are.

The poor have to fight for their living. The rich have it given.

The castle were the beginning and ending, and our rights were simply not.

To have money or a prick gave you power. To have neither left you bereft.

These are things that every child knows. Aye, the rich might deny, justify, tell us that being rich is a virtue and poor a vice, but Mum were working the land all on her own before the prince taxed her twice for being a woman. There'd been no reason to turn to the likes o' Kump if the world had not made her weakness its trophy.

And had I not been "sold" into slavery to the men who set me free, I might've been locked into that world, that same sky, that same taste, because I had no words for the familiar but "it simply is."

But I *were* sold, and my familiar changed as well.

I do not remember much o' that first day. Diarmuid greeted us at breakfast with a bandage around his forearm and a determined smile on his face.

He'd made eggs.

I were sunk in misery, but I ate every last bite. Not often, but sometimes we know what things are worth even in our ignorance.

After that, it were a blur o' fetching water, fetching implements, learning what things went where. Cairsten, who were patient as an angel when I'd skewered his journeyman, suddenly became a roaring, barking demon, and the only thing that kept me from tears were the hope that the angel would be back in the evening.

Diarmuid apparently knew that fear.

"Where's the water, boy?" Cairsten demanded. "Dammit, we need the fuckin' water or the barrel'll catch fire—it's not a fuckin' whim!"

I were working hard, but my legs weren't long, and the pump in the kitchen weren't easy either. I had to stretch on my toes to reach it, and it were harder to prime than all that.

"Sorry," I gasped, sloshing water on me breeches. "Oi! But I'm sorry, Cairsten, so sorry—"

"Easy," Diarmuid said, as placid as always. "Here, let me." He took the bucket from my numb fingers and dumped the water in the big oaken barrel where they quenched the heated metal. A gush o' steam erupted, and I jumped back, frightened because it were scalding hot. Neither Diarmuid nor Cairsten jumped much, but then, they were used to such heat. The smithy itself were an oven, and my much coveted eggs had near to been vomited out right after breakfast when I'd tended the bellows an hour.

Now, Diarmuid looked at Cairsten and said, "We're done here. I'll bring another bucket and make lunch."

Cairsten, for his part, blinked like a man coming from a dream. "Lunchtime? Is it lunch?"

"Aye. And if we dinna want Teyth to run away after lunch, I think he needs a rest."

"Of course he needs a rest," Cairsten rumbled. He looked at the swords set on the wall and nodded. "We worked a fair bit today, boys. Teyth, much o' tha' speed were yers to claim. Well done. Aye, D. Get tha' bucket. Teyth's good for the day."

I gaped at him, stunned at the praise, at the thanks, at the pleasant master as opposed to the barking demon. Diarmuid smiled wearily and ruffled my hair. I were so tired I didn't even flinch.

"'E's like this," he said, hefting the bucket for me and walking down the close, hot corridor that separated the infernal smith's forge from the cottage and the snug kitchen. "In a job, when he's taken by his work. He yells, he curses, he demands—but when he's done, he's all tha's kindness. Much o' it is for safety, ye ken? The barrel catching flame, the bellows going too fast or too slow—these things'll kill a boy who's not wary, yeah-yeah?"

I nodded, understanding some now. "Aye."

"Is hard work," he said, opening the door. "Dinna ye worry, though, Teyth. Yer doing fine." He winced when his wound hit the door, and my heart quailed.

"I can carry the bucket," I mumbled.

"Is naught," he said firmly. "I'll fill the bucket again if ye can cut bread and cheese for lunch, yeah-yeah?"

I would have to take it. Forgiveness had been offered for neither silver nor gold. I'd be a fool not to buy it with my gratitude.

"Aye."

Diarmuid and Cairsten went back to work after lunch, leaving me to clean up. They told me to look at the picture book while they worked in the afternoon, and to be prepared for Cairsten's thorough discussion after dinner.

There were no bath before dinner this night, but Diarmuid took a cloth to himself and his bare body then rinsed the cloth out, swished it in the pot of warm water, and gave it to me. It were not the sweetness of the bath, no, but it were still a relief after the sweat and grime of the day.

Also, it seemed to make the food more pleasant as we prepared it, and that, to me, were a wonder. (That pleasure got even better when they taught me to clean my teeth.)

This night were different too in that I helped Diarmuid clean up afterwards, and when he went to sit down he took out his own book—something smaller, with smaller words—and sat down to read while Cairsten quizzed me.

"What's tha'?" I asked, and Diarmuid's smile were shy and secretive.

"A gift," he said softly. "The bookseller's boy—he's about my age. 'E loaned me the book so he might have someone to speak with about it, an' I liked it so much…." He waved the book sheepishly, and Cairsten looked over from his place on the end of the couch.

"He's a sweet boy, D," he said, sounding hesitant. "His folks… they've got their hearts set on a girl from Gladstone, across the river. Ye know tha', right?"

Diarmuid looked down at his book. "Is a gift," he said. Blood were still seeping through the new bandage on his arm, but his voice never sounded hurt until now.

"Aye," Cairsten conceded, and the word had an odd ring to it, a painful tone. He grimaced at Diarmuid like he wanted to say something but couldn't. "Ye savor gifts," he said at last, and then turned back to me and my book.

That night I slept sound, tired from work, happy from food, comforted by clean sheets. The next morning, Diarmuid's voice woke me, and we started the day all over again. And what were strange became familiar, and what were familiar became so much a part o' my world that I had no words.

FALL PROGRESSED to winter. One day during my second sevenday, Diarmuid let me sleep in. After I awoke, stunned by the sun coming in through the uncovered window, I joined him and Cairsten in the kitchen for breakfast and discovered the tub there as well. I were the last to bathe, being the last to waken, but when I were dressed in a new set o' clothes made special for *me,* they'd taken me to the marketplace on the other side o' Cairsten's garden.

I'd merely *thought* I knew the marketplace, given what Kump'd dragged me through. This day they took me around the muddy street with the blacksmith's house to a whole new wonder. Our street had a joiner's cottage, a wood smith's, a city stable, a cart builder's, a tinker's cottage, and a potter with a brick kiln and a brick cottage. Aye—wonder o' wonders, all those folks lived and worked there, and when I clambered to the top of the garden wall I saw that all o' them had a little bit o' green heaven in their backyards as well.

On the other street, behind the brick-enclosed gardens, were the bazaar, where the trade wagons and tents set up shop. The bakers were at the end o' both rows, which is why I saw them as we entered the gates with Kump, but that were only the beginning. Silk scarves, stuffed poppets, leaded glass, a weaver's, a millinery, a candlestick maker, a sweet maker's…. The list went on, and there were a double row o' stalls through the town.

Diarmuid pressed five copper pieces into me hand and closed me fingers over them carefully.

"These are yers to spend," he said, making sure I could meet his almond-shaped brown eyes squarely. "Ye earned them. Ye have more, yeah? Ye've seen Cairsten—'e puts 'em in the pewter ewer on the mantel." His voice thickened, and I listened up. That usually meant it were important. "Whate'er ye spend yer copper on, tha's yers. But ye canna take it back. So if ye spend it all on sweets, tha's fine, but ye 'ave no poppet. If ye spend it on a book, tha's fine, but ye 'ave no sweets, ye ken?"

I stared at the coppers, awed. "Me choice?"

"Yeah-yeah."

"Maybe a big thing, and sweets for the leftovers?"

He smiled prettily and ruffled me hair. "Yeah. Tha' sounds like a plan. Keep an eye on us, Teyth—we're going to the soap makers, the spice stall, and the lamp-oil stall. Every time we come out o' a shop, we'll look for ye, and we willna go back in until we see ye, yeah?"

"Aye."

"Good lad."

I grinned at him, and a little more respectfully at Cairsten, and then set about exploring the marketplace. There were so much!

One stall had knitted poppets o' yarn, and I petted those reverently, near afraid the calluses on me worked hands would snag on them. Another stall had small carts made o' wood. I were too big for those—they were a small boy's things—but I remembered how much I'd loved the one I'd had before Kump burned it.

As though summoned by thought, I looked up across the marketplace, through the milling crowd, and saw them—Kump, Mum, and Aubrey in the last, clinging to Mum's hand.

Such a rush o' feelings then. Terror the foremost, for Kump. Wistfulness next, for Mum. And tenderness for Aubrey, who were crying softly. Mum turned to him and smiled, tired as she always were. She reached out her arms and hefted him into them, although he were getting big to be carried.

Kump turned to her then, saying, "Keep tha' brat still, ye stupid bitch!" and Mum soothed Aubrey and ignored him.

I swallowed. Would Kump turn on Aubrey next? Cairsten had asked, and it were likely. Suddenly the idea o' being "sold" to the smith were a comfort. Somebody had silver for me. It would be good o' me to go put meself between Aubrey and Kump, but I could not. I were *sold*. I *belonged*.

But still—here I were, in clean clothes, newly made, with five coppers in me hand.

I turned to the toymaker and found a cunning little cart, painted brightly red.

"Three coppers," the toymaker said kindly, and I lit up brightly. I could afford sweets, too!

I thrust me coppers into his hand and ran with the cart, making sure to approach the family from behind. Aubrey were hanging over Mum's shoulder, and he started to wriggle when he saw me.

"Tay'! Tay'!" he cried, and Mum had to put him down or drop him.

I ran to him, holding out the little toy, and he ran into me arms.

Gods forgive me, the first thing I noticed were the smell.

His skin were rancid with it, and I could not fathom the last time someone had washed his arse. But his weight were sweet in me arms, and his greasy hair didn't fettle me.

"Stay away from 'im, ye little turd!" Kump snarled, and I looked up, suddenly fearful. Diarmuid and Cairsten were buying lamp oil, and their backs were to me. I pulled out the little red cart and thrust it into his hands.

"'Ere, Aubrey," I murmured. "Remember Teyth gave ye tha'."

I felt a hand—gentle and filthy—in me hair, and I looked up. Mum smiled weakly before her hand were knocked away.

"I said git!" Kump yelled, and it had only been a fortnight, but I were fed and healthy and rested—I dodged and laughed as his foot lashed out.

"Stop drinking, coward!" I shouted and turned and weaved my way through the crowd.

I weren't looking where I were going, and I had just cleared the oil vendors when a fire-hardened hand reached out and hauled me into the stall by me collar.

I recognized the smell—o' heated metal that never washed out, and cedar-scented soap—and I didn't panic.

"Diarmuid?" I said, turning, hoping it were he.

"Other guess," Cairsten said grimly. "Were ye courtin' trouble, boy?"

I shook my head. "Nay, Cairsten—I swear. Diarmuid said I could spend me coppers on anything I chose. I bought a little cart for Aubrey."

Cairsten's stern expression softened. "Tha's sweet, lad. How many coppers it cost ye?"

"Three."

"Good. Here's three more coppers. Go buy yerself a book, aye?"

My face lit up. "And one for sweets leftover?"

"Aye. But let Diarmuid take ye, aye? Diarmuid?"

Diarmuid looked up at us from where he were giving the oil-seller's daughter a copper to deliver the purchase in the afternoon when we'd be home. She were near to an age with me, a pert girl with freckles and a turned-up nose. She winked at me, and I startled.

"Boy, ye hear me?"

"Aye, Cairsten. I hear ye."

"Good. Take 'im, D."

At that moment I heard a cry—distinctive, even among the chaos filling the market. "Aubrey!"

I darted out of the canvas tent, but just as I cleared the entrance, I felt Diarmuid's hand on me shoulder.

Together we looked out and saw Kump grinding the wee little cart into the mud.

"*No!*" I cried, bolting toward them, and Diarmuid?

Diarmuid did the surprising thing then. He wrapped his arms around me middle and hauled me up, limbs flailing, taking me toward the one solid building at the end of the bazaar.

The bookseller's.

"*Aubrey!*" I screamed, thrashing away. "*Aubrey! Au—*"

I stopped then, watching as Cairsten strode up. He snagged a cart at the toymaker's even as he walked, and dropped a coin in the toymaker's hand without so much as stopping his stride. Kump's hand were flung back as he were about to clock Aubrey into the mud, when Cairsten stopped his arm and handed Aubrey the cart in practically the same motion. Then he grabbed Kump by the collar and, leaving Mum and Aubrey to comfort each other, dragged him out of sight behind the nearest stall.

I were sobbing quietly watching this, and Diarmuid, using the strength I saw daily, grabbed me around the ribs with his big hard hands and threw me up, spinning me toward him. He caught me under the arms and carried me, much as Mum had carried Aubrey, but Diarmuid didn't miss a step.

I hiccupped into his shoulder—the bright day, the promise o' me own money and me own book and sweets all forgotten.

By the time we walked into the bookseller's, I'd stopped me puling and were boneless, sorrowful in Diarmuid's strong arms.

"Yer not gonna run away from me, are ye?" he asked grimly, and I shook me head.

He settled me down. "Teyth, ye need ter stay away, ken? Yer stepda's a bad'un. 'E'll hurt yer little brother fer spite, yeah?"

I nodded, suddenly exhausted and cowed. "Aye," I whispered, and that were all.

"Always silent," he muttered, and then were distracted. "Kaspar!" he said with genuine joy. I looked up and saw the prettiest boy I had ever seen in my life.

His hair were blond like sunshine, and his eyes blue as a clear lake. He had a scatter o' freckles across his fair cheeks, and sweet-berry lips.

I near to hated him, and all for the way Diarmuid glowed when he said this new boy's name.

"Dermott!" Kaspar said pleasantly, and I scowled at him.

"Diarmuid. Can ye not speak?"

Diarmuid scowled at me. "Dinna be rude, Teyth—e's from the south, yeah?"

"Aye," I grumbled sourly, but I filed it away. Diarmuid were *my* boy.

"This must be your new apprentice. Hello there—pleased to meet you."

It were hard to be grim in the face o' that much sunshine, but gods know I tried.

"Hey."

Kaspar laughed. "Silence, indeed," he said, winking at Diarmuid. "What can I do for you two?"

"'E's readin' primers, Kas, but summat wi' a challenge, yeah? He dinna like ter be bored."

"An' pictures," I spoke up and then remembered I were limited. "I have five coppers." Och! There went my visions of sweets, didn't it? But now that we were here, the books lining the shelves called to me. And oh, did I love the pen and ink, the lovely hand-painted illustrations. Often the illustrators used filigree drawings to separate text, and I had a love o' that. I wanted to *make* it, but not in pen and ink. I wanted to make it live and grow, palpable, cool, and climbing, like Diarmuid's most delicate weapons work but finer.

"Five coppers we can do," Kaspar said jovially. Then, as though he *meant* to buy my soul, "But here, young master. Have some sweets while you look. It makes the time pass quickly, yes?"

He held in his hand an assortment o' the candy maker's newest paper-wrapped sweets, and my whole body simply melted at the sight.

"Aye," I whispered, appalled. I would *have* to like him now, whether he held a claim to our Diarmuid or not!

But that knowledge did not keep me from reaching out my hand and accepting the entire fistful o' candy. I stuffed it carefully in my pocket and looked up at his open, expectant face.

"Thank ye," I said grudgingly. I took a breath. "Tha' were kind." Oh gods. My best manners here—this were someone Diarmuid liked. "May I see the books now?"

"Yes, young master. Here—follow me."

I did, past shelves and shelves o' books that went clear to the ceiling. There were a ladder along one wall, a wide one, built like a flight o' stairs on wheels. Two men could sit abreast on the step o' it. Adjacent to it were a long double shelf, shorter than the others, full o' leather-bound primers. Kaspar pointed to a quarter o' the top. "These here are our five-pence, yes, Teyth? I'm afraid the others are for silver."

I reached out a tentative finger and stroked the bindings. So *this* were what Diarmuid were warning o' when he pushed the coins into my hand. This wanting, a helpless yearning. Where once I thought a full belly and warm clothes were all I could need, I felt a gnawing in my stomach for more.

Well, today my five pence would gain me more—but this feeling o' want, it would return, o' that I had no doubt even then.

I spent a blissful hour in the bookseller's, lost among the riches. I'd forgotten Aubrey and Mum, and even my heartbreak over the little cart, and my hero worship that Cairsten had replaced it. I sat in a corner and compared two primers, one o' which were far more challenging than the other, and the other o' which had the most beautiful illustrations I'd ever seen.

I'd just decided on the difficult one, so as to make the most use o' my five pence, when I realized that Diarmuid and Kaspar had been having a hushed conversation sitting abreast on the ladder at the end o' the building.

"I'm sorry, Dermott," Kaspar were saying, his voice aching. "I know… you and me, we're…."

"Special," Diarmuid whispered. I heard the word and looked between the shelves and saw them, fingers twined.

Kaspar raised Diarmuid's battered fingers to his strawberry lips and kissed.

"You are," he said softly. "So special. But my parents—they've arranged the marriage and everything. It's not a question o' them liking you or not liking you, or caring if I love men instead of women. It would be the same if you were Kerrigan, the baker's girl. They gave their word when I was small." His voice broke. "I would have given it to you if I had it free o' my own."

"Yeah," Diarmuid murmured. "Yeah. I ken. Is naught ter fettle ye, yeah? Dinna fret, I ken it all. I'm but a dalliance, an yer off ter better—"

"Stop," Kaspar choked, and I sat on my knees now, watching them in shock and a little bit o' horror. Diarmuid's voice were thick, his words nearly unrecognizable, and hearing him pour out those rough country words on Kaspar's highbrow accents were almost a sin. How dare this boy hear my Diarmuid this naked? How dare he break his heart?

I'd stood, hardly knowing what I'd planned to do, when I felt Cairsten's heavy hand on my shoulder.

"Have ye made yer decision, then?" he asked softly, and I nodded, mute.

"Aye."

"Do ye have yer coppers?"

"Aye," I said, aware that they were saying more quiet, passionate things to each other and I had no way of stopping it.

"Good boy. Is that it?"

I offered him the book I'd chosen—the one with the challenge, that I thought I might try to illustrate on my own—and he took it, leafed through it, and checked the price on the corner. "D, young Kaspar—we've found our book," he called, deliberately loud. I watched them startle and then followed Cairsten past the raised platform where it appeared Kaspar usually did business. "We're leaving Teyth's coppers on the counter, aye?"

"Yes, sir. Thank you, Master Cairsten," Kaspar said, and even I could tell he were holding on to his politeness through his tears.

"Yeah, Cairsten, I'm—"

"Me and the boy'll go home and fix lunch," he said. "Ye come home before dinner, aye?"

"Yeah-yeah," he said, and I knew he were crying same as Kaspar.

Cairsten pulled me out the door, holding on to my precious book, and together we stumped around the block to the cottage I'd come to know as home.

"That were awful," I said as the bookseller's disappeared behind us, and I couldn't tell which part of the day I meant.

"Aye," Cairsten agreed. "Did ye get yer sweets after all tha', Teyth?"

Surprised, I reached into my pocket and pulled out two o' em, the ones that tasted like root beer. "Aye!" I said and offered him one.

He took it gravely. "I'll have to go get a whole bag o' these," he acknowledged after the little bit o' sugar patched some of the pains o' the day. "Do ye think so?"

"Aye," I murmured. There were so much I wanted to ask, so much I wanted to know—not just about how Aubrey and Mum would fare, but about how Diarmuid and his friend would do without each other. I still did not like that he called my Diarmuid "Dermott" and that he looked and smelled like sunshine. But I *really* did not like the heartbreak in Diarmuid's voice as they sat and spoke, either. I would spare Diarmuid that. I would do *anything* to spare him that, and in the coming years, it would be my only salvation.

But in spite o' all I wanted to ask, in the end I asked none o' it. I would wait for Diarmuid to get home, somber and red-eyed, and serve him the dessert Cairsten had gone to fetch from the bakers while I were reading my new book.

I would tell him a riddle I'd heard from the toy maker and treasure the way his lips quirked up, almost a smile.

And I would listen with burning ears as Cairsten asked when Kaspar were leaving, and breathe a sigh o' relief that it weren't until spring.

Anything. I would do anything to spare him—even if that meant sharing him until the frost left the earth.

A WEEK later the village gathered for the Samhain fires, sending offerings o' burnt bread and meat to the gods, hoping for the blessing o' lasting through the winter. It were the first time I'd gone, although Kump went every year, grumbling all the time about the pittance I knew my family added to the sacrifice. In truth, only a little food were thrown into the fire. Much o' the rest o' it, in particular preserves and salted meat, were put in the village stores to give to the poor. More than once, I knew, Mum had stopped by the stores on her way home with the laundry in order to feed us when Kump had drunk away her pay.

But this were my first time, and I enjoyed it. I'd come to know the people here. I knew Kerrigan, the baker's girl, and Vidar, the toy maker. I knew the sweets maker and his round boy, Abel, and I knew the girl who delivered small decanters o' lamp oil, Clancy. We'd been to the market one other time, and although I'd not seen my family, I had seen all the others. Kerrigan, Abel, Clancy, and I had sat in a small circle on the bookseller's porch and played a game o' jacks with Abel's rubber ball.

Us children ran together, playing tag and screaming at the Samhain masks worn by the elders of the village, and tried to avoid the shadows cast by the flames of the great fires.

Clancy, Abel, Kerrigan, and I were slightly braver than the rest, especially when Clancy tripped over two writhing bodies behind one o' the tents outside of the town square.

We stopped, all o' us, and stared as the girl lowered her skirts and the boy pulled up his breeches, and both o' them betrothed to other people.

"Not a word," snarled the boy—the carter's son. "Not the lot o' ye."

"Not ter worry," Clancy said pertly. She had blonde hair and freckles, much like Kaspar, but her nose were snubbed and not straight bridged, and she were as much o' our village as I were. "This 'ere is Teyth. His name means 'silence.' He tells no one's secrets, isn't tha' right there, Teyth?"

I stared at her, appalled. Aye, I weren't talkative, but that my own silence had become something to tell a story of were terrifying.

"Aye," I said weakly, and the others nodded as if it were a given.

"See?" Abel said, grinning. His heart were as sweet as his father's stall, and I could see why he were a popular boy. He never had a sour word, not in the time I'd known him.

"And ye, Kerrigan?" asked the boy. The candlemaker's girl had long since disappeared into the shadows, probably to pretend it had never happened.

Kerrigan, the baker's daughter, looked at him archly, as though they had history. "I am ever silent, Llant. But ye'll tell me sister on yer own. Ye have no stomach for secrets."

With that she flounced off and we followed, but I admired her. Brown hair, brown eyes, a little plain but with a spine as straight as her speaking. I'd not had friends in our little cottage, and I were coming to like the ones I had, even if I simply tagged along the fringes o' them in silence.

My feeling o' well-being cut off abruptly as we passed one o' the other close shadows with bodies writhing in the frosty air.

I knew those shoulders, that broad back, and even that arse as it pumped back and forth.

I knew the sound o' Kaspar's voice, ragged against the wall, as he begged for more.

The others chattered, praising Kerrigan's bravery, and it seemed I were the only one who knew Diarmuid were coupling in the darkness.

Well, let him, I thought, trying to be generous. Kaspar would end up with no baby in his belly, and whatever moments o' happiness they smuggled, it would only be until spring.

It weren't until we returned to the fire, the elders in their masks dancing in grotesqueries around the base o' the fire, that I realized my eyes burned from more than smoke.

I found Cairsten then, easy to see in his barrel-chested vastness, and separated from my playmates with a murmur. It weren't just a pained heart that led me there. I'd also seen Kump, drinking with his own cronies in the corner where the shadows hugged the stone wall surrounding the village, and I didn't want to stray too close.

As I drew near, Cairsten put that strong, fire-hardened hand on my shoulder and squeezed, and I must have made a sound.

He bent down and said softly, "What'd ye see in the patterns of the dark, Teyth? Ye look brokenhearted."

"Diarmuid an' Kaspar," I murmured, because it did not occur to me to lie to Cairsten. "They were coupling."

Cairsten rumbled. "Wish 'em well, boy. There willna be many chances before they part for good."

I nodded and wiped my eyes on my shoulder and then allowed Cairsten to draw me against his great body. I swayed there, mesmerized by the fire, lost in the flicker o' flames, allowing this very strange autumn to pass over me like smoke.

THE NEXT morning, after the Samhain fires burned to the ground and the embers were left to cook the last pig o' summer, a group o' men from the village and surrounds went into the woods for a final hunt. Cairsten went with them, and so did Kump.

Kump did not return.

"What happened ter him?" I asked when the frightened group o' villagers came back, a boar slung on a staff between 'em. The news had preceded them—Abel, in fact, had cut over the back wall of the garden to give it to me as I pulled out the last of the tomato plants. (I'd come to love that red vegetable as Diarmuid cooked it, and I looked forward to planting more o' those in the spring.)

Abel hadn't been able to give me details, and Diarmuid and I spent the rest of the afternoon fretting as we went about the chores that would make our little house safe and cozy for the winter. Things like furs on the floor and the walls had never occurred to me until Diarmuid started giving instructions, but once I blocked a draft with a stuffed bit o' linen, I began to understand why he were so intent.

"The bloody fool ran into the woods," the butcher spat when we were finally able to ask him. "Scared to the death, I s'pose. We heard him screaming and found blood, but nothing. There were nothing there."

"Aye," Cairsten rumbled. "It were in the center o' the forest, the part we dare not go these days, and for good reason."

The rest of the villagers mumbled assent, and it seemed that not one o' them doubted that Kump had met a nasty and well-deserved end. But I saw Diarmuid and Cairsten exchange a long glance, and Diarmuid pulled me inside from the frigid night air.

"Cairsten thinks summat got him," I said flatly, because Diarmuid had never lied to me yet.

"Yeah-yeah," Diarmuid said. "Take off yer jumper and yer jerkin, Teyth. Is warm in the house, and we've furs enow on yer bed." His voice thickened, became harsher, more alien with his accent.

"But what? What in those woods—"

"There be old magics in there," Diarmuid snapped. "Ye dinna go violating long-established paths. There be reasons there are things men shouldna do!"

He stopped and we stared at each other, my shock at his saying those words not more than his look of shock that he'd said them.

"Nothing would punish him for tha'," I snarled. "Tha' happened, and it were proof tha' no god cared!"

Diarmuid turned away, his shoulders slumped. "Perhaps," he said gruffly. "Perhaps men pick up where the gods give up."

My knees went to water and I practically fell backward upon my own bed. "Cairsten wouldna do tha'," I muttered, my own voice thickening. I'd learned this from Diarmuid, I thought blankly. I'd eaten at his table for nearly a month, and already some o' his words had become mine. But I needed his words. I'd been willing to consign that'un to all the fires o' a demon's forge, but Cairsten? With his kind words, his gentleness? Nay.

Diarmuid glanced behind him and then flickered his eyes away. "Aye, boy. Yer probably right. Cairsten wouldna. But then, ye must know the other thing is true."

The woods. Where Diarmuid had been found wandering, naked, covered in blood. Well, Diarmuid would know.

"I feel naught for him," I said, not even a little surprised. "Naught. Only… how will Mum and Aubrey see clear through the winter?"

They knew, both o' them, what Aubrey were to me.

That, o' all things, were what reassured me in the end. They knew. Aubrey'd been my one sweet moment when living with Mum and my stepfather. They would not let bad things happen to a helpless one, not even to rid the world o' Kump.

Diarmuid grunted, standing in front of the window and looking out into the night. His arms were still crossed as though I'd hurt him somehow. "I dinna know. But give Cairsten some time. He may have a better story than all tha', and a way for them ter see it clear."

The silence descended, hard and heavy as the largest hammer, and for a moment even I were cowed by it.

When the voice rang through the room, it frightened me. I were hardly aware it were mine.

"Wha'd yer parents do, Diarmuid? That ye were left alive and they were taken?"

Diarmuid looked behind him again and smiled slightly. "I wondered if ye'd figure," he said softly. "I dinna know. But Cairsten took me to the villages north o' the woods, and not a soul would so much as look at me. His wife had just died, and their child with her— summat about an illness, but 'e dinna talk about it. But 'e took me in. Trained me. Were kind."

"Like me?" I asked. Diarmuid were so competent—his metalwork were beautiful, superlative, and his hinges and handles were as intricate as his sword hilts.

"Yeah-yeah," Diarmuid said, looking back outside. "And nay. He were ready for ye. He dinna know what ter do with me."

I were used to Cairsten now. The fear o' his sharp words that had so skittered me in September were now but background noise, like the clang o' hammers and wheeze o' bellows. Not pleasant, of a certain, and me ears would ring for an hour after we called it quits and put up our tools, but it were merely a part o' our day.

I'd been told that the first things I made at the forge would be shite. They'd be mangled and twisted, scarred by what I did not know, unable to be salvaged by the things I did. I would wonder, as the years passed, what scars Diarmuid would bear, being the first boy made at Cairsten's forge—scars and errors Cairsten didn't mean to make, but that people made just the same.

"Do?" I said now. "What were there ter do with ye? Ye pretty much do everything."

Diarmuid laughed some and came away from the window, ruffling my hair. "Is not yet bedtime, yeah?"

No—in fact, the hunting party had come back right after dinner. I assumed Cairsten had been eating the leftovers Diarmuid kept for him on the table.

"Do we need ter go to sleep?" I asked in horror, Kump forgotten. My lesson time—did I not get lessons?

"Nay. Let me bring one of the oil lamps. Ye can read in here. Me'n Cairsten'll talk."

I were about to agree when I realized that I'd allowed myself to be distracted. "Diarmuid!" I protested, feeling betrayed. "Ye'll... ye'll tell me, right?"

Diarmuid sighed and then nodded. "I'll tell ye, yeah. But only if ye promise not ter run away."

I thought o' me mum, o' Aubrey, o' the dead look in her eyes as Kump dragged her through the marketplace. I could give her my silver now that Kump were gone. It were a better thing. I no longer had to be the boy who deserted his family; I could be the man who went to support his kin. I liked that. I did not need a pocket full o' sweets if I could be the man Mum had needed before Kump came along.

I let that comfort me as I sat at my bed and carefully copied the letters from my primer to a piece o' parchment. I'd chosen a passage from a story about little folk to copy: *Their fathers are the old gods, the takers of blood, the givers of joy, the ones who mete justice of bone.*

I copied assiduously, and when I were done with ten repetitions, the words etched into my brain, my penmanship growing more steady with each sentence, I set the book down and stretched.

Diarmuid and Cairsten's voices had carried to me down the hall this time, and although they'd been low and intense, they'd never raised. I took comfort in this when perhaps I should not have.

Diarmuid had given me an old pair o' slippers, leather on the outside, fleece on the in, that were too small for him, and I loved their comfort now that the days grew chill and snow threatened. I slid them on and padded down the hall to see if it were safe to come out.

As I stood still in shadow, I heard a snippet o' conversation that made me pause.

"I say it again, D—I didna!" Cairsten's voice thickened like Diarmuid's, but I heard his sincerity in the country accents as well. "I wouldna. He were evil, o' the worst kind, like the...." Cairsten spat on his own floor. "Like that'un in the castle, but I got no stomach for killing, not in cold blood."

Diarmuid sat, head bowed, fingers steepled and pressing into his brow. "I hear ye and believe, Cairsten. But ye be false summat, and I dinna... I canna fathom. It's eatin' at me, willna let me leave it be. *Please,* Master Cairsten, *please*—could ye no be tellin' me?"

Cairsten's sigh shook the table.

"I spilt blood," he muttered apologetically. "Me own." He shook his head and held out his hand, with a quick and dirty bandage on it. "See? I lingered back—them farmers, they never look out for the other, and I been minding you, boy, and Teyth. So I lingered back, looking for stragglers, and that'un—he talked evil, he did. Things about Teyth, things he planned for the little'un. Just… trying t'get a rise out o' me, I suspect, but evil, nonetheless. If I were a blood-spilling man, then's when I wouldha spilt me some blood. But I clutched me spear, blade-up, because there were boar scat everywhere." Cairsten laughed, and it had no humor. "Almost drowned out the stench o' that'un, that be the truth. And sliced me hand." He held out his hand with a fragment o' fabric wrapped around the middle, very like a spear slice. "Me blood… it dripped down the staff and leached into the earth, and the whole time, I were thinking, 'Please… please… just let him be no more.'"

My heart, cold and still in me chest, began to beat slowly, through thick blood. It were no worse than what I'd thought, and better perhaps, because Cairsten had the means. He *could have* taken Kump's life. One swing o' his fist, and the man would be dead at his feet. But he held his tongue and his fist. A part o' me knew this were a better man. The man who would not strike down Kump were the man who only spoke sharp while we worked and never used blows to make a point.

That were Cairsten.

I looked up to the table and watched Diarmuid cover Cairsten's hand with his own. Not in the way he and Kaspar touched, no. This were like Aubrey, who patted Mum's knee.

What occurred to me then were so simple, I should've thought it sooner.

Diarmuid's his. His son. His flesh and blood.

Oh gods. Perhaps I would be one day too.

"So ye wished?" Diarmuid said, a quirk at his lips.

"Aye, boy. I wished. And no sooner had three drips o' blood soaked into the earth than Kump screamed as though he saw devils in a horse cart coming for him with a crook. He screeched, running past me fer the woods, and he were pursued by a…." Cairsten shuddered in the silence he'd left. "A fetid wind, boy. I have no more words for it. Warm and rank, full o' blood and shit, it blew after tha'un, pursuing him to the heart of the woods. Two others saw him run away screaming; they witnessed it and ran in after him. Half the market street—if tha'. We fought our way through the brush, and found a clearing no bigger'n this table, and it were full o' blood. We stayed clear o' tha' space, D. It had the same charnel-house smell, ye ken?"

Diarmuid's eyes were the size o' dinner plates—and for that matter, I could feel my own drying in the draft o' the corridor.

"There were no doubts," Cairsten finished, and the part o' me what knew I were young were relieved. I could remain a boy for just a bit longer. I would not have to choose between a home I loved and a thing I knew were wrong. Cairsten had made a bargain, like the books said. The small folk, the ones who drank the leftover beer Diarmuid left in the tin plate every night—they made small bargains.

The heart o' our forest, that were different, I reckoned. That took the big bargains, did the dark things.

The things that did that, they didn't care about niceties, about right and wrong: they were only there for the bargain.

Cairsten had given it blood, and it had given him the same in return. It were a fair trade as far as I were concerned. I would not gainsay it for all the world.

I walked in then, mindless o' the sounds I made, and came to sit at the table. The two grown men looked at me in surprise.

"Is there cake left?" I asked, still intent on that, after all. "I know there be milk, but I'm hungering for cake."

Both men blinked slowly, as though coming out o' a dream. "Yeah-yeah," Diarmuid said, breaking the silence first. "There be cake. Ye know tha', Silence."

I met his gaze, uncaring. "I do. Cairsten, would ye like me ter serve ye some cake? It be good stuff. Has the honey an' butterfat an' chocolate, aye?"

Cairsten smiled briefly, his lips and cheeks gaining back some color I'd not known they'd lost. "Aye. Sounds like good cake."

"An' sweets make things better," I said, remembering that sad day from the market.

He smiled again, this time stronger. "Aye. They do."

We ate then, and the world, which had gone sideways, with a sky o' green and grass like a red sea, returned to normal, with things o' iron and metal beneath our feet, not the thirsty earth o' the gods.

I asked what would happen to Mum and Aubrey, and although it were a tremendous thing to demand o' Cairsten, I were hoping that Aubrey might come and live with us. I am shamed now to know I had already consigned Mum to the cottage by herself—this haven here at Cairsten's had become men only, and there were something in me already that didn't imagine a man and a woman together to make a household, not when it were my fantasy coming to life.

Not once in all o' that did I think Mum and Cairsten should marry, although we all knew he'd had a wife he'd loved very much. It weren't that I didn't want him to have another one. It were merely that Cairsten were strong and Mum were not. It didn't seem fair to Cairsten to put Mum in his life. A mate o' his would need to be his equal. A woman his equal, a man—but equal.

Not Mum.

Cairsten didn't say anything o' that, though. He said he'd see if she needed help through the winter, and if she could keep her little cottage and the farm Kump'd never worked.

The next day, Mum walked away from the cottage and the few things inside. She walked by the smithy where I were working with Diarmuid and Cairsten. Aubrey were on her hip, and her few things were in a satchel on her shoulder. She didn't even stop to say good-bye.

She waved, careful not to wake Aubrey, who were sleeping, and pointed to the castle, the great stone framework that drenched our village in shadow at the sunset and reflected the light of the sun in our eyes when it rose.

She were going in, to live. I stood helpless and waved back, wondering if, before Da had been killed, before the prince had taxed her endurance with money, before Kump'd destroyed her spirit—sometime in there, had there ever been a time when she'd loved me?

I watched her grow small in the shadow of the great cylindrical tower that made up the part of the castle that faced the village, and I watched her knock on the great oaken door.

Guards ushered her inside and she disappeared, Aubrey sleeping on her shoulder.

Cairsten's hand descended on *my* shoulder, and I looked up at him, feeling as old and wise as he were.

"Ready to go back to work, boy?"

"Aye."

"They'll make it through the winter in there," he said kindly.

I looked away. We all knew what living in the castle meant. It meant they owned you. I were lucky. Kump'd sold me into freedom.

Mum had just sold her and Aubrey to the hulking great stone shadow that ate souls for breakfast.

And I could not fix it. All I could do were go fetch another bucket o' water and be grateful Kump'd thought all men were like him.

STORMY PASSAGE TO SPRING

THE SNOWS came, deep and lush over the farms. The farmers had their preserves in their root cellars, their salted meat, and hopefully enough amusements to keep them from the throats o' their family until going outside were not a death sentence.

I remembered those days, snowed in with Kump and Aubrey while Mum worked in the castle. Not good times, really.

In town it were different. Even the deepest snows were tramped down eventually, and while our little household were tranquil, that didn't mean Cairsten didn't go out for a pint o' ale at the tavern sometimes, or that Diarmuid didn't visit the bookseller's boy until it broke his heart.

Me own free time were spent with the books, o' course, and with my cronies, Abel, Kerrigan, and Clancy. I'd say we were terrors, but it were not true. I knew want and were grateful. The others had known nothing but kindness. We fed stray animals and made up games for the smaller children. There were no stealing pies for us—Abel's father gave us sweets, and Kerrigan's da were free with the pastries. Clancy always had a copper earned for a meat pie, and for that matter, I pitched my own in to keep us occupied.

A few days before Solstice, I were hauling everyone to the booksellers—because not all the parents were like Cairsten, bent on teaching lessons, and I wanted to show them what the magic were all about. As we entered we saw Diarmuid and Kaspar behind the counter together, hips touching as they looked out at the lot o' us.

I carried a low, dull ache at the thought o' Diarmuid and the beautiful boy. I'd not seen it, but I were sure they'd found other times to couple, and a part o' me thought that if anyone were to rip me in two like Kump had, it should be Diarmuid, who at least had a beautiful soul to shove inside me.

But Kaspar were too kind to hate, and he were leaving. I could forgive him if he were leaving, because Diarmuid would be here with me, and Kaspar would marry a girl he didn't know.

I really did have the best o' the bargain; even I could see it.

So this day, I pulled my crew in to the five-pence books and opened one o' me favorites, one that I'd sold back because I'd wanted one longer, with bigger words.

"See?" I said excitedly, opening the book carefully. "The illustrations help ye know—ye can learn to read looking at the pictures and the words together. Is easy!"

Clancy eyed it suspiciously. "But why canna ye just draw the picture cat when ye want a cat?" she asked.

I waved my hands, realizing that I'd been caught in the trap of the familiar. This—words, meaning, sounds, pictures—it had all become so familiar it twined together in my head, and true to silence, I had nothing to explain.

"It's... there are things ter speak o' tha' ye canna see!" I stammered, not realizing how much like Diarmuid I sounded. "Dinna ye ken?"

Clancy looked taken aback—and we might have come to words—but at that moment there were a clatter on the porch o' the bookseller's shop, and *he* stepped in. The one who'd changed our lives when I weren't much older than Aubrey. The one who'd ordered the village militia slaughtered when they went to fight for their homes.

He were terrifying.

In his thirties, he had hair gone to silver already and a thin face. I could see the bones in his jaw, and his cheekbones jutted out with arrogance. His lips were as thin as his face, and his nose were thinner than both—one twitch o' lips, with an arch o' transparent eyebrows over heavy-lidded eyes, and the world swooned at his disdain.

His clothing were rich. It weren't spangled with gold and jewels, like I'd imagined, but he wore a fur coat, cut and sewn like a regular coat o' wool, and a wool jumper underneath that were white as sparkling snow.

He came to town occasionally, his name like the flutter o' starlings' wings among us. *Were he here? Did ye see him? Aye, did ye? Nay, he drove right by! He were wearing indigo today—nobody here dyed that wool. Well, none o' us shoe his horses, neither, but he were happy to tax us on iron.*

This time, he came into the bookseller's, and Diarmuid and Kaspar stood there, so cozy, looking up at him blankly.

They met eyes, and Kaspar stood to do his duty, approaching cautiously.

"Milord, may I help you?"

The prince's eyes fell on him—plain brown eyes—and they glowed like a cat's eyes in the dark.

"Yes," he purred. "Yes, indeed. I have need of a rather special volume." He pulled out a small piece o' parchment and handed it to Kaspar.

Kaspar's fair face reddened, and sweat appeared on his forehead. The next look he gave the prince were an exquisite look o' both embarrassment and fear.

"I'm afraid we don't have this one," he said quietly. "We know the printer, though. We can order it."

"Wonderful," the prince said pleasantly, and for a moment I thought that would be the end. Kaspar would not have to worry about incurring the prince's ire by not having the book on hand—he did not seem that put out. "Perhaps you can deliver it when it arrives?"

Kaspar's mouth fell open, and his throat bobbed convulsively. He stood there, stricken, when Diarmuid spoke up.

"He canna!"

Strong, like they were equals, Diarmuid strode from behind the counter. "He's leaving to be betrothed tomorrow. He willna be here when the book comes in."

The prince's mouth pursed, and the glare he cast at Diarmuid were truly terrifying. He wanted my Diarmuid dead.

And Kaspar—Kaspar's eyes filled as he stared at his lover. I knew that he were not supposed to go to be wed until spring. Diarmuid could not lie to the prince—it would be found out. Whatever had just happened, he'd sent his lover away months early.

"Will you?"

"Will I what?" In all that followed, it were Diarmuid's only moment o' confusion regarding the prince.

"Deliver. The. Book."

A wash o' color took over Diarmuid's brown face. "Oh," he said, and after a moment of horror, he composed himself. "I'm the smith," he responded squarely. "Odds are, 'twill be his da come to serve."

That bland, almost otherworldly face contorted into a snarl. He snatched the parchment from Kaspar's hand.

"I shall have to search elsewhere, then."

With that, he whirled, leaving his own layer o' frost in the little store.

Kaspar wiped his eyes with the back o' his hand. "Dermott—"

Diarmuid's throat worked. "Go pack, Kas. Tell yer da. Cairsten'll tek ye if yer da canna."

"But… we had until spring!"

Diarmuid shook his head and wiped his own eyes. "Better yer married tomorrow—better yer married *tonight*!—than deliver a book into tha' one's clutches, yeah-yeah?"

"No," Kaspar whispered. "Not if it means—"

"Dinna say it," Diarmuid said thickly. They were standing apart, the shadow of the prince lurking between them, holding a space. But Diarmuid's voice broke and Kaspar threw himself into Diarmuid's arms while my cronies and I stood, forgotten, witnessing their pain like a poppet show.

"I thought we had until spring," Kaspar wept, and Diarmuid buried his face in that fair hair and shook.

I backed out of the bookseller's and left them to their parting. My friends looked at me as I closed and locked the door from the inside, none o' us speaking until we'd walked silently off the porch.

"That weren't fair." Abel spoke first, saying the obvious.

"Life ain't fair," I snapped. Diarmuid were crying in there. It seemed like the height o' tactlessness to voice the thing that hurt him.

"He… he just *does* that," Kerrigan said, her voice full o' hatred. "My sister's man—he weren't never the same after he came from the prince's bed. He doesn't even *like* men."

I stared at her, my mouth opening and closing. For the first time, I contemplated which one I'd *choose* if there'd been a choosing, and it occurred to me that Diarmuid had become the center o' all my dreams.

I'd never dreamt any different.

"I… I need ter find Cairsten," I rasped through a dry throat. "Diarmuid'll need 'im."

Cairsten were in the pub, which were not his usual place, but I didn't blame him. He rarely drank more than a pint, but same as Diarmuid and Kas, or me and my cronies, he had need for his own people.

My friends stayed put when I ran in and tapped him on the shoulder, getting his attention. I whispered the situation in his ear, and he reared back, then looked at the doorway.

"Ye three!" he called, gesturing my friends inside. "Ye stay here. Yer folks'll tek ye home." Then he called to the pub, "Everybody—the prince were out, looking for a playmate. 'E tried the bookseller's lad, but the boy were to be betrothed and Diarmuid fettled 'im. Ye should see ter yer children an' kin if ye 'ave 'em, aye?"

There were a startled silence. Then most of the men drained their ale in one gulp and gave a distracted "Aye!" as they ran for their families.

Clancy and Kerrigan were seized by their fathers as they left. Clancy, for all she were a tall, strong girl, were hoisted in her father's arms like an infant and rushed away, looking irritated and frightened and unhappy.

Cairsten didn't even stop to down his ale. He clasped my hand and hauled me through the street, heading for the in-town stable.

"Canda!" he hollered as we entered the surprisingly warm, wide space. "Canda! Are ye 'ere?"

"Aye—what's the news?" Canda emerged, a lean, leathered woman who could cow a horse with a scowl.

It took a moment only before she had two of the stable's stock horses ready and hitched to a sled that she apparently let out to town members when it were needed.

"I'm taking Teyth home ter pack," Cairsten told her, looking anxious.

"He's a little young," she said, looking at me worriedly.

I stared back, startled. "'E wouldna want me," I told her. "I'm too plain. Diarmuid is pretty, though. Can we go, Cairsten?" I were anxious too now, the fear of the townspeople infecting me like plague.

Cairsten nodded, seizing my hand like he expected the prince to materialize from nowhere and whisk me away.

"I'll have the sled at the gates!" Canda called, and Cairsten thanked her on the way out.

Diarmuid and Kaspar were waiting when we returned, and what followed were the most flurried bout o' packing in me life. I were terrified o' whatever nameless horror the prince seemed to embody, and then, as we threw our warmest clothes in duffels, I were suddenly terrified o' leaving my home.

"We'll be back, aye?" I asked repeatedly as Diarmuid told me time and time again that I could not take my books with me, or my favorite hammer from the forge, or the slippers that had once been his.

"Teyth!" he said finally, putting his hands on mine.

"Aye?" I asked, panting.

"We'll be gone a week at the most. We're spiriting him away, we're sayin'"—his voice hitched—"good-bye, an' we're comin' back to our home, hopefully after the prince's ire has passed. Ye ken?"

"Aye," I murmured, all misery. "Tis no' fair, Diarmuid. Ye didna do nothing wrong."

"Yeah-yeah," Diarmuid said wearily. "We dinna. But it were to end soon anyway. Now is good as then."

He looked away, as he should, because he were lying and it weren't fit he look me in the eyes when his heart ached with the truth.

IF I'D had even a minute to spare, I would have been excited about a trip through the snow, and for the first hour or so, it were a wonder. The farms spread out before us, a picture before the solstice, white and muffled in the fog.

But even the fleece-lined mittens and coat Cairsten brought for me could not seal out the cold, and the lap robe he tried to spread over our laps kept falling off me, simply because he were such a giant o' a man.

I would have complained—I yearned to cozy between Diarmuid and Kaspar, simply to be sandwiched between their warm bodies— but one look behind me to the back o' the sled, and I could not. They were happy. It were as though they pretended this were but a sleigh ride through the country. They talked about books, about the candlemaker's son, who could tell a pretty joke, about the horses, and how Diarmuid would like to learn to shoe the beasts, but Cairsten feared because he were so slight. (Cairsten judged all men against his fearful mass. I am not sure if Diarmuid ever knew he weren't child-sized, even as a grown man.)

We rode hard through the rest o' the day, snacking on dried meat, cheese, and a giant loaf o' fresh-baked bread Kerrigan's sister had tucked under me arm as we fled the village.

I thought we would pause to rest somewheres, but it weren't snowing and the horses were sound. Cairsten just kept them up steadily, resting them when we came to streams. Naught were frozen over, which helped. It were cold, but we would live.

Our bodies would live.

I didn't know if Diarmuid's heart would live much past this eerie, moonlit good-bye.

Diarmuid took over the reins when Cairsten were too tired, and I fell asleep next to him, the horses still keeping a steady rhythm, their feet crunching through the few inches of snow. My last thought as I drifted off against Diarmuid's warm thigh were that I could finally keep the lap robe on.

I awoke near dawn. Diarmuid had taken refuge in a small copse o' wood while I slept. He and Cairsten must have taken time to spread a canopy over us; the resulting shelter were close, colored gold like the sun from the canvas overhead.

Cairsten were snoring in the front o' the sled, and I sat up and stretched, looking behind me. Diarmuid were awake as well. Kaspar were asleep against his chest, and he were leaning on an elbow, gazing about him thoughtfully.

"D, I need ter piss." Of a sudden, I missed the water closet right outside the back porch. There were pipes that led underground, Cairsten said, and some folk had their outhouses on the inside, but he hadn't been the one to build the house. His master before him—his father—had, and he'd built before the pipes. I frankly didn't care—a piss pot that flushed away the piss were a luxury after the little tin chamber pot my family had used.

Diarmuid smiled slightly and lifted Kaspar up gentle, laying him down again as he got out of the sled. Together we ventured a little deeper into the copse. He'd brought a shovel, and the ground weren't that hard. We took care o' business and covered up right quick, all in the silence of the woods.

When we were done, we stretched our hands over heads, and almost as one, we raised our faces to the thin sunshine that were beginning to climb the horizon.

"Teyth?"

"Aye?"

They were the first words spoken between us since the day before, when I hadn't wished to leave what had become our home.

"I'm glad ye'll be with me when we're back at t' house," he said, eyes still closed, face still toward the sun. "I'll... yer good company. It'll...."

He reached out and fumbled for my hand through the gloves we'd only just put back on. I clasped his tight and closed my eyes.

It'll hurt less.

I heard the words as though the forest had said them, and I said a silent *Thank ye!* to the surrounding woods.

It never occurred to me that something might have heard us speaking, or that the tears we both shed might be accepted as an offering too, no matter how small.

THE VILLAGE where we took Kaspar were large and prosperous. Kaspar asked the village smith—perhaps trusting him innately—for the family he were looking for, and Cairsten drove us, tired horses and all, to drop him off at their doorstep.

The world stopped. Time froze, like a drop o' water on a branch.

Kaspar and Diarmuid looked at each other, stricken, aware that whatever they'd had, whatever they'd been doing, it ended here. Both o' them were good boys. There would be no running, no shirking responsibility.

Diarmuid moved first, kissing Kaspar on the forehead and then swinging out of the sled, pulling out the case o' belongings that Kaspar had put in the back of the cart.

Kaspar took the belongings from him, and they both nodded soberly. Then Kaspar walked up the stairs to the great house—greater than the smith's and the bookseller's put together, and painted white, with columns and all—and knocked on the door.

He were greeted warmly—if with a bit o' surprise—by a man who looked his father's age, and ushered inside.

The three o' us left in the cart looked at each other wearily.

"The inn, the stables, and the pub," Cairsten said gruffly. "We all need food and rest, and Diarmuid here needs a drink."

The pub were smoky and full o' the smell o' beer, just like our pub at home. I ate my stomach full and fell asleep in Diarmuid's arms as he knocked back his third pint, and he and I woke up crammed into the same small bed in a room with Cairsten.

I remembered opening my eyes and burrowing into his arms. All the thinking I'd done about mothers and fathers, and liking boys not being a thing that must be, and I closed my eyes in one conclusion.

Someday, when I were grown, I must wake up with Diarmuid's arms around me again. In that moment, before falling asleep once more, I remember thinking that he were right. Home would be there when we sought it. Home were always where he were.

THE FIRST DROPS O' BLOOD

HOME MIGHT have been where Diarmuid were, but Diarmuid, Cairsten, and I weren't destined to go directly home.

There were soldiers in the way.

We left the inn early and arrived in our land before dusk. We saw the men trooping out o' the castle from a distance as we neared the walls around the village. Fortunately, the village sat in a valley, and the river—routed and rerouted—passed before it. We were above them, and they weren't looking at the ridge.

Cairsten suspected they thought the story o' Kaspar's betrothal were fancy and fabrication. Diarmuid thought they were all buggers.

It mattered not what I thought. We were all driven to the woods to hide, although Cairsten fretted that the underbrush would not let us stay hidden long. Snow had fallen in the two nights we'd been gone, which were good and bad—it allowed us deeper into the woods in the sled, but the woods didn't hide us as they might have.

Cairsten were driving tensely, and Diarmuid and I ducked into the bottom of the sled, our heads below the frame.

"We'll never do it," Diarmuid muttered. "They'll see us, sure."

"Maybe the forest'll save us," I told him hopefully. "It has before."

Diarmuid gaped at me and then tapped Cairsten on the shoulder. "Stop," he muttered harshly. "Stop, and pull out yer knife."

Before the sled had even drifted to a halt on top o' the crispy snow, Diarmuid spilled over the side, the small shovel he'd used to dig our privy in his hand. I saw what he had in mind and scrambled out too, getting on me hands and knees and digging snow between his shovelfuls.

In the background we heard a shout, a "Ho, there! Who passes?" but we were close, so close to the ground.

My hands were chilled even through my gloves, and the water'd soaked through my knees, but I did not stop. Diarmuid must have been as driven as I, because as he hit ground he said, "Gimme the blade!" and I didn't even flinch as the scarlet hit the snow and then trickled onto the bare ground.

Nothing happened, and I heard Cairsten grunt, and more blood added to the spell, and without being asked I took off my gloves.

"Gimme," I muttered.

"Nay, Teyth—yer too—"

"*Gimme!*" I snarled, because we could see them approaching.

"Ho, there! Who goes there? Be you the smith and—"

Diarmuid seized the blade from Cairsten, fell on his knees, and grasped my hand. Very carefully he cut at the meaty base o' the thumb, and three drops o' blood joined the rest to mingle with the water and the earth.

The snow, the gray sky, the shouting soldiers, the frigid black pine trees with their snowy loads—all disappeared.

We were surrounded by earth, warmed by the sun in late spring, and by tree roots forming a hollow. We could see the horses, separated from us by a thin veil of... other. A fine silver mesh, on the other side o' which were snow and soldiers and fear.

But not around us.

The cave we found ourselves in were close, and it were real. We were still crouched, the cold o' snow soaking into our flesh and bones, the wet o' it seeping into the earth. Our blood were pooling in the ground before us, swirling, spinning into a design, a filigree, a picture, sure as the cat, the house, the hammer, and the plow were pictures. I extended my finger, still dripping, to touch that pattern as it etched itself into the earth, but Diarmuid's rough hand on my wrist stopped me.

I met his eyes, and both of us looked at Cairsten. He nodded. To touch it were to break the spell, whatever enchantment bound us to this secret place—this warm, blood-beating heart o' the wood—and we dare not break it.

The soldiers were descending upon the horses.

Diarmuid and I gasped. We watched a spear point go into a flank, just deep enough to shed blood, as the soldiers shouted harsh questions into the air.

The horse reared up, the blood spattered, and the cart were abruptly in the cave with us, frightened horses and all.

Cairsten and Diarmuid secured them, calming them down, murmuring softly. We could not tell if the soldiers could hear us as we could hear them, but we did not want to risk it.

I stayed crouched by the ground, watching the pattern spread. Then I heard a breath that Diarmuid and Cairsten could not quite contain.

Unbidden, my glance wandered to the veil.

There were a giant looming behind the soldiers.

Not a giant, I thought, containing my own terror. A *spirit*. It were greater than them that violated this place—taller, stronger—and through the veil it appeared solid.

But the soldiers were looking right past the thing, and they could not seem to see.

We saw.

We saw one of the mighty arms pull back and release, and one of the soldiers flew through the air.

I could hear his bones crack, his skull mash as he hit a tree. The body fell to the ground as close to the veil as Cairsten's outstretched arm, and the soldier stared sightlessly through his helmet, his dead face slack. Before I could worry much about his death, about the spirit that had left his flesh and the darkness that must swallow us all, I saw that his blood were seeping through the snow.

"Oh, no," I whispered.

If our blood had started this spell, what would their blood do?

The spirit—great and brown and green, the shape o' a man with suggestions o' twined branches for limbs, growing twigs for fingers and toes, and tangled vines through animal skins for hair—he must have known.

He set about the soldiers in a hurry, the spirit o' forest vengeance, and soldier after soldier were tossed about, smashed, and, in one dreadful splash o' crimson and viscera, ripped in two.

And the whole time, I watched as the blood pool o' ours ran, formed rivulets, and grew into that twisting, pixilated filigree, the incantation o' forest soul.

At the same moment, the raw blood o' the first dead soldier dripped steadily in our vision, running through the thickness o' snow.

The last soldier wearing crimson and gold livery flew through the air. Before he landed, the first soldier's blood hit the earth.

And we were with the fettled horses, breathing harshly in the snow in the glade, surrounded by dead soldiers.

The earth around us buckled and heaved, and we were moved again, plopped like poppets at the hearth on the north side o' the woods—a two days' ride from our village, no soldiers in sight.

There were naught to say.

We met eyes, and Cairsten and Diarmuid settled the horses almost by rote. We stood in the unfamiliar whiteness, the slice marks throbbing on our chilled hands, and simply breathed white puffs into the air.

It were that, perhaps, that moved Cairsten to action.

"It's getting colder," he murmured, staring at a sky that had lost its fog and gained clouds. "A blizzard is coming. Probably be here Solstice Eve," he said, matter o' fact. "I ken the beasts are fractious and tired, but we've no time to cosset them."

Diarmuid and I nodded grimly, and we piled back into the sled.

The rest o' that day and the next were a blur o' snow under the runners, and hunger. We hadn't brought enough food for the extra two days, and we had no time to hunt. At one point, as we rested the horses and gave them melted snow, since the streams had frozen over, we saw two rabbits venturing out from the forest. They sat, noses quivering, staring at us with limpid eyes that practically begged us to eat them.

"Nay," Cairsten murmured, and Diarmuid and I heard the thread o' panic in his voice. "'Tis nice o' ye ter offer, but we have no time for skinning and roasting, and no blood to barter for. Thank ye—we shall have to manage on our own."

The conies shrugged, as though 'twere our loss, and hopped back into the forest, leaving the three o' us to throw ourselves into the sled.

The horses must have been feeling some panic o' their own, because they stretched themselves out in a long, ground-eating trot even as the snow started coming down, adding to their burden on the earth.

There were no soldiers left in front of the village as we pulled in through the great gate. Usually there were gatekeepers, sleepy soldiers who'd pulled sentry—not that anything dangerous ever tried to enter our village. It were more a sign o' power, Cairsten said. A signal that they *could* keep people out if they wished.

'Twere a waste. Such a waste. Why bother to keep people out unless they were a threat? I did not understand, but then, I didn't stand in the great stone tower that cast its icy shadow over our home this Solstice Eve, either.

We stabled the horses with Canda, and Cairsten asked her to pass on the news that we were safe and Kaspar were duly delivered to a place with its own prince where nobbut could touch him. We slunk exhaustedly into our home, and the first thing I noticed were the chill.

It were as though we were the heart in the body of the house, and without us, it had died.

Cairsten started the fire and all good things began.

He and Diarmuid brought in the tub and extra firewood, starting a fire in the wood-burning oven as well. We went through the food, bringing out the salt pork and pulling some potatoes from our stores and some tomatoes that Diarmuid had apparently preserved as well. I measured out flour, yeast, and salt, and for a comforting hour we moved about the house in established patterns.

We filled the tub from the icy pump and added kettles as fast as they heated. The men let me go first, and being clean were blissful. Afterwards, as I ran to my room wrapped in a bathing towel and holding an oil lamp to light the shadows, I remembered something.

When I returned to the kitchen, clean, dry, and dressed in a nightshirt and breeches (it were a compromise, since we weren't quite going to sleep), I produced two handfuls o' sweet candy.

"I'm sorry," I said, putting the wrapped sweets on the table. "I were… I mean, I'd been going to buy a candle to eat by for you, Cairsten, and…." My voice dropped as I spoke to Diarmuid. "I were going to buy ye some oil, the kind that smells good, for when ye went to see Kaspar," I whispered. "I'm sorry. I have no Solstice gifts but candy here. But… ye know, it be gifts, right?" My last Solstice gift had been the wee cart from Da. The first thing that Kump had destroyed.

I looked at them hopefully, needing their smiles, their cheer, because they had sustained me, grown me warm inside, from that day in early fall when Kump'd dragged me, frightened and deluded, to Cairsten's forge.

The next thing I knew, Cairsten had caught us both in a bear's great hug. "We're alive, Teyth. Yer both alive, me boys, and untouched. I'd give…." His voice choked, lowered. "I've given me blood—I'd give more—to know I've got me boys in me home, and their hearts are warm and beating."

I found myself engulfed, cared for, and loved.

Not even I could doubt it were love.

Diarmuid clung to us both, his hands bunching my nightshirt in his fist, his head buried against Cairsten's great chest, and although he did not cry, I felt the fine trembling in his hands.

Eventually we sat down to hurried stew and bread.

Afterward, Diarmuid disappeared into his room and came back with a book for me and a new, hand-tooled apron for Cairsten.

And Cairsten disappeared and came back with a shoer's pick for Diarmuid, and a small hammer with a hand-carved handle for me.

Both of them said, with all the veracity in their formidable souls, that the sweets, eaten at the end of the hard-fought meal, were the best part o' our night.

THE STORM continued through Solstice and the week beyond. On the fourth day after our return from Kaspar's hasty betrothal, Cairsten treated us to a dinner in the pub. We'd been hard at work since Solstice morning, catching up on necessary things. A trivet were not a small matter when ye were heating water for dinner during a blizzard, nor were a stovepipe nor a sled runner.

We'd worked hard, and were still tired from our journey—and tired o' bein' confined in the snug house, with the furs over the windows to keep out the freezing cold.

I watched Cairsten digest the news as we sat in the pub. Clancy's da, the candlemaker, had joined us, and he were full o' the scary days when the soldiers had taken over the town.

"There were soldiers out?" Cairsten asked ingenuously, and Diarmuid and I gazed at him with innocence in our eyes.

"Aye," said Fisher. Like Clancy, he were small boned, with an upturned nose and ginger hair. His freckles had faded, become part o' his ruddy face, but he were as obviously Clancy's da as Abel's round and jolly da were his. "It were frightening when ye left," Fisher added. "The prince sent out people looking for tha' boy all o'er t' village. We were lucky—we'd all been hidin' in our own homes—we hadn't seen him. They asked about yer boy D as well, and even about a passel o' brats getting underfoot."

Cairsten glowered, and Clancy's father nodded. "Aye. We 'ave no brats underfoot, which is what all o' us said. And as fer D—well, we all knew he'd been summoned to a job in the south."

Cairsten nodded. "Tha's the truth," he said, although everybody in the room knew it for a heinous lie. "So what happened to these soldiers? Did they find what they were looking for?"

"I know not," Fisher shrugged. "They disappeared. In fact, a whole squad o' them went into the forest. They didna return."

"Strange," Cairsten grunted into his ale.

"Aye. Well, tha' forest is strange. Ye doona antagonize the great spirits o' the world. Air, earth, fire, sea—ye feed 'em blood an' fear, an' they repay you a thousandfold."

"An' love," Diarmuid said, surprising us all. "Blood an' fear, or blood an' worship—it dinna matter ter the forest spirits, yeah?"

"Aye, son," Cairsten nodded, suddenly as sober as he were drunk. "An' love. I buried me wife an' son in tha' forest. I wanted them somewhere they'd be cared for."

Beside me I heard Diarmuid gasp, and I knew me own eyes were the size o' saucers. Blood an' love. Whether Cairsten knew it or not, he'd fed that forest spirit years before.

"If tha's wha' happened ter them men, it were too good fer 'em," Fisher said, meaning it.

Cairsten and Diarmuid drank to that, and I hefted my own root beer and joined them.

No more were said o' soldiers after that, nor forest spirits neither. No more were said o' Kaspar neither, unless we went to the bookseller's—and we still did. Diarmuid would take news o' Kaspar with polite interest, as well as free books from parents who seemed as kind and understanding as any I'd ever met. And my interest in the pictures and the words, in the symbols and the meaning, continued.

Together, we made it through until spring.

In the spring, we spent many hours digging the garden out and replanting. Since I'd come to love the produce the garden gave before I put the labor into it, I were not so oppressed by the labor. My friends came to help, and even brought treats and sang songs as we dug, and Cairsten paid them in coppers as well.

When that were done, there were planting an' watering. The same pipes to the water closet also sprayed out o' an oilskin hose to keep the garden wet when the rains did not cooperate.

For the most part, everything cooperated.

After the garden were watered, there were work to catch up with. One morning, while Diarmuid ran errands, Cairsten thrilled me by having me go get my own hammer from my room.

He thrust a piece o' iron into the freshly pumped fire and pulled it out glowing red. "Shape it," he told me. "Tha's low-grade iron to make a coat hook," he said. "Now pound away!"

Diarmuid returned an hour later, and I'd heated the thing three times over. It were a jagged, sorry piece o' metal without even a bend in the middle, but I'd labored over it something fierce.

Cairsten, in the meantime, had turned out twelve such hooks, and I looked at the mangled, twisted thing on my anvil, practically in tears.

Diarmuid took one look to assess the situation and had me put the piece o' metal in the crucible above the fire.

"'Tis brittle now," he said gently. "Too many trials for strong mettle."

"Ye warned me," I said stoically, crushed by all my dreams o' being a genius with the metal as I saw Diarmuid and Cairsten be every day.

"Yeah, we did. But ye think ye see, right? Ye think, 'I know a way ter make it not so.' Humility is good in a smith. It means ye'll plan every hammer stroke, so as ter not waste yer metal or yer effort."

I smiled at him, relieved. This winter, he'd been more o' silence than I had. As the earth quickened and the sky turned to blue, he'd begun speaking more at dinner and had even begun to read me his coveted storybooks at night.

Until then, I hadn't realized how much I missed the Diarmuid o' the fall.

He were back again—quieter, aye, but still sound and gentle, as sweet and humble as he'd ever been. His skin tanned in the summer, and he reminded me o' one of the trees in the forest: strong, growing, gentle, and brown.

I'd listen to him pass gas in the morning with an eager heart, but his instructions on metalwork were far more useful.

By the end o' the day, with his help on the tongs, I'd hammered three passable hooks, and two that were simply beginner's shite. It mattered not. For brief moments, I'd held power in me hands, and it were sweet.

That night, as I sat and listened to Diarmuid read, the patterns in my head began to swirl, to lengthen. I saw a filigree, like the one in the storybook, but powerful, mysterious. I saw it in silver and iron, in gold, platinum, and bronze, sprinkled with jewels. It were shaped much like... almost exactly like....

The whorls of blood as the forest shaped them in the earth.

My eyes flew open, a pound o' excitement in my veins. I wanted to do that. I *yearned* to do that. To create a *thing,* a frieze, a screen o' metal, all in the shape o' the runes the forest had traced in the ground with our blood.

Suddenly, as though I were looking at a picture, I saw the ruined and mangled metal o' my day's endeavors. My excitement eased, and my breathing leveled.

I had much to learn, I realized. I could do it, perhaps, but not now. Not as a child o' ten winters.

But Cairsten had no intention o' stopping my instruction, and Diarmuid would be here—would *always* be here—and I would learn. I could create something, something beautiful, something destined to last beyond time o' flesh and youth.

That thing I'd begun to fear, the blackness that came when yer flesh were rent and yer blood spilt—that were pushed into the recesses o' my mind then.

I had a way, I thought, a purpose, a spirit that would keep my heart beating even when my body failed.

I could be immortal.

WATCHING BAIRNS GROW

I KEPT this ambition secret and close for the next years. I'd sketch the design in the borders o' my parchment as I worked on my letters, and I took any quiet moment at the forge to learn from Cairsten or Diarmuid's able hands.

They were good teachers, both o' them, and while Diarmuid were the more patient, Cairsten were the more zealous, and both o' their souls tended to perfection in their craft.

I saw naught o' my mother or brother during this time, although some days, in one o' the windows on the side of the tower, I would see a small boy looking out avidly over the village. Hoping it were Aubrey, I would wave like mad, and the boy, seeing me—even across houses and shops, across the washing square and in the midst o' crowds— would wave back.

It were Aubrey, I would think, warm and happy in the knowledge. It had to be. And he remembered me. And he were safe, and fed, and given that joyous waving, the castle had not yet devoured his soul.

Diarmuid grieved for a time, but he recovered himself. He were, as always, steady and kind, with surprising humor. As I grew, I found my eyes followed him in quiet moments. I simply liked to know where he were, who he were talking to, what he were doing. I watched for two years as he politely refused company—both girls and boys—during the Solstice, Beltane, or Samhain gatherings. No coupling in the shadows for Diarmuid, no. In the third year, Kerrigan's older sister gave up on her faithless, ruined fiancé and drank too much ale. Diarmuid allowed himself to be coaxed into a corner by her. I saw their gentle movements. Too sad to be coupling, mostly it were comforting, and I thought mournfully o' my own growing limbs.

I were not yet Diarmuid's height, but we all knew I would pass him up soon.

I were not yet Diarmuid's width across the shoulders, and I never would be.

I were not yet Diarmuid's age, when he had risked his life and ours for the boy he loved—in fact, I were three years shy. But I were getting there. He would have wed Kaspar if he'd had the chance—and no one else seemed to have caught his fancy. Three years I had before I could be wed at Solstice (although coupling were common before then).

Then two.

By my fifteenth summer, I'd passed Diarmuid up in height by half a handspan, with more growing in me. That Beltane, Clancy were forward, spiriting me away to a corner before I knew what were happening. Kerrigan joined us with Abel, and what followed were awkward and hilarious and the kind o' coupling ye can only do with good friends on a night o' drunken revels. When the night were over, Diarmuid found me half-naked in a corner—with Clancy bared to the waist and asleep on me shoulder, Abel with his head still in my lap though my cock were now sleeping, and Kerrigan, fully clothed by now, curled under Abel's arm.

Diarmuid regarded me soberly. I grunted and politely disentangled myself, then helped to cover Clancy's breasts so I could tuck her in. It looked as though she and her friends were merely sleeping.

Silently we turned and left the dying party, the warm spring night fading to gray light as we walked.

"Did ye enjoy yerself?" he asked dryly, but I gave it my honest thought.

"I dinna think Abel likes men like I do," I said after a moment. His mouth on my cock had been goodhearted, but mostly reluctant. No—Abel had not been excited to do that, but since I'd done it to him, to show the girls, it had seemed only fair. He'd needed more ale in him than were probably wise.

"And ye? Ye dinna like the girls?" he asked curiously.

I adjusted my stride so as not to make him trot. "They dinna...." I looked at him sideways. "They dinna make me hard," I said apologetically. "I.... Ye know, Clancy, she fancies me. It would be...."

Ah, hells.

"It would be convenient," Diarmuid said, his voice as regretful as mine. Kerrigan's sister had been an occasional visitor for dinner this last year, but if he'd been with her this even, it would be more in the nature o' farewell.

"What I want…." I wanted to drape my arm over his shoulders and hold him to me—anything but this curious desolation. "Is not convenient."

"Nay," Diarmuid said, stopping in the lane before our house and meeting my eyes. I turned to meet his. "Is not convenient. Not now."

I swallowed. "When will it be?"

Diarmuid's smile were shy, and the ruddy crescents on his cheeks were not from the redness o' his skin at the forge.

"I thought I'd wait 'til ye knew I were not the only one out there," he said apologetically. "But there be young men yer age who like men, and ye dinna like them. Ye'd rather frolic with yer playmates than look fer summat ye dinna know."

"Aye," I murmured. The boy who worked for the carter, the one who'd helped Diarmuid learn to shoe horses—he'd ignored Diarmuid, which astounded me, and flirted with me at every chance. Another boy, one who came in from the surrounding farms for supplies for his family, he'd flirted with both o' us. And tonight, I'd seen him in company with the carter's boy, which were only right since we were not game.

"'Aye' what, Silence?" Diarmuid said, sounding exasperated. "Tha's not enow o' an answer, not for this. This…. Me heart, it canna do this again, not if I'm a passing fancy, yeah-yeah? I dinna want a child in me bed, I want a man in me life. Ye ken tha'?"

"I'm near ter grown!" I protested, although my heart knew it were not true.

He smiled kindly, and I thought my truthful heart would be broken.

"Not in body nor in spirit, not yet," he said, and insult o' insults, he reached out to ruffle my hair.

I caught his hand. "What… what're we ter do?" I wanted him so badly, even exhausted and smelling o' Beltane sex. There were a warmth to Diarmuid—the knowledge o' sweet soft earth, o' iron, o' strength, o' warm hands on my shoulder whenever my heart were sore—it rent my stomach with longing.

"We wait," Diarmuid murmured, turning his hand to squeeze mine. "Yer not grown yet, 'tis true. But soon. When me heart says yeah an' yer heart says aye, we'll know. Yeah-yeah?"

I pulled his hand to me mouth, knowing o' pictures o' princes and princesses. I had no use for them mostly, but the courtly gesture—*that* appealed to me. Softly, remembering the touches o' my friends the night before, I brushed my lips over his battered knuckles. He let out a shuddering breath and reclaimed his hand. When I looked up, his eyes were closed.

"Aye," I whispered, and watched as one corner of his mouth turned up.

I followed him around the canvas we pulled over the forge when it were cold and empty, through the hallway, to the front door of the house. It were only as I grew that I saw most houses didn't have a storefront as a house front, but I could not imagine any other home.

We were just opening the door when Cairsten rumbled up behind us. I'd been so busy with my own "frolicking," as Diarmuid put it, that I hadn't noticed where Cairsten had gone.

Diarmuid and I turned to him in surprise.

"Cairsten!" Diarmuid said, half laughing.

And even as we entered the house, the bright light o' morning filling it, we could see the flush that traveled his cheeks under his great black beard.

"Beltane is not just for the young," he murmured, "but staying up all night is." He yawned this last, while Diarmuid and I retired to our room.

Over the years, Cairsten and Diarmuid had become less apprehensive about frightening me with their nakedness, but this morning, Diarmuid turned his back toward me as he slid his nightshirt on.

This morning, I did the same.

"D?" I murmured after we'd fallen into our separate beds.

"Yeah?"

"Who do ye think—"

"Cairsten?"

"Aye."

"Canda, o' course. He's been sneaking out t' bed her fer years."

"Huh," I wondered to myself. "Fancy tha'."

"Ugh," Diarmuid murmured, surprising me. "Would rather not. Thinking o' yer elders in bed is no good way to sleep."

I laughed, remembering that Diarmuid were good at making me smile, and on that note we fell asleep.

IF I thought anything great and terrible would follow from a conversation when I were fifteen and stumbling from exhaustion an' lovemaking, I were to be sorely disappointed.

But I had no such hopes. Diarmuid were as steady as ever, and that were something I needed—*had* needed, if truth be known, since the day I'd shown up on their doorstep. I'd needed Diarmuid to be kind and Cairsten to be firm, and together, they could have the raising o' me.

What that conversation did—what it needed to do—were make me *aware*.

I were aware o' the carter's boy, Jad, who flirted and touched my arm, and o' how he followed me with his eyes.

I were aware o' Amben, the farmer's lad, who stared with hunger at both Diarmuid and me. I watched Diarmuid be kind to him in a way that left him with no hope, and I used the same gentle rebuff when it were my turn.

I were aware that the frolicking I'd done with my mates were best saved for Samhain, and that Abel should maybe not be pressed into the lot o' us if my body didn't excite him.

I spent the next year judging my moves regarding my cock and my mouth with the sense o' how I would look Diarmuid in the eye if I did it. So when Jad threw me against the back wall of the smithy in a sudden lusty abandon, I returned his kiss and withdrew.

"Nay," I said breathily, and not without regret. He were blond an' muscled and pretty as they come, but Diarmuid's almond-shaped eyes mocked me. "Yer pretty, but yer probably bedding seven other lads on yer route. I'm nobbut special."

Jad chuckled a little and backed away. "Well, ye are *now*," he said with some feeling, and I turned from him back to my work.

"I'm nobbut a blacksmith," I told him, thinking o' the wrought iron on the roster for the day. Gleefully I pulled on my triple-layered leather gloves. "But I do love my work."

Jad left, chuckling, and Diarmuid walked into the stall from the street, nodding his head courteously as they passed.

"'E fettle ye?" Diarmuid asked, his voice as casual as could be.

"'E tried ter shag me up agin the wall," I told him soberly as I pulled the first bar for the frieze out o' the fire with tongs. The hammer were heavier than my first by far, and I wielded it with a certain skill. Diarmuid and Cairsten left me the artistic work, because I seemed to have an eye for it, and because every time I designed something pretty, I begged for the leftover metal, be it silver, gold, or iron. I kept sketching on parchment, but my handwork with the pen didn't seem to equal my handwork with the hammer and tongs, so I had done nothing with my metal hoard yet, but I dreamed.

"Did 'e really?" Diarmuid sputtered, staring at me as I worked. "Did 'e think tha'd work?"

I finished pounding the curve into the metal and thrust it into the oaken barrel with the water. Now that I were no longer the water boy, we took turns—whoever weren't working an anvil were in charge o' filling the barrel.

"I doona know," I said, not wanting to talk too much about it. "I were naught but an open arse ter 'im—that'un, he has no shine."

Diarmuid were stacking steel bars next to the forge, and stoking the forge with more coal and pumping it as well. When it were hot enough, he put one o' the wide, flat iron bars in and began to heat it fast and hot to make strong metal. For all he wished to be a horseshoer, Diarmuid were a swordsmith, and nothing could make that gift go away.

"Yer interested in the shiny, are ye?" he teased gently. "There be a goldsmith in the next village. I hear he favors lads!"

"Aw, shutyerbit," I muttered, but I were smiling.

He laughed, and for a while we worked together, our companionship a perfect thing.

THAT WINTER were particularly trying for me. Diarmuid and I spent night after night turning our backs when we dressed, or making sure when one were in the tub, the other were in another room, or even in the privy outside. It should not have been so difficult, aye? Near to seven years we'd been sharing a room. I used to look with admiration on his muscles, his tight stomach, the compact, fit form.

But this winter, through one forbidden look after another, I began to memorize more o' Diarmuid than I thought to be comfortable with.

It did not make me fear, though. It only made me crave.

Diarmuid had seen twenty-three summers by this time, and although he'd never be as broad as Cairsten, and not near as tall as me, he would always be solid. Were he some other profession—candlemaker, carter, farmer—he'd be slight and stringy. Were he a runner who took mail and packages from one town to the next, he'd be lithe.

But he were a blacksmith, and he were trim and solid, his shoulders, waist, and hips joined together like two triangles, overlapping at the waist. The triangle that were his hips were small and narrow, and the one that were his shoulders were wide at the inverted base. His arms bulged, his thighs too, and his face were weathering some from the heat of the forge.

It did not matter.

What were left under the muscles were a brown man. His hair streaked gold in the summer, yeah, but it were sand brown most other times, and his eyes were still shaped like almonds and colored that quiet, earthy brown. They crinkled in the corners when he smiled, and his nose were almost a little thin for his short, square jaw.

Jad said he were a little plain, but I didna see it.

Ambren, the farmer's lad, said he were the prettier of the two o' us, and I didn't see that either. Diarmuid, he were all that were beauty. That were all.

His patience were exquisite—and excruciating.

One evening Cairsten were gone to the farms. He did this in the early spring, loading a cart with his tools and a pump bellows and using a deserted forge at a long-departed crofter's. He'd ply his trade there, fixing plows, horse tack, horseshoes, and pots and pans, all in a span o' three days. He made a great deal in copper coins then, and the people didn't have to leave the business of planting to service the tools o' their trade.

Diarmuid and I set up the tub, a habit so ingrained in us we would not dream o' changing it. Diarmuid bathed first, remembering his bathing sheet and drying off before retreating to the bedroom for his clothes.

It were my turn next, and this time….

Well, I conveniently left my sheet lying on my bed.

I scrubbed quickly but thoroughly, using the cedar-scented soap in my hair and scrubbing three times the usual before rinsing off. I scrubbed me creases extra good as well, not locking in my head why I were doing these things but doing them all the same.

When I were done, feeling as sweet and as soft in skin as I had after my first bath, I stood up and let meself drip as dry as I could into the tub.

"D!" I called. "D! I left me bath sheet in there. Can ye bring it? And the mat as well!"

"Ye forgot?" Diarmuid grumbled as he wandered into the kitchen. He had breeches on, but no tunic, no jerkin, and although the shadows were long through the windows, the balminess o' the air let me not be quite so cold. My nipples were pebbled, aye, but my equipment weren't shrinking any.

"Aye," I lied, taking the towel from his hand. I used it to dry off my hair first, and while I were still standing, seized the wooden comb from the counter and dragged it through my straight black hair. I had a rather long face, so letting my hair grow in shaggy bangs around my eyes and layers over my collar were a becoming look for me. It weren't why I did it—like Diarmuid, I weren't overly fond of the barber—but it didn't look bad.

I knew my eyes, looking through that fringe o' bangs, were blue-gray and enormous.

I made sure to turn them on Diarmuid as I combed my hair back from my forehead.

"Cold chicken fer dinner?" I asked. Diarmuid had fried a bloody great batch o' it the night before, in order to see Cairsten off in style. Cairsten had taken a goodly portion with him, and what were left would feed us until he returned.

"Yeah-yeah," Diarmuid said, but he hadn't moved, and his hooded brown eyes lingered on my body. I'd passed him up in height two years ago, but my shoulders were less the width o' his. I would never be as brawny as Diarmuid, but my ranginess suited me.

Clancy still fancied me, and although I'd been gentle but firm with her, the keening of her battered heart made me not so likely to run with my friends as I had been.

"Is no fair," Kerrigan had told me bitterly not more than a week before. "Yer hidin' from us like ye've done summat wrong!"

"I doona want her ter suffer," I said wretchedly. "Just… when she doona look ter me with such longing, Ker. I'll be her friend, aye?"

She patted my cheek. "Yer a nice boy, Teyth, and is a sweet notion, but maybe ye should try ter find the words ter tell her."

"The words? The words are I like women fine, but not in me bed—but those aren't the words she wants ter hear. So I have no other words 'til she do."

I stared at someone's front yard then, grass thick and filling in after the winter snows.

"Silence," Kerrigan humphed, and I had naught for her but a shrug.

"Is me name," I said with dignity.

But now, naked and catching Diarmuid's eye, I wished for words. I wished for seduction, for promises, for a plan for us, but all I had were all I ever had.

My name.

"Ye 'ave something ye wish ter say, Teyth?" Diarmuid asked softly.

"Everything," I muttered, miserable. I set the comb down and dropped the sheet on the floor so I could step on it and dry my feet. I stepped out and into his space, and Diarmuid didn't step back.

"Yer prettier this year than last year," he said, a slight smile on his lips to let me know he were teasing.

"Am I pretty enow?" I asked tentatively.

He met my eyes, and his tongue, pink and vulnerable, darted out to moisten his lips.

"Yer very pretty, Teyth." As though he could not stop himself, he reached out with one hand and traced the ridge of my collarbone until it ended at my throat. My heart about ceased its beating and then resumed, triple time.

The touch of Diarmuid's hand on my bare skin shuddered through me.

"Ye want me," I said, satisfaction saturating my voice, my body. Between my legs, my member began to swell and ache. I'd touched it in the night, when Diarmuid were sleeping. I'd imagined his hands on my body and found quiet, glorious release in my own fist.

"Aye," Diarmuid said now. He leaned closer, his breath dusting my cheek. "I do. Yer... yer not yet grown, though, Teyth. Not...." His hand were still at my throat, and my pulse throbbed against his skin.

"Aye," I murmured, because I had no other words. He were there. Right there. Our lips touched briefly, his eyes searched mine, and I nodded, then closed my eyes before I could betray anything— nervousness, exultation, the tiniest bit o' fear.

His mouth on mine were sweet. Bitter tea were on his breath, but his tongue were gentle, tracing my lips, seeking entrance into my mouth like a gentleman courting a virgin.

I were no virgin.

I parted my mouth and pulled him in. He groaned, a needy sound, and his hands cupped my cheeks on either side. He held me, and repositioned his mouth, and kissed again. I could barely hear our breathing, my heart thundered so loud, and I reached my hands down and cupped his arse, squeezing, pulling him into my body.

The vibrations o' his moan in my mouth vibrated straight in my groin.

I cried out and buried my face in his shoulder, thrusting against him, feeling his cock through his homespun pants and his smallclothes. My whole body shook—the need, the want appalling—and he soothed me, stroking my hair, calming me, until only the ache of arousal remained.

Our breathing were still harsh, but less rushed after a moment, and I turned my face on his shoulder and gazed coyly into his eyes.

"Is like fire," I breathed.

He raised his hand to my face and stroked my hair back, a bemused smile on his face. "Is like air and water," he murmured. "Fills me, Teyth. An' I not be filled in so long."

He were lowering his face to mine again, to kiss me one more time, when a girl's voice called through the smithy. It grew closer, hollering my name, which meant it were someone we knew to go through the canvas tent flap and come to the door. After a moment, a heartbeat, I whispered, "Kerrigan! Is Kerrigan!"

"Go change," Diarmuid ordered tersely. He'd brought his tunic in with the towel, and he were sliding it over his head as I grabbed my bath sheet and ran for the back bedroom.

By the time I'd pulled my breeches and tunic on, and grabbed stockings so that I might venture out if need be, Diarmuid had let Kerrigan in and were currently holding her arms as though trying to keep her calm.

He lifted his head as I entered, and I took a hurried breath. "Is no' good news," he said, face so sober I felt my knees wobble.

"Wha'?" I asked, slipping on my stockings and handing Diarmuid his own pair. He took them with a nod and began to don them.

Kerrigan had grown from a plain, sturdy girl into a lovely young woman o' eighteen winters. Her face were an elegant oval, and she had large brown eyes to add to the impression o' serene strength. There were no serenity today, though, and although we were dressing as she spoke, she were bouncing on her toes, her simple skirts swirling around her ankles as if we could not dress fast enough. "The prince," she said harshly. "Hurry. We have no time!"

"What o' im?" I asked, hopping. He'd been quiet, mostly, since he'd lost a passel o' soldiers in the woods. Every so often he'd take his cart through the town, and we'd hide our young'uns. He had an eye, it seemed, for over fourteen and under twenty.

The last time me and Clancy had spoken, we'd heard the shouts of warning through the street and spent a breathless, almost happy moment scrambling through the back of the oil seller's tent and into Canda's garden. We'd crouched there, between Canda's pear tree and the wall, listening to the village rousting itself like a hornet's nest and waiting for the man to go back to his great cave o' a castle, and kissing for sport. At the end, when the skies were growing dark and the late winter were getting too cold, she'd tugged my hand, smiling.

"Come with me ter bed, Teyth," she whispered. "Me parents'll let us handfast, an' even if there be someone later, for now we can frolic together, aye?"

I'd pulled away regretfully. "Nay," I murmured, remembering Diarmuid's warning o' not breaking his heart. "Nay. I.... It were only in fun, Clancy. I told ye I'm not... not made fer girls, aye?"

"Then kiss someone else under a pear tree," she'd snapped. We'd vaulted different stone walls then, each to return to our own homes, and we'd been avoiding each other since.

"He came by to purchase oil today, and she were dressed... ye ken, like a boy?" I did ken. Her hair were often pulled back in a rough tail, then doubled back on itself, and she wore her da's old breeches so she didn't soak her skirts in oil. She were a plain girl, still freckled, and it were her openmouthed and lusty laughter that made her fun as a mate. Truth were, when she were dressed for her work, Diarmuid were almost prettier by standards o' girls.

"So what? She looked like a boy, an'—"

"It were reckless! She assumed, I think, aye? She wouldna be wanted, e'en though she know he doona care."

"He dinna do it fer pleasure," Diarmuid said harshly. "He ruts ter show he owns us. He seized 'er then, yeah?"

"Aye," Kerrigan said, miserable. "He seized her, an' her da had the townsmen block the cart with barrels. The prince—he's sayin' she's not wed nor handfasted. He's got rights ter 'er, ye ken? Like offerings."

Diarmuid and I met eyes, and he nodded. "Boots," he muttered, and together we ran for the front door, hauling on our boots and doing the laces on the run through the smith's corridor.

It were dark and growing chilly in the early evening, and we followed Kerrigan through the streets to the end of the market near the baker's stall.

Every man in the village were there, along with any woman not hiding in fear at home with her children. They were all sitting on barrels or washtubs or, in the case o' Canda, on a borrowed cart pulled by a placid gelding. Looking at the lot o' them, I felt a sense o' pride. These were strong people, and they would not let one o' their children disappear.

"Get out of the way, or I shall run you down." The prince's carriage were pulled by two enormous draft horses, not native to this land. It were brightly painted royal blue, and thick, baroque scrollwork marked the sides with gold.

"Ye canna take our children!" Clancy's da cried. "Tha's me girl there!"

"She was dressed as a boy, and I seized her as help. This village *owes* me a tithe of workers, remember? Consider her my Beltane offering."

I looked at Diarmuid worriedly, but he shook his head. "He can take her if she's unattached, but only if he's short on washwomen." The prince had been gifting his friends with the farms he broke. The farmers usually went to the castle—the likelihood o' his being short on any help at all were thin.

"What were our elders thinking?" I blurted, angry.

"They were thinking we'd lost several o' our men on a nearby field in the fall," Diarmuid snapped, and my mouth opened and closed o' its own. So much o' this life had been forged when I were a child at my mother's knee. For a moment I floundered, lost in the unfairness o' a world under the tower o' stone.

Diarmuid, fortunately, remembered why we were there.

"She's not unattached!" he shouted. The populace fell silent, all o' them staring at Diarmuid through the thickening dark. Diarmuid looked through the crowd and met eyes meaningfully with Clancy's father. The man closed his eyes and swallowed, both in gratitude and sorrow.

The prince squinted through the encroaching dark as though he didn't believe what he heard.

"You only like men," he said, and he sounded almost hurt.

Diarmuid turned a grim face toward me. "Our apprentice, young Teyth. They be handfasted this Solstice, yeah-yeah?"

This last he aimed at the crowd, and they all looked at me with eyes that said they knew exactly what this were, and they'd go along with it ter save one o' theirs.

"Aye!" they all shouted with one voice, and they all turned to the prince with new resolution.

The prince's face hardened as Diarmuid and I met his eyes.

He inclined his head slightly. "My mistake," he said smoothly. "I shall have to check on the new couple periodically, to make sure they are happy."

"We dinna hold our young'uns ter a handfast like an indenture," Diarmuid replied tartly. "They fast in hope, not fer fear, then. If they be findin' another ter wed, then tha' be their own mind, yeah-yeah?"

I don't know what the prince would have said, but the townsfolk were geared to answer now. To a one, they all opened their mouths and said, "Aye!" in unison.

The prince glared, the expression clear even in the dark gray. Suddenly, his eyes were drawn to my face.

"You—apprentice. Do I know you?"

"Nay," I answered.

"Nay? That is the only answer you have to give me?"

"His name be Silence," Diarmuid said, and I very carefully didn't look him in the eye. Aubrey. Those glimpses o' him in the tower, growing, showed a boy like me, with straight black hair, a narrow face, and probably blue eyes to boot. "Tha's nearly the only words ye'll get. If ye dinna ken 'im, ye dinna ken."

"I 'ken' him," the prince said thoughtfully. "I shall figure where."

"An' what?" Diarmuid challenged, while my heart stuttered and rolled like a runaway barrel.

"The people in this village seem to run wild," the prince replied. "I shall… mentor the boy."

My heart froze in my mouth. The boy. He knew. Diarmuid's hand locked on my shoulder, and I swallowed.

I were Silence, after all.

"Ye be doin' tha'," Diarmuid said easily, like it weren't no pain for us. "Ye be mentoring. But ye shouldna bugger what aren't yers. The girl, Yer Highness. She be not yers."

The prince disappeared. In a moment, a girl, naked past the waist, her breeches dragged off her hips, were thrown out of the carriage. She fell in the mud, her hair tumbling from its knot in the back o' her neck, her face bloodied and bruised.

Her father got there first, an' then us and Kerrigan. Kerrigan were wearing a cloak, and she pulled it from her shoulders and wrapped it around Clancy's body, while Clancy yanked her breeches up.

"Our house," Diarmuid murmured. "Teyth—ye, the girls, Fisher—tha's all." To the crowd he called, "We be goin' home now!"

Canda waited until all the others were gone and far off the road before clucking to the horse and getting out of the way.

The driver whipped the horses then, his lash sharp enough to raise red welts on their tan backsides, the blood appearing black in the dim light.

None o' us lingered in the road. In fact, most o' us were out o' sight before the wheels had gone round even once.

Clancy were crying so hard I lifted her up ter carry her for a few houses, and by the time I got to the forge, everyone were waiting for us. I wanted so badly to talk to Diarmuid—to thank him, to blame him, to cry on him—name an emotion, and that were what roiled in my heart.

But Clancy, my friend, were losing her composure, violated, frightened, and hurt.

Diarmuid had added the kettle o' water to our bath, an' some o' his oil for scent as well.

"Ye want ter bathe, now, Clance?" I asked softly.

Her answer were to sob harder in relief.

"Kerri?" I said, and she nodded back.

"I'll look to 'er. Ye...." She closed her eyes. "He'll know where the blacksmith is. The look on 'is face when ye were speakin', Diarmuid—he'll not be takin' kindly ter either o' ye."

Diarmuid and I met eyes, and then Clancy's father spoke up.

"Teyth?" I looked at him, the small ginger man with all the freckles. He seemed smaller now, grief stricken, and I wished I had a better way.

"Aye?"

"We... I mean, she wept on 'er mum 'bout ye. At first, I thought ye were... lettin' 'er down easy, but... ye care fer my girl. An' ye jus' gave up a future—"

"Not a future, Da," Clancy spoke up, still leaning against my chest, her voice clogged. "A year. Can ye find me a place in a year? I...." Her shoulders shook again. "I doona doubt Teyth loves me, Da, but is not fair if he canna love me like...."

Kerrigan stepped forward and looked at all of us, taking Clancy from my arms. "Go set up the bedroom," she ordered. "She'll need ter sleep 'ere fer some time."

"Willna Cairsten be surprised," Diarmuid said softly, but he led us down the hallway, lighting an oil lamp from a taper as he went.

In the bedroom, the two beds on either side of the room seemed to mock us. I'd had a thought, as Diarmuid's mouth had closed on mine, o' pushing the two o' them together and sleeping next to a body for the first time since my little brother.

Now I were sleeping with the equivalent o' my sister, and I were not pleased.

But I would not send Clancy out in the world with no protection, either. Still, I heard Diarmuid sigh as the two o' us got behind me bed, lifted it, and shoved it next to his.

"But D," I said after a moment, looking at our handiwork, "where will *ye* sleep?"

Diarmuid shrugged, but I could feel the sadness in him too. "On th' couch, Teyth—where'd ye thinkit?"

"I thought…." I thought that kiss would be the new place in my soul where we'd live. "Ne'ermind," I muttered, closing my eyes and turning away.

His hand, warm and firm on me shoulder, surprised me. So did his voice near my ear. "A year, Teyth. It were prolly—"

"If ye say is fer the best, I'll…." I couldn't finish that sentence, but his hand tightened on my shoulder, and I did not imagine the kiss on my head.

"Nay," he murmured. "I canna say tha'. Were not fer any good whatsoe'er."

We separated and turned toward Fisher, who were wiping his face with the back o' his hand.

"A year," he vowed solemnly. "I'll go get some clothes fer when she gets out of the bath, an' let her mum know how she's doing."

"Her mum can come here tonight," Diarmuid said, surprising me. "Teyth an' I, we'll sleep in Cairsten's bed—'tis big enow fer two. Let Clancy have her mum an' Kerrigan. Ye can sleep on the couch. Let anyone come knocking who wants—no man can say they're not living here."

I looked at him and swallowed. One night, maybe two, lying together in Cairsten's bed. It would have to last us until Clancy's da found her a husband in another town.

Fisher left, and Diarmuid and I stayed in the bedroom, leaning against the headboard side by side, waiting for the grieving and healing of the women. Our bodies were pressed together, knees to thighs to hips, and Diarmuid surprised me by leaning his head on my shoulder.

"Comfortable, are ye?" I asked dryly, and he flashed me a sweet smile from gentle brown eyes.

"Yeah-yeah. Do ye object?"

"Nay."

I gave in to comfort and wrapped my arm around his shoulder because he let me.

"This isn't what I wanted," I felt compelled to say, thinking painfully on that kiss, on our bare bodies in the kitchen.

"I'm sorry," he murmured, brushing my face with his hand. I closed my eyes and that moment came back, because as often as we'd sat in the same room together, we'd never sat like this.

"Doona be," I said shortly, and he pulled his hand back in hurt. "Ach! No, be not angry!" I begged. "I.... Ye were marvelous, standing up ter the prince, there. Ye thought so fast, an' spoke so well."

He looked away. "I did what I must. Is not enow. Ye wouldha done the same, yeah-yeah?"

"Nay," I said, feeling it. "I watched ye speaking, and I only had one word. The forest word. Murder."

I thought he would pull from me, but he regarded me soberly instead.

"Is not the only word," he murmured.

"Nay?"

"Nay. Murder wouldna get ye here. It wouldna get me this." He pushed up and our mouths met. I let him lead the kiss while I were threading my fingers through his hair. Tongue, mouth, teeth, kindness. Were such a simple thing, but I could not stop. He pulled back after a few moments and rested his head on my shoulder again. Both o' us were breathing harder.

When he could speak again, Diarmuid's voice ached into the silence.

"I always loved ye," he said softly. "Yer body grew, yer heart grew, the love grew. Were it tha' way with ye?"

"Aye," I whispered. I had the words in my heart, the carefully hoarded moments o' us working side by side at the forge, o' looking up and seeing Diarmuid, face intent on his task, and knowing all the world were well when we were side by side. The physical moment o' seeing his muscles heave and wanting him, and the moments o' kindness too numerous to count. Even that moment in the forest, after taking a piss, when his soon-to-be-departed lover slept in the sled. All the moments, all the stories he'd read, all the times he'd looked at my careful sketchings, tracing them with a callused finger and saying, "This'll be summat, Teyth. I ken it deep."

There were no words for that.

I kissed his temple, and repeated it, those images driving behind my eyes. "Aye." And then, the words I could think ter say, the ungrateful ones. Always with me, it were the ungrateful ones. "I resent this year," I told him. "I doona know how ter change it, but it festers under me skin."

He cupped my cheek, and my chest swelled with the yearning— not just o' this moment, but o' all the moments before and after.

"Dinna be angry," he murmured. "Dinna resent it. Be grateful for this moment here, for the others stolen from time. Be happy because ye want me back. I know I feared fer the longest time. I woke ye up last Beltane, and yer eyes searched mine out, and suddenly ye wanted me. There ye were, covered in sex an' bodies, and ye wanted *me*. I couldna stop wanting ye, not fer a thousand years."

Ah! Gods, he could make it sweet. My Diarmuid—he could make pain and waiting sweet. I closed my eyes against the surge behind them, not sure where it came from, this thick emotion clogging my head.

"Yeah-yeah?" Diarmuid whispered, stroking my cheek.

"Aye."

There were no more words after that. They clogged in my throat, and perhaps Diarmuid had used all his good ones. I did not know, but when Kerrigan came knocking, we were simply sitting on the bed, Diarmuid in my arms, listening to our breaths, grateful.

We parted when Kerrigan entered, but not as though we'd done summat wrong. That morning, when Diarmuid and I had helped Cairsten load his gear, Diarmuid had brushed up against me, his body hot and live. Even before that kiss in the bathtub, I think we'd both cleaned ourselves o' any wrongdoing about the plans we had for each other.

Kerrigan didn't measure us as she walked in, but just burst out with what she had on her mind. "I feel ungrateful, Diarmuid, but I think we're all starving."

"Yeah-yeah," Diarmuid said, smiling slightly. "There be chicken in the cold box. Ye want we should come in and dish up some supper?"

"Aye, tha'd be lovely." Kerrigan smiled gratefully, her brown eyes shadowed.

She took my arm as Diarmuid led, and I said quietly, "How is she?"

"Angry. Fiercely angry. But grateful ter ye, fer being her friend after all. This...." She looked up to where Diarmuid had entered the kitchen and were setting about making supper with his usual quiet efficiency. "I interrupted summat, didn't I?"

I grimaced. "Aye."

"How long have ye an' Diarmuid—?"

"About five ticks of the clock, Kerrigan. But we willna mention it ter Clancy, aye?"

"Aye," she sighed, leaning her head against my arm. "Abel and me, we'd like ter handfast at Beltane. Would it make it all less awful if we were in it together?"

I smiled and stroked her hair back from her face. Unbound, it fell to her waist in soft brown waves. Abel were a lucky young man. But he were also a young man with a big heart and an easy smile. Husky and wide, he liked to laugh, and he looked at Kerrigan with utter devotion. She could have any boy in any village around, we knew. Her father had taken her with him when he went to trade, and she'd come back blushing to the sound o' her father telling o' one young man after another, helpless before her beauty and her fine manners. But she'd chosen Abel because once he'd made her a rose out of hard red candy, and another time he'd bought a stuffed poppet and learned to sew that he might stitch a lollipop to its paw. Because he kept a pocketful o' sweets so when he walked through the village, no young person might pass disappointed. Because he worked much o' his roundness into muscle helping his da build a house for them on a nearby patch o' land, and he'd asked her opinion for every joist, every room, every color o' sanded board.

She'd chosen Abel with every belief that she were reaching up for him, and only gratitude that he should fall before her feet with joy.

I did not know if I could love like that. I knew I loved Diarmuid, but their utter selflessness were terrifying.

I realized these were the words blocking my throat earlier, the silence Diarmuid needed me to fill.

But first I should answer Kerrigan's question. "Aye," I said gratefully. "If Clancy an' I can be children fer another year yet. I think tha' would save us all."

We ate quietly. When we were done, Diarmuid showed everyone where the water closet were, and we both pulled our nightshirts from our dresser and disappeared into Cairsten's room with an oil lamp. As I closed the door from our bedroom to the hallway, I saw Clancy sitting on the bed with her mum on one side and Kerrigan on the other. She were weeping quietly and they were soothing her, and her da were making himself comfortable in the sitting room.

It were the best we could do.

Cairsten's room were the size of mine and D's, but his bed were bigger, and the quilt on top were, well, womanly in a way. It were mostly white, with a Bridle Path pattern in black and red, the likes o' which dominated the whole room.

The mattress were feather ticked, and the sheets were clean. I watched curiously as Diarmuid pulled the covers back and laid a dry bath sheet down before pulling on his nightshirt over his bare body and crawling in.

"Tha' were no fair," I joked feebly. "I might've wanted to look a spell before ye hid all o' tha'."

Diarmuid rolled to his side and leaned upon his elbow. He'd loosed his queue and brushed his hair back, and I smiled at him shyly.

"Yer... yer damned handsome," I said, delighted.

He grimaced at me and shrugged. "Yer the prettiest boy I ever saw," he said, and his heart were throbbing there in his voice. Suddenly I quailed. I couldn't live up to that, could I?

"Kaspar were—"

"Nay," he said gently. "Kaspar weren't prettier'n ye, Teyth. Dinna... dinna pretend yer not a bigger piece o' me heart."

My face heated, and I stripped without looking at him. I pulled my nightshirt on over my head and slid into bed on top of the bath sheet, mirroring his position with my head propped on my hand.

"I'm...." Och! But he were beautiful. I reached out gently and ran my finger across his chin. The stubble rasped my calluses and I wanted more o' him, so I cupped his cheek in my hand. My hands ached to touch more, but I remembered Kerrigan, remembered Abel, and thought that for all o' Diarmuid's kindnesses, I owed him the words I'd found for what I were not.

"I'm... I'm not a good bet fer a lover," I said frankly.

"Yer young," Diarmuid said, his mouth twisting. "Ye dinna need ter do this, if yer not sure."

I shook my head and ran my palm over his chest because he were letting me. "Sure that I want ye? Aye. I... I've wanted ye afore I knew what it were. When Kump died, I thought, 'Good. Diarmuid can do tha' ter me, an' I can forget what tha' bugger's touch were like.'"

Diarmuid's face wrinkled, and he quailed back from my touch.

"Oi! *That's* what ye think o' me?"

I grasped his muscled arm and shook me head. "Ye dinna ken. I *wanted* ye. Ye were... are.... Even before I came, when Kump were sayin' evil things o' Cairsten, I thought that if anyone could do summat ter a man as fine as ye, he must be evil indeed. And then I were here and I kenned Cairsten were the best o' men, and ye? Ye were…." Och! No words! "Aye—I been Silence my whole life, and now I need some fuckin' words and they're rusty in me throat. I *love* ye, Diarmuid. That frolicking I did with me mates, that were… were practice… were making *sure,* that no other man, no other person, were who I wanted. No one but ye. But…."

I buried my face in Cairsten's great pillow, and Diarmuid stroked me from the top o' me hair, down over me shoulders.

"But what?" he whispered, his voice even. I turned my head sideways, saw his almond-shaped eyes intent on my face.

"I'm not Kerrigan—"

"Thank all the gods and the moon and stars," he burst in.

I laughed softly, like he meant me to. "And I'm not Abel, and I'm not Kaspar."

"I be knowing," he replied, serious as I were. "Yer harder, Teyth. Ye use one word when ten'd be better. Ye close in on yerself and keep the world out. When yer reading yer books, ye look up and dinna see me, and when yer deep in yer ironwork, ye do the same thing. Tha' speech ye just made me—ye've gone a season an' not said so much, ye know tha', right?"

I buried my face in the pillow again. "I *know!*" I said in exasperation. "I want ter be… Abel, courtin' Kerrigan wi' sweets. I want ter be *you,* courting Kaspar with kindness and kind conversation. But… but I'm *not.* I'm all hard want, and the things I feel about ye, about ye being taken from me—they're not gentle, loving things. There's *violence* in me, the way I want ter keep ye next ter me skin, me heart. Is not gentleness, D. Is not courting like ye shown me—even like I seen with me mates. Ye need ter know—"

He stilled me with a kiss and then gave me a gift.

He let me take over the kiss.

I rolled him over, taking his mouth hard and clumsy with me own. He let me—opening, accepting, being all the things I knew Diarmuid to be. Kind. Soft o' heart, hard o' resolve.

It were so clear. He'd resolved to let us be lovers.

I kept kissing, framing his face in my hands and pressing feverishly against his compact, muscular body. When he spread his legs and wrapped his thighs around my hips, pressing against me with his heels, I thought it were all over.

I ground into him, rutting, *needing.* I sobbed breath into the hollow of his neck, breathing in the clean, smoky scent of his hair. He kept thrusting against me, and his cock were large and hard enough through his nightshirt to hurt the both of us.

I were shaking, I wanted that pain so badly.

He soothed me then, hand in my hair, whispering, "Sh…. We've time enow, yeah-yeah? Time enow?"

He took over the kiss, quietly changing my urgency to tenderness. My cock still ached for him, but it were an ache I could hold on to. With hands that were *not* patient, he reached to the hem o' my shirt and ran his hands up my backside, kneading it, stroking my back.

I sighed and went boneless, collapsing on top o' him.

"Here," he murmured, rolling so we were side by side again. "Let me. Not too fast, not too much. Ye'n me, we… we *know* each other, Teyth. We lived like brothers, but we were none. Ye, touching yerself at night? Ye think I dinna hear?"

If he were not so near, I'd have hidden my face in mortification, but he *were* near, and my nightshirt were rucked up to my waist. His languorous, drugging stroke down my hip and flank soothed me.

"Slow," he murmured. "Ye do whatever ye want ter me, but I know ye like it slow."

I caught my breath and nodded my head, shaking. His touch continued, and I took his cue, rubbing my hand up his thigh slowly, appreciating the things I'd seen. The rasp o' fair hair, the hip bone that thrust up from the solid muscle o' his stomach—these were parts o' him he'd hidden at first, and then showed without thought, and then….

Hidden again.

And now they were revealed to my skin, and it were like seeing a sunny day in yer mind and then walking out into it. It were *better* against my skin.

I slid my palm up his ribs, his chest quickening under my touch, and he flattened his hand against my stomach. I closed my eyes, bucking my hips because I could not help it, and tried to remember the moment I'd first known my wanting were an adult thing. I could not. The first time my cock grew hard, I'd thought o' Diarmuid. The first time I'd seen him and Kaspar coupling, I'd wanted it to be me, and I hadn't known coupling could be a good thing then. Good, bad, it didn't matter. If it were Diarmuid, I'd wanted it to be me.

"Wait," he murmured and then turned and blew out the oil lamp. Before my eyes adjusted to the dark, his hands were back on me, a little more urgent, a little harder. We hadn't draped the furs over the window, and I could make out his face as he lowered his lips to my ear and spoke.

"Quiet, yeah-yeah?" Because of the other people in the house.

"Quiet, aye."

I turned up my face for a kiss because I could drink them like sweet spring water, but he didn't kiss me. Instead he kissed his way down my chin, lingering to tease the skin o' my throat. It were vulnerable, exposed, and I held my breath, wondering when I would curl in on myself like a bug to keep him from my tender spot.

But his kisses felt good, lovely in fact, and my chest relaxed first, then my limbs. He pushed at my nightshirt until what I'd just put on were taken back off and I were naked before him. His mouth moved across my chest, and there were so many tender spots—my ribs, my nipples, the indentation near the crease in my arms. I held his sturdy shoulders and panted, waiting for the next nibble, the next suckle on my flesh.

The touches to my ribs made me gasp, and to my chest made me moan softly, but when he took my nipples into his mouth and suckled, I grabbed two fistfuls of his hair and bucked, biting my lip to stay quiet.

His low chuckle made me smile even as I ground against him. He lifted his head and played with the bit o' flesh using his forefinger and thumb.

"Ye like tha'?" he whispered.

"Aye," I breathed into the darkness.

"Ye like a mouth on yer cock?" Oh, Abel had tried—all in good faith and fun, yes. But he hadn't the will. "Oh, aye," he murmured, hearing my breath hitch, the little whimper come from my throat.

He kissed my stomach, finding the little trail that led to my root, and his tongue dipped briefly into my slit, then lapped at the fluid dripping from the head.

I bit my hand, wanting to shout, wanting to gasp and beg, but having no recourse for that. Diarmuid were merciless, teasing, flicking his tongue, cupping me sac and fondling me stones.

When I were shaking with need for him, his mouth opened intimately and he engulfed me. My body slid into the wet, heated dark, and behind my closed eyes I could see my frieze, the pattern I would forge—the stark beauty o' it, all in silver and gold, pure, shining, unsullied by error, as clear as a mountain lake on a fall morning. In that moment, Diarmuid and I were wrapped in that beauty, taken in, and it glowed around us, pressing into our flesh, becoming a part of our bodies, spirit, and sex.

Then Diarmuid's grip around me tightened, and his mouth put pressure on my cock head. The pleasure spiked, rolled hard, and I became too aware o' my body to hold on to that vision.

But it didn't matter.

Because the vision weren't more important than Diarmuid's mouth, or his hands playing with my chest, or his breath, which caught me skin every time he backed off o' my cock.

I were going to come. Oh gods, I needed it. I needed it like I needed to breathe, and my stomach felt punched it were flexed so hard.

And at the same time—"Lemme touch ya," I begged, but for once Diarmuid ignored me.

"Nay," he whispered, breath frissioning on my cock some more. "Nay. I want ter taste yer come, Teyth. I need yer ter fill me, so full. I been empty so very long."

He pulled me in then and squeezed, and the frieze exploded behind my eyeballs, but only for an instant. Everything else were me body, and I'd come before, but this... with this man I'd loved, had yearned for... this were the clang of the forge, the rising of the sun on yer face, the taste o' life-giving water, the smoky air o' autumn—all in this man's touch.

I gasped and arched my back, and came.

Agh, gods, I couldn't stop. My stones clenched up, my stomach too, and I buried my hands in his hair, fisting them, spilling my seed, my dreams, my life into Diarmuid's willing mouth.

I lost time, coming aware when Diarmuid moved up next to me whispering, "Sh, sh," at the same time he were wiping his lips with the back of his hand.

I didn't think I'd been talking, or loud, but when I heard his voice I realized little sobs were escaping my chest with every breath. I gazed at him, silhouetted in the moonlight from the window—feeling soft inside, when I never felt soft, and worshipful, when I thought the gods had died.

He nuzzled my neck, my jaw, my temple, and I caught my breath against his chest.

"Ye good now, Teyth?"

"Aye."

I heard a rare sound of impatience. "Ye be wantin' ter touch me now, yeah?"

"Oh, *aye!*"

I rolled, wrestling with his nightshirt in the dark. After a flail o' solid limbs and linen, he were naked, bare to me, vulnerable on his back, thighs slightly spread and legs raised, looking at me with eagerness and shyness, the mixture o' which tore my heart.

I were young, he'd said. Repeatedly. And he'd been hurt and bereft before. I returned the favor o' kissing down his body, paying attention to his nipples, which popped against my tongue. He gasped and kneaded my scalp through my hair, and I looked up his body.

In that moment I saw him in hues o' silver, lead, and glass. I wondered what it would take, what I would have to smith, what I would have to learn, what metals I'd have to steal in order to make a medallion with his likeness—head tilted back, mouth opened, lines drawn in his face to show the exquisiteness o' the moment.

And then his hips bucked at me, and I released his nipple regretfully.

I had no patience for teasing.

I grasped his cock and pulled it in, swallowing it down until I gagged. I tried to still my breaths so I could hear his, and he didn't disappoint. Ah, his body were so sensitive. I coated his foreskin with spit and slid it up and down, licking at the slit when it were down, pulling it between me lips when it were up.

Diarmuid's fingers in my hair grasped frantically, and I stopped for fear o' hurting him, but he whispered, "No! Dinna stop!" and I went back to it. He tasted clean, with the faint musk o' sweat, and I loved that he couldn't seem to keep his breathing even, didn't know what to do with his hands.

This man in my mouth, under my hands, with muscles in his stomach as hard as forged iron and biceps like cannonballs and alloyed steel, *this* man were coming apart in a house full o' people, losing sounds into the air around us as fast as I could suck.

He reached behind him and grabbed a heavy feather pillow, hauling it over his face. That were when I dribbled some spit on my forefinger and traced it back between his stones. His groan didn't make it much beyond the pillow and my own ears, but as I thrust my head over him, I thrust my finger inside him, and the way his body stretched taut like a lute string would forever make my stomach ache with the things I wanted for this man.

I couldn't court him gentle or smile sweet, but his cock in my mouth, my body in his—that made him snap tight, it made him break, it made him come.

He flooded my mouth, and it weren't honey and coffee. It were come—viscous, salty, bitter—and I didn't care. I gagged some, let some slip from my mouth, but swallowed some too. The leavings dripped between his thighs onto the bath sheet, and now I knew what it were for.

I wanted more. The core o' me wanted to shove his legs up, to taste all the places his seed dribbled past, and to explore them. But I made a mistake and let out a sigh o' my own completion. My body, seeking rest after my own climax, suddenly sagged against the sheets, and I pillowed my head on that taut stomach and licked his cockhead lazily.

He tugged on my hair, and I stopped so I could heave my body up to the top of the bed.

The look he gave me were limpid and agonized at once, and I could do naught but stare at him in the darkness.

"What?" I asked, my voice scarcely a scratch in the air.

"Ye'll be careful o' me, yeah?" he murmured, and I recalled that moment, his head tilted back, his body at my mercy. His warmth, his gentleness, his strength—he were all that were beautiful.

"Aye," I told him.

I meant it. I meant it with all o' my fiercely beating heart. I didn't know then that the heart lies so we may tell our lovers the things they need to hear. My heart were duplicitous, cunning. I'd had another secret lover this entire time, and I never knew. This moment, precious and sacred, with Diarmuid—I'd shared it unknowingly with Beauty, and my gross lust for that vile bitch would gnaw at the promises I'd spoken, almost rendering them lifeless and dry as the dust o' bones.

BEAUTY'S TEARS

CAIRSTEN WERE none too pleased to return home and find a female in our midst.

Diarmuid and I got one more night o' silent passion, and Clancy got one more night o' pretending she were sharing a cot with Kerrigan and her mum while they visited friends. But Cairsten returned home when his stint as traveling smith were done and found the lot o' us at the breakfast table. It were here that Diarmuid and I asked Clancy if she would mind performing chores while we were working at the forge.

She were not skittish about being part o' our household—she offered to deal with the washerwoman and visit the market for us if need be. She even offered to clean, but we told her cleaning would be all o' us, as it always had been. She conceded, and her da were more than happy to have her help at his stall when she were idle here.

I were relieved, and I think Diarmuid as well. She were a nice girl—my friend—and I were coming not to regret saving her from the horrors that had lain in wait for her, but still.

Diarmuid, Cairsten, and I had our home. This were *our* home. It were our sanctuary. It felt invaded by this woman. While I did not want to sand her skin with the salt o' our circumstance, I didn't wish for her to intrude any more than necessary, either.

We were in the middle o' hammering out details when Cairsten barged in. Upon hearing o' our new arrangement, he called Diarmuid and me into his room to talk.

We went, meeting eyes gratefully. We'd changed his sheets that morning, because the second night had been as passionate as the first and no bath sheet alone would absorb the smell o' our come.

"Ye...." His beard were long enough by this time to bind in small leather thongs, and when he shook his head in agitation, that long wave o' thongs rippled over his barrel chest. "Ye... ye two. Ye did this ter save yer friend?" His beard wavered again, and Diarmuid, as it always were, answered him.

"Yeah-yeah, Cairsten. She were… she were in the carriage. She were a mess when he threw 'er out. We couldna… we knew tha' girl since she were born, ye ken?"

Cairsten nodded, sorrow in his eyes. "Aye, I ken. Remember, she were born in tha' late spring storm? Ye an' me, boy, we fetched the midwife from the farm cots, but by the time we got the poor woman 'ere, that'un were squallin' on 'er mom's tit, aye?"

Diarmuid cast a shy glance at me, red crescents appearing on each cheek. "Yeah-yeah," he said softly. "I couldna. She's part o' our town, yeah? She's Teyth's playmate since he arrived here, and she's delivered our oil since she could walk."

Cairsten wrapped his rope o' beard around his hand and let it uncoil again, then eyed us again. "Aye, Diarmuid. I'm not arguin' any single point 'ere, I'm just…." He met Diarmuid's eyes as though they were speaking a secret language. "I had hopes ye wouldna get yer heart in another fix, aye?"

Diarmuid looked at me and reached for my hand. I reached back.

"Yeah-yeah," he said softly. "We ken. We'll be… findin' reasons ter visit the forest, I think. I hope ye dinna mind."

Cairsten grimaced. "I doona. Just make sure the forest doona mind, aye?"

Both of us nodded, but it were Diarmuid who said, "Yeah-yeah."

Just as well. The forest always liked him better.

CLANCY AN' I were handfasted next to Abel and Kerrigan not two fortnights later. The town knew—there were no illusions about us growing old together and bearing babes. Nobody said anything, and there were no coarse jokes in our hearing, but the gifts we got were separate, things we could each keep one of, so that our parting would not be bitter. For our part, we made all the joy we could o' Abel and Kerrigan's troth. There were no lies in those vows, and there would be no parting.

From the smith's household, we gave a thing I were very proud of.

After all those years o' sketching a frieze o' metal in the margins o' my books, I finally made one o' wrought iron. It were not delicate or soaring, because it were to block a window in the upper stories so that they might have infants and tykes running in and out and not worry about one going too far. The delicate triskele o' iron were brought to mind by the idea o' two parents and a child, so it were a prayer for children as I knew they wanted.

The function for it were brought about by worry.

I'd been watching that boy, the one I thought were my brother, looking out over the town more and more often. Two days before the wedding, I saw him looking out at us, and I waved.

Then an adult with white hair and rich clothes put a hand on the boy's shoulder as though to whisper something in his ear.

I saw the boy reject whatever were being whispered and walk away, but I also saw him come back and look wistfully over the town.

This boy wanted to be a part o' us. He wanted to fly.

The triskele were a prayer for his safety, pure and simple. I had no power o' me own, an' no magic either. All I had were this sweat-earned gift, to make metal as I willed.

I willed that boy safe up there in the castle tower, looking wistfully at the people he did not know.

THE WEDDING celebration went long, as it were Beltane. Clancy were in the middle o' drinking too much wine and flirting with Llant, who drank too much and fucked too much too, when Diarmuid tugged gently at my sleeve. I left them to their comforting, knowing they'd be coupling in a corner before the night were over and not wanting there to be awkwardness.

She deserved coupling in a corner and too much wine.

To my surprise, Diarmuid didn't take me to a corner, or even to our bed in our own house. Instead, he tugged on my sleeve and whispered, pulling me from shadow to shadow toward the gates. Two guards stood duty, spines stiff, eyes wistfully on the great Beltane bonfire in the square o' town.

Diarmuid pulled me deeper into the shadows, one arm around my middle, and waited. My breath were still because of the arm around my middle when we'd so very carefully not touched this past month, and I heard the girl before I saw her in the shadows.

She were old enough to deliver ale, but too young to flirt with. Instead she stood and told jokes to the men, keeping their attention fixed on her and explaining our traditions to men who were told to keep the peace over us but very often knew nothing o' our ways.

Their conversation were playful, friendly even, and I had cause to wish that these men under command o' the great castle could, perhaps, be some o' us if they ever stopped taking the castle's orders. Diarmuid tugged on my hand again, and we departed as silently as we came.

We flitted through the dark like moths, our feet flying down the cattle path that led out from the village and then split near the wood. We ran right through the split path into the shadows of the wood itself, until we found the clearing where we'd last seen the forest spirit spilling blood.

There were no signs o' that battle now—no blood, no spirit, just us, happy and laughing as Diarmuid whirled and attacked my mouth, devouring me and thrusting me against a great pine tree, one o' the ones with smooth bark that fell off in little puzzle pieces.

I wanted so much o' him. I bent a little, cupped his arse in my wide hands, and pulled his hips up so we could grind against each other. He fumbled with our breeches, and the shock o' skin ter skin were not enough to make us stop. In fact, it spurred us on.

After a grunting, fumbling moment, he thrust a small tin in me hand. I recognized it—'twere balm, that came in cake form but would spread and make things slick and soft and....

Penetrable.

Ach! Coupling. I wanted it badly.

I stared at the little tin, excited and uncertain, and he whispered in my ear, "Where ye want it, Teyth. 'Tis yer own choice."

Ah... I couldna decide, aye? I wanted Diarmuid, mine, his body under mine, me inside o' him.

But I couldn't rid myself o' that bittersweet moment when I were but a child and I saw two figures coupling in the shadows. I'd wanted so badly to be Kaspar then, to be owned by Diarmuid—even though not even that act could promise ownership, not o' another soul.

Hands shaking, I took the tin and scooped out a fingerful, rubbing it with my thumb to melt it slick.

Diarmuid stared at me, face lit up by the Beltane moon, eager as a pup. I reached behind me and rubbed, pushing the slick around my crease, and then one finger, two. The sensation were far different than when I were a frightened child. My fingers didn't rip—they danced, they slid, penetrating gently. My breath caught, and shivers rippled up my spine and into my stones. I made a sound, loud, a wanting sound, and Diarmuid sank to his knees in the forest loam and took me in his mouth.

I closed my eyes and saw sparks and fire looping, swirling into that pattern that had haunted me since I were a child. It were clearer now, touchable, and every lick o' Diarmuid's mouth upon my cock made it light up and sparkle, a metallic rainbow of colors in the hues of soap riding the surface o' water.

My skin were alive with the sparks. The design—I felt like it were carving its way into my flesh, every nerve ending alight with the lightning strike o' pleasure.

He pulled back when I were on the verge o' becoming, and I groaned, shoving his mouth on me cock again until he gagged. For a moment, I feared—my gentle Diarmuid, gagging on my cock as I fucked his mouth. How could I?

But he let up, stroking with his lips only, and thrust forward, gagging again, like he couldn't get me far enough to the back o' his throat. A low, dark joy knotted my groin, and I massaged his scalp through his hair, knowing he'd do anything, *anything* I asked.

The forest rose behind my eyes, suggesting him bent double before me as I ravaged his helpless bunghole and he screamed in pain, loving it because it were me.

The image repelled me—I couldna.

I dragged his head back and pulled him up to me to kiss, and I tasted my precome in his mouth. It inflamed me even further, and I wanted nothing more than to have him deep inside me, ravaging me as I'd dreamed o' ravaging him, but with gentleness.

My Diarmuid could never hurt me.

I whirled, leaning forward and thrusting my stretched, slippery arse out. His hands on my flank, my buttocks, my back, both cooled and aroused me, and I were making sounds, words, by the time he thrust his cock into my opening and stayed, waiting for my ring o' muscle to open.

Some o' his sweat dropped upon my backside, and I groaned— loving the feeling, fearing the pain, waiting, just waiting, for something to give.

Unexpectedly, it did.

The entrance o' my body opened, and I pushed against him as he pushed through, and he slid in slowly, every vein popping against my tender flesh.

I groaned again, the sound ripping through the forest, and he responded, thrusting all the way to his root and breathing harshly in my ear.

"Yer good, yeah-yeah?"

"*Aye, D—fuck me!*"

Ah! Aye! Aye! The pleasure inside me built and built, and at the same time, I registered where we were, what we were doing. Our cries echoed into the listening darkness, and the forest grew fat and heavy with our sex. Every stroke o' D in me arse made the pregnant spring stillness quicken further with life.

Diarmuid's hands were everywhere—my hair, my neck, my shoulders, my throat, my hips—and every new position felt like the only way he should ever touch me, a pleasure so perfect it were pain.

We'd given up with quiet. 'Twere just as well. Our cries and snarling were feral, like beasts, and anyone listening would assume the truth—that we'd become the forest in our coupling, the offering o' our souls into the waiting Beltane night.

Diarmuid howled then, biting my shoulder blade in his passion, and I dropped my hand to my cock and stroked, gasping, gibbering, dying for release from this breathless capture o' the precipice.

Then he let out a whimper, a plea, and like that, his need sent me over and I plunged into darkness, spasming around the intrusion in my body, feeling the wet splash o' seed on my insides and then, hot and sticky, over my hand and spattering on the tree and the loam below.

He collapsed against me and I let the tree bear my weight, trusting the forest would catch me as we plunged trustingly into its depths.

I came to when my knees buckled, and Diarmuid pulled out o' my body. His seed spattered between my arse cheeks and down my thighs, some o' it landing on the forest floor too. That were funny to me for some reason, but I were panting too hard to hold the thought in me head.

Diarmuid's arm wrapped around my waist, catching me and bearing me up, and we leaned for another moment, and another, eyes closed, catching our breath from the enormity o' rutting in the woods.

I opened my lids with my eyes downcast, and I "hmmed" in my throat as something caught my eye.

"What is it?" he asked as I bent down, still arse naked in the forest.

"Is... odd...." A spatter o' silver against the tree—tiny drops, as though spurted through something when liquid, then dried solid. I stood, pulling my breeches up so I could squat and search for more. As I turned on the loam I saw that under me were more spatters, but this pool—just a bit, a teaspoon or two of each—were gold.

The last night in Cairsten's bed, the last night we'd touched each other before this, Diarmuid had kissed me while stroking my cock, until I'd spattered seed all over my chest.

The pattern, the tracery o' come in the moonlight, had looked just like this.

Embarrassed, thrilled, wondering, I began to pick up the little gifts, a teaspoon full o' silver, and one o' gold, o' what used to be our bodies. Not blood, nay, which apparently did dark and dangerous things, but come—which, with us anyway, were about the joy o' doing.

"Look," I murmured as Diarmuid pulled up his breeches. "It's us. It's...." Saying it out loud made me blush, when I'd just been fucked naked in the middle of the woods. Diarmuid stood behind me, reaching out a finger to stroke the cooled spatters of molten metal. I closed my hand, suddenly seeing my design, my frieze, and I turned to Diarmuid, feeling clean and beautiful and newborn.

"Feeling covetous?" he asked, but there were naught but humor in his voice.

"Aye," I told him, spreading my palm again in contradiction. "Aye. I have plans for this."

D's voice grew sober. "Well, then, we must be sure to slip away here and make more."

I looked at him, and the coming year loomed with an aching sort of loneliness. We'd been promised a visit by the prince's guardsmen the next morning—they'd been kind enough to write. But until Clancy were found a new home far away, our home, our bedroom, our little family would be under scrutiny.

Diarmuid and I, we could only touch when nobody were looking. Tonight? Tonight were stolen. Odds were, the next time we came together, we would be here again, in this very space, with only the forest to bless us.

"Aye," I told him softly, pressing my lips against his.

I heard it, though. I heard our vow, echoing through the forest. This would not be the last time we sorted silver and gold from the forest loam in that long year. It would not be the last time we spoke hushed promises into the night air of the old wood.

But it were the first night, when we still believed the glittering promises o' the spend I held in my palm.

THE NEXT day, it were not a guardsman who were led through the forge to Cairsten's front door: it were the prince himself.

His carriage showed up as Diarmuid, Cairsten, and I had just gotten to work. The fires were hot and the oak barrel full, and Cairsten and Diarmuid were laboring fierce on parts for the carter. I were in the corner with a crucible, pouring tiny ingot bars o' silver and gold. Not just what we'd found on the forest floor, but what I'd been hoarding. It were tricksy work, and I ignored the prince for moments while I filled the mold an' then put the crucible back over the fire.

When I were done I put down my tongs and took off the face mask Cairsten made me wear, as well as the heavy leather gloves.

"I'm not accustomed to waiting," the prince said coldly as Diarmuid and Cairsten both took time to leave their projects in a good place.

"We aren't accustomed to stopping a good day's work," Cairsten said bluntly. "We apologize for the wait. Would ye like ter see where the children be fucking now?"

The prince gasped in shock, and Diarmuid and I met amused eyes. Aye, well, Cairsten had not been pleased at a home visit.

"They do not seem to be rutting in there now," the prince said mildly, and my stomach knotted.

Clancy had needed to go to her mum's. She'd taken to our home so sweetly—we gave her privacy and the first wash on bathing day, and she helped keep our home while we worked. She were pert and sassy, but grateful, and we did our best not to ever remind her o' that day in the carriage with the man who claimed to rule us.

Every night, we put on our nightshirts and slid under the sheets. Once the initial awkwardness had passed, we remembered we were mates. We spoke o' our neighbors often, in the shared darkness, o' the farmer who cheated us for his strawberries when it were time to make preserves, and the carter's child who were growing so big. We spoke o' Abel and Kerrigan, who were hard workers, but who seemed to be working hard in the bedroom too. We wondered when Kerrigan would grow ripe with child, and when we'd be able to hold it.

Same conversations I'd have with Diarmuid, truth be told. But whenever Diarmuid and I spoke intimately in a darkened room, our hands were on each other's skin and our mouths were busy tracing patterns on the other's throat, his chest, his stomach.

We could not have those conversations when anyone else were home.

So we spoke as brothers at the supper table, and we'd always worked well together.

And Clancy and I were forced into a partnership that had friendship but no passion.

Those ingots of gold and silver were glowing star bright in my mind, and perhaps it were that vision that gave me the courage to speak.

"She doona wish yer company."

The prince eyed me as though he'd never seen me before. Perhaps he hadn't. "How very quaint. She 'doona' wish my company?"

Cairsten stepped in front of me, literally, and for the first time I realized that I were as tall as he were, if a third as wide.

"I doona wish yer company either. Are ye satisfied? They be living in handfast, and unless they choose ter separate, ye've no claim on either o' them, aye?"

"They are my subjects—"

"As long as yer presence be less intrusive than war," Cairsten snarled, and the prince jerked back as though slapped.

The men behind him flinched too, and the older, more grizzled guardsman on the left looked haunted and horrified. I could read it in them—nay, they weren't excited about a war over a pair o' feckless children and what they might be doing in their bedroom.

"Well, then"—the prince smiled thinly—"now that I know the law is being followed, I shall leave you to your... smithing."

"Thank ye," Diarmuid muttered. "I dinna know how we were to continue without yer bless—"

That quickly, the prince were on top o' him, pressing him to the door with an arm at his throat.

"I am your *monarch*!" he snarled.

My stomach clenched and all o' me froze, like silver in the river.

"Yeah-yeah," Diarmuid confirmed, not flinching nor backing down. "So ye tell us. Are ye done being king, or will tha' girl need ter clean up me blood when she returns from her mum's?"

My vision blackened. I thought o' Diarmuid dead at our feet, and realized the terror o' making another person more important in your heart than your own well-being.

He could… right this moment….

The prince backed away. "It would be a shame to blacken my garments with blood," he said coldly. In a moment he'd left, and we heard him and his men stomping through the forge, knocking over equipment as he went.

Cairsten took a breath. "I'll go make sure they doona burn us down," he growled. "Ye two—ye two tell each other what ye need to that ye not be mouthier 'n me next time around. He willna threaten me, ye ken—but ye, he doona fear ye yet."

"He should!" Diarmuid snapped, and I'd never seen a finer man.

"Oh, aye," Cairsten agreed, although his blood were still up. "He *should* fear ye, D—yer the best an' smartest o' us lot—but tha's not the point."

"Care ter tell me wot tha' is?" Diarmuid snapped, voice thick, but he were losing some o' his ire. We were not, when all were said and done, angry at each other.

We heard an ominous noise outside—not the roar o' flames, but the clanging o' something still falling after it had been disturbed.

"The point is tha' yer our secret weapon agin' him. The less he know o' ye, the more he fears!" Cairsten roared—but he roared it on his way out the door, with us on his heels.

The smithy were in shambles, finished products, materials, all o' it spilled across the ground. They'd been careful enough to leave the forge untouched, but we spent the better part of an hour picking up implements and hanging them up just right, since Cairsten couldn't abide an untidy space.

I did not know about the other two, but for me, I spent that time clanging about with the hard iron implements o' our comfort place, dwelling on Cairsten's words. Diarmuid had a future, he'd implied, something greater than just being ours. It were something I should have seen from the very beginning.

TWICE MORE we visited the woods in the bright of the fullest moon. I never knew if Diarmuid planned it that way, or if his blood always thrummed to the forces that drove the world. Did the oceans roar in his veins? Were his arteries full o' river water? Did he dream from the eagle's view?

I do not know, but I do know he were the one who suggested in council that we start a secret cache o' preserves in the fall that the prince would never see. He were also the one who suggested a bridge across the river and a community well upstream o' the town. And he were the one who suggested we act as a community and make sure everybody had plumbing, and that our sewage flowed into a cesspool far away from the village and the neighboring farms. The farmers would break the waste down and use it as fertilizer, and as that project raged, I were never so glad I were not a farmer or a digger o' ditches.

But for this year—the painful year o' Clancy in our midst—he had proposed those things, and those ideas would come to save us eventually.

He were already more than all o' us combined.

I saw it taking shape, and I still didn't see. My eyes were bright-blinded. By Diarmuid, aye—he were always in my sight—but he were sharing vision with the tiny bud o' silver and gold tendrils I were forging with my jeweler's hammer whenever I had spare time.

It weren't just any spare time, though. No.

Specific spare time.

The times I looked at Diarmuid and wanted him like a slug to the gut, and he wanted me in return—both o' us knowing we would go into our home, our *sanctuary*, and be separated by a wall. Those times I stayed late at the forge, working on my escape into beauty. Some nights—many nights—Diarmuid came outside and sat, reading through the noise o' my working. It did my heart good to look up and see him. Felt as though we were in this misery together, somehow.

The days, few and far between, when I looked up and saw the young'un who *must* be Aubrey staring wistfully out of the battlements o' that monstrous great tower o' gray stone—*those* days I were driven to pour my yearning into the gold an' silver we'd gleaned, smuggled, and honestly spewed in those few moments in the forest.

It were coming along, a delicate frieze o' maybe two hands high by three hands wide. It curved, sensuously in places, trickily in others, and when it were cool, it were so finely pounded, so lovely, I could sit and stroke its lines, watering my soul in the sweetness o' craftsmanship.

Diarmuid loved it too, then, and Cairsten as well. I would watch them after I'd spent a late night tapping, and they would run their fingers over it as I did, closing their eyes and shivering because the metal were so bright, and so soft and cool.

I worked on it through the summer, while the townspeople started on the extra well that would take them into the winter, and the sewer that wouldn't make us all sick. I worked on it through the fall, while the farmers and townspeople put up the extra preserves as Diarmuid had suggested. An' I were working on it in the wee hours o' the night when the soldiers claimed dire need and rode through the common pantry, taking most o' what were there and breaking and destroying what were left.

Four days later, the prince tried to sell us grain and fruit he'd bought from a southern kingdom for cheap.

We weren't buying. Not one o' us bought his food. We'd scrape sugar barrels and eat winter deer first.

Bastard.

Were a good thing Diarmuid had the hidden stores, so we didn't need to resort to any o' that.

But spring came, and with it, Beltane approached. Clancy, bless her, were excited about the spring bonfire. Her da had found three lads who wished to help them run the oil trade, and who wished to meet the smart, competent woman who had been so willing to make her home with men she didn't wish to live with.

Diarmuid and I could barely stand to brush up against each other in the hallway, we were so wound up.

Handfasted—we would handfast the very moment Clancy were taken. We would share a bed, touch each other in public and private, be acknowledged by the council. We'd been visited three times, random hours, by the prince's guardsmen. One o' the times had been late at night. If Diarmuid and I *had* been coupling, we would have been disturbed by the men knocking and invading the tidy little home.

Clancy and I had been, as our habit, sleeping cuddled together like children. And like children, we blinked warily up at the guardsmen as Cairsten thundered in behind them.

"*Gerrout!*" he'd roared, loud enough that our neighbors for three houses came running. The guardsmen were booed out of our home with half the village at their heels, and it were the last time they came to visit, but the point were made clear.

Were only our village if we actively sought ownership o' it.

Diarmuid's ideas for how to keep the town independent and functioning became as gold, and more and more people sought him out. He gave his time and his patience, and freely so. I were proud o' him but at the same time I knew that at some point I'd want him to myself, and that the people clamoring for his attention now would drive me beyond anger.

Mine. Weren't he mine?

I were thinking that one cold spring day, the night before Beltane, when I looked up at the tower. The polished granite were particularly matte that day, and it were a dark and foreboding missile thrusting at the sky.

Ach! But there were my brother waving at me, and he seemed to be smiling.

I put down my hammer and waved and smiled back, and for a moment I had a dream. Someday, Aubrey would be old enough to leave the castle, and he could come out and visit. I would tell him o' Diarmuid and Cairsten, and how we'd given him a cart all those years ago, and how he had a brother who loved him.

My musings were interrupted by the sight of the prince—as I knew it must be, in the rich clothes and with the prematurely white hair.

He leaned over and whispered to my brother, and even from across the town and far under the tower, I could see the uncertain nod of the head.

Aubrey looked out at us again and waved more slowly, and then, to my horror, scrambled up onto the stone ledge that stood at his waist.

"No!" I screamed, but my voice didn't come. I tried again, desperate to get his attention. Diarmuid looked up from the discussion he were having with Kerrigan's father and squinted in the same direction I were.

He stood up straighter, and it were his throat that made the sound mine could not. "*No!*" he screamed, just as Aubrey looked behind him and nodded, and then spread his arms like a bird.

And plummeted to the earth in full sight o' me, Diarmuid, and the village.

Diarmuid and I were running side by side, but I scarce knew he were there. I heard him swear, and we both looked up to see a hysterical woman, and we could hear her screaming from the battlements as we ran. We turned the corner, the last few shops by the entrance to the castle, and the still body....

I couldn't look, and in that moment, that moment I couldn't look, the screaming stopped.

We both heard the impact as my mother's body hit the ground.

I were inconsolable. Screaming, sobbing, carrying on. I flung myself into the mud where the boy's blood seeped in and screamed his name over and over again until Diarmuid's arms wrapped tight around my own, stopping my breath, crushing me into silence.

I looked up to see guardsmen—the same two, older and younger—who had invaded my bedroom one night to see if I were really screwing my wife, and they couldn't look me in the eyes.

I could see Aubrey's face in profile. He looked so like me at ten, I'm sure Diarmuid had nightmares for months.

I didn't think o' Diarmuid then, damn me.

But he were thinking o' me.

"The forest," he whispered harshly in my ear. "I dinna want 'is blood on the prince's damned mud. He feeds on our misery, I willna feed 'm wi' yer grief."

That made sense. *That* penetrated.

The wood. Our holy place. My brother could be in the wood.

I scooped him into my arms—the slight body horribly liquid, blood pooling from his ears, nose, and mouth. Behind me, Diarmuid grunted. He were bringing my mother.

The two o' us trudged through the town, and the townspeople lined on either side o' us. Nobody challenged us—not guardsmen, not prince. We carried what were left o' my family out o' a silent village. Nobody touched us. Nobody dared.

BREAKING HAVEN

THE WOODS were chilly on this cool spring day, and the ice in my bowels made it worse. The horrid burden in my arms were fluid in a way that no flesh should be, and as we drew near to the heart o' the forest, a voice like a heartbeat pounded near the base o' my brain.

He does not belong with you anymore. Give him me.

Blindly I walked, Diarmuid silently at my heels, until my foot hit a place that seemed to set up the toll o' an invisible bell.

Here. Here were where I should leave him. I knelt and set that body gently down, thinking I would need to dig a hole in a moment. My heart died a little more at the task.

Diarmuid knelt across from me, and together we stared at the casualties of the great gray tower that dominated our home's horizon.

My brother... child's face. Beneath the blood, the distortion, that's all I could think of. Were a child's face, a face much like mine had been the first time I'd seen myself in a mirror.

My mother, under her clean homespun dress, were old. Her blood-soaked hair were gray, and not even the warping o' her features with her death from a fall could obscure the deep and bitter lines etched into her skin.

"She jumped," I said, a question I'd answered in me head already, since I hadn't looked up.

"Yeah," Diarmuid replied, and the sound o' our voices hardly interfered with the stillness o' the wood.

He reached out to me over the bodies o' my blood kin, and I clasped his hand because I knew enough to cling to a thing to keep myself from drowning.

Our fingers wove together, the blood on them mingling, and the forest awoke beneath our knees. The blood spreading from Aubrey and Mum began to whorl, to form patterns in the loam. I knew these patterns—they were the same ones I tinked out with my little hammer in the forge night after night, only these patterns were barbed and bloodied, like brambles that impaled some unlucky creature in their embrace.

Diarmuid and I watched as the whorls extended out, etching themselves into a blood-and-earth frieze embedded in the forest floor. It swept wide around us, circling us, binding us together, and the shock o' spirit passed through us as we clasped hands.

The bodies o' my mother and brother began to sink into the ground, pulled inexorably inward by the twisting frieze, bound by earth, blood, and sorrow.

Both o' us startled and met eyes, and the forest disappeared.

We pulled in our breaths and smelled dirt and water, but for a moment could see naught but darkness.

Diarmuid's hands tightened on mine, and he spoke first. "Underground," he said calmly, and I let out an explosive breath.

"Aye?"

"Yeah-yeah. Wait. Our eyes'll fix in a moment."

He were right. My eyes'd been feeling a wee bit dimmer in these days, doing such fine work in the back of the forge, and it took some time before I could look around us.

It were a cave, like the last one, but this one had a stream running through it. The cave itself were much the size o' mine and Clancy's room back at the house, and tall enough for Diarmuid to stand up, although I had to stoop. We wandered for a bit, coming to meet on the far side away from the stream where it ran underground, and then, without speaking, sat.

"How do we leave?" I asked ruminatively. I were not frightened.

"Same way we got in," he said, leaning his head on my shoulder. The gesture spoke o' simple trust between us, and I wrapped my arm around him. I didn't know—how could I?—that I'd be the one to violate that trust. I took it for granted in a way we never should.

"I didna bring a knife," I said.

He shrugged. "I have one." He pulled the little leather pouch he wore at his waist. He carried balm and silver, as well as a knife at his belt—because that were D. "Do ye really want ter leave just yet?"

"Nay."

"Yeah, then. We'll stay."

"Aye."

"Yeah-yeah."

We sat for a few more moments, and then D stood, stripping his shirt and breeches off without shame. While I watched dumbly, he stood in his smallclothes and started rinsing the blood out of his jerkin and breeches. He were right, I realized. We were filthy with it, reeking in things not just blood. I stripped with him, and the two o' us worked silently in that cave o' magic until the water ran as clear as we could see it. When we were done, we wrung our clothes out, each one o' us at each end, twisting until the excess water were all dripped out, and then we hung them on a protruding root.

We worked in silence. When we finished, we sat down again at the far end of the cave, and Diarmuid made a startled sound.

"Look! Lunch!"

I turned toward him, bemused, and saw he had a mat o' maple leaves in his hands, covered with berries, nuts, and even some wild tubers. Diarmuid rinsed off the tubers while I parceled out the berries and nuts, and we leaned against the cave wall in the cool silence and ate.

Just when the earth bore heavily on me, and the silence more so, Diarmuid spoke.

"I ha' so few words fer ye, Teyth. Fer a time when ye first came, ye were my little brother. I'd wake, frightened, fearing ye'd left us—ye were skittish back then, ye ken?"

"Aye," I whispered.

"I'd lie in bed and imagine what'd happen, what I'd do, should tha' un get hold o' ye, should summat awful befall ye, and I'd come unmade. It'd destroy me, it would. An' tha' were when ye were but eleven, twelve summers. It weren't even when ye'd grown ter now. I dinna know how ter fix wha' must be in yer heart at th' mome—"

I buried my face against his bare shoulder and wept. His arms around my shoulders anchored me inside this sacred place, and his kisses in my hair reminded me that I were loved.

The sobs tore me apart, and when they eased, the silence and my lover's arms bound me back together. Diarmuid pulled a cloth from his little leather bag and wiped my face carefully, and I looked up into his eyes with a sort o' burgeoning gratitude that I'd never felt before.

He *were* larger than just him and me, but here, in this haven, he were mine.

He moved first, and his mouth on mine were sweet, tender, healing. I opened my mouth to his, sure, so sure I were deserving o' that sweetness. I took him in, let him warm me when I could o' sworn my bowels would be cold, so cold, for all our days. When it were time, he laid us on our sides and took the balm from his little leather pouch. We didn't fumble anymore, and he eased himself inside o' me with gentleness, one arm pillowing my head and the other wrapping around my chest while he ebbed and surged like tide.

My body bucked and shuddered, and the forest rippled in and out o' existence around us as I spattered my seed on the ground. He groaned softly and climaxed in my clutching portal, and I were greedy. I wanted it all in my body, and none o' it on the ground.

But he had to withdraw, and I felt the flood o' warmth from my backside dripping onto the loam. I closed my eyes for an exhausted sleep, and that must have been when it happened.

In a moment, a shiver o' time, we were naked on the forest floor with our clothes neatly folded under our heads and Diarmuid's little leather pouch clutched in his hand. We woke up slowly, looking in surprise at the sky, trying to fathom how long we'd been gone, safe in our little bubble o' earth.

In a moment, we were both on our knees, touching each other's faces in a sort of delirium o' joy. We were the same. He were my D, his hair were loose from its queue, and his almond-shaped brown eyes crinkled a little in the corners as he smiled in shock.

"The next morn?" I asked, looking at the mauve sky, and he shook his head.

"Nay—the next night, I fathom. Lookit the moon. 'Twould ha' been full last night, and 'tis waning in the west."

He were right, and my stomach rumbled to prove it. I swallowed, because the world, grief, anger, want—those things were waiting for us back in our village, and I hated, suddenly hated with the viciousness o' the beast, that one man, one entitled person, should so take from us, that the home we'd made o' love were a place we now feared.

"No one must needs know," he said softly. "Ye an' me. Clancy, she be finding 'er new husband, an' ye dinna need be wi' me in handfast if ye dinna want to."

I reeled. "Doona want to? Are ye mad?" I remembered yesterday morning, when that full rise o' joy had threatened to overwhelm me. "Nay, nay. O' all the things I'm festering about, being with ye, beloved… tha' be sun an' moon an' stars."

He smiled slightly, troubled about something. "I'll take tha' as a vow, ye ken," he said solemnly, as the last rays o' Beltane sun kissed our skin. "Ye an' me, we're elements—metal, earth, blood, fire, water, air. We twine together like yer frieze, an' no line o' tha' design must be parted from the other, ye ken?"

I nodded, eyes burning, because he saw that in my art, saw that it were him and me twined together, and all we loved and hated twisting us this way an' that.

"I ken," I whispered. "Ye an' me, Diarmuid. Tha's as it should be."

We dressed and looked around the clearing we'd been left in. It were unidentifiable from any other part o' the forest—only here, under our feet, were tiny drops o' silver an' gold.

It had taken our offering and given us preciousness after all.

WE WALKED into town summat after dark, and when the two guards challenged us, we glared at them until they backed down. Our rough wash in the underground stream hadn't completely succeeded in rinsing the blood off our clothes—they knew who we were, all right.

We walked past the town square to find the remains of the bonfire were already cleaned up, and we looked at each other in surprise.

"Three nights," Diarmuid murmured, because the bonfire were never cleaned up the day after Beltane. "Cairsten must be worryin' himself sick."

We hurried to the forge. It lay quiet, and we made our way to the front door, opening the door hesitantly because it were so dark an' lifeless without us.

Cairsten were sitting alone at the table, his shoulders slumped, three days' worth o' feasting prepared on the table and grown cold.

He looked up at us, his mouth slightly parted in relief, and for the first time I reckoned how many grays had threaded through his coal black hair in the past eight years. It must've aged him, watching the boys he loved grow into men during fractious times.

"Ye took long enough," he growled, standing heavily to his feet.

"Be all tha' food fer us?" Diarmuid asked, an edge o' plaintiveness to his voice, and Cairsten closed his eyes and opened his arms.

It were not until he enfolded us both that I realized how much I'd been yearning for this moment, when the final blessing o' our home wrapped around us and kept us. I never knew there were goodness in the world, but this gruff, great, brawny man who could flay the hide off a fly with his tongue—he were good.

It were that last thought that brought the tears again, and Cairsten's gruff comfort were another sort than D's. Ah, gods, spirits, and ghosts—how were it that he could make us feel safe, when we knew the world to be anything but?

I did not know then—and I'm not sure I've ever learned.

But I do remember that night and how Diarmuid and I were on our second round o' bread and melted cheese when Diarmuid started with the questions.

"Clancy?" he asked, after a great swallow o' bread.

"One lad stepped out to offer her condolences, ye ken?" Cairsten said soberly. "One lad. The others wanted ter know what we'd done ter anger the prince. He weren't the most handsome lad, aye—plain as a potato, mostly—but she took 'is hand an' held it to her face, weeping. I were standin' wi' 'er da, ye ken? An' she hugged me hard, turned to him, an' said, 'Yer kindness is more beautiful than gold, sir. If ye'll still 'ave me, I would give a marriage contract my blessing.'"

For a moment, I were stricken. For a year, I'd resented what circumstances forced on us—but I'd enjoyed the friendship. She'd been playful and kind and warm at night. Knowing I hadn't desired her in the least had left her feeling safer in my arms than in any other place, and there were a comfort there I'd taken for granted.

"I'll miss her," I said, surprised to find I meant it.

"Aye, well, she were a sprightly lass," Cairsten agreed.

We both looked at Diarmuid, who rolled his eyes. "If is necessary, I ken," he muttered, casting a sideways look at me.

I smiled, patting his arm, and he caught my hand and then released it.

We both went back to the food, and Cairsten apprised us o' more.

"The village brought most o' this food," he said. "An', oi! Were they worried when ye two doona show up today. I told 'em ye were still grieving, an' they let up, but I had ter hide yer work, boy," he said to me.

I looked at him in surprise. We had never been, none o' us, covetous. Theft were not a problem, not o' gold or silver. Baker's goods, aye, or tykes stealing toys—it were simple human nature, and most children were schooled away from it. But folks on the whole did not look at things o' art and shout "gimme!"

"Whyfor?" Diarmuid asked.

Cairsten's shrug were more accepting than baffled. "It gave 'em comfort, I think. They know ye through tha' piece, Teyth. Ye doona speak much, but if ye can create something like tha', they're proud ter call ye theirs."

I blinked hard and chewed another bite—this o' meat and bread—thoughtfully. That my twined folly would be o' greater interest, that had never occurred to me.

I were still chewing when Cairsten spoke up, apparently not expecting any more conversation from my end o' the table.

"So, ye know what happened while ye were gone—"

"The prince?" Diarmuid interrupted. "Did he fettle wi' any bit?"

From the expression on Cairsten's face, I almost thought he would spit at his own dinner table, but he held back—just barely. "Nay. Nothing. No addressing the people, no apology, no condolences. Just looked down at ye as ye walked away."

Diarmuid shook his head and set down his food. "'E just walked away... like tha'un had no control over what happened there? We saw him, aye?"

We all nodded slowly, but no one wanted to put it into words. Surprisingly enough, I were the one to break the silence.

"I wonder," I said slowly. "What could 'e say ter a boy that age tha'd make 'im think ter jump?"

Diarmuid looked at me in sorrow, but it were not until much later that I realized he knew. What lies would a man in power tell a child to get him to remove himself out from underfoot? Diarmuid knew.

The silence that descended were thicker than sorrow, and it were Cairsten who bludgeoned through it with a smith's hammer.

"Are ye gon' ter tell me where ye were?"

Diarmuid spoke. "Remember the sled, then? After we took Kaspar ter his bride?"

Cairsten blinked hard, breathed, stood up, and knocked his chair about. He sat down while we waited patiently, and we regarded him, waiting ter see what he'd say.

"Were that all?" he asked after a moment. "Ye stayed in the cave, fell asleep, and woke up? Did it give ye anything? Any gifts?"

We looked at each other.

"Food," Diarmuid murmured, and then we both grimaced. "And trade," he added.

I reached into my pocket and pulled out the silver and gold droplets, pouring them into Cairsten's hand.

He blinked at them, and then at me, in surprise. "I've seen these shapes, in Teyth's art. Ye've gotten this from the forest before," he said shrewdly.

Diarmuid and I both looked away and blushed.

"Aye," Cairsten muttered. "Well, no more harm than ye've already done, I gather. But," he reached out and poured the metal back into my hand, "be careful. A gift is precious, aye? But ye better not go expecting ter always be so gifted."

"But we come ter ye fer food and work," I burst out, only to have both of them stare at me.

Cairsten spoke. "Aye, boys. But I give ye outta love. What be the spirit giving fer—answer me tha'?"

I had no answer, not then. Behind my eyes my work throbbed, begging me, *pleading* with me to resume it, to go pound on it, and to temper it with what were new in my hand. It wanted me, I thought in wonder. We'd sealed the bargain, the woods and I, with me, Diarmuid, and our seed on the earth. It would grow in me, along with the art I labored over, and we would create beauty.

I didn't go out that night—I wanted to, but it wouldn't be seemly. Tonight of all nights were the first time Diarmuid and I would share a bed under Cairsten's roof with his blessing.

That thought lured me away from the new metals and the call of the art. It were Diarmuid. Should not he always come first?

HOW LONG did we have then, when happiness were perfect? Tinged with melancholy, perhaps, with bittersweet, with grieving. For a bit, I would look up from my work instinctively, over the rooftops to the tower, expecting to see Aubrey from one o' the windows. Every time, there were a shock o' hurt, like snow down my shirt on a knife wound, and eventually I stopped doing that.

We did as we had been doing. In a way, our lives were no different. We worked the forge—Cairsten and Diarmuid on the sturdy things, the practical things, doing their jobs with craftsmanship and pride. I took the finer jobs, the decorative ones, because as my frieze grew, apparently so did my fame.

The project grew to the point where it were no longer practical square, and I began to shape it. A tube, yes, but one that twisted, flared, rippled. Sometime it were flame, sometime it were water, sometime it were wind, but always made of the precious metals of the earth. People walked the muddy streets, strangers journeying to our village to trade, just to see it take shape above me. For an hour past closing time, when I'd used to do lessons and read, I worked on it, lost in the beauty, the curves, the great fascination for what it would become.

For an hour. Then two. Then three.

I got used to cold baths, cold meals, the delicious crowded solitude o' my mind and my work, as the object in the forge, the piece o' art grew.

Diarmuid would come out, wait until after I'd quenched the piece, and tap me on the shoulder.

"Peace, love," he'd say quietly. "Peace. Come in. Bathe. Eat. Be with us. We be missing ye."

Most times, it were enough.

Most times, it called me from my madness, from my grief and my anger, and I would enter the haven I'd known since I were small, and perhaps loved the more because it were never taken for granted.

Most times, I'd go in, bathe in the cold water, and sit under a woven blanket and eat fire-thickened stew while Cairsten and Diarmuid talked around me, reminding me what people were like when they were at their best.

Those times I would pull from my waking dream in time to respond, to smile, to laugh, to remember the people coming and going from the shop. Those times I would respond to the brush o' Diarmuid's hand on my hip, my waist, my back. I'd clasp his hand

and smile at him, kissing the battered knuckles and promising with my eyes.

We'd fall into bed, keeping our embrace as quiet as possible in deference to Cairsten in the next room. O' that year I have few memories o' flesh-and-blood people, o' human interactions that meant anything o' substance.

But ah! I remember my lover's face in the moonlight. I remember the way his eyes locked with mine before we kissed, the way he seemed to search me, to peer into my soul.

It did not occur to me until later that he were possibly looking to see if the boy he'd fallen in love with still lived within my skin.

That year the boy did, mostly, live within me. That year, when pulled from his fragile, blooming obsession with the gorgeous twistings o' metal, he were as in love with his lover as any boy had ever been.

Diarmuid, for his part, worked as hard as I did on his own obsession.

His obsession were finding a way to protect the people o' our village from the shadow o' that dark granite tower.

Some nights, I would come out o' my waking dream on my own and find Diarmuid sitting on a little stool with a book in his hand, as he read about governments in far away lands and the way some people were not at the mercy o' a prince with no soul.

Some nights, I would come in and find him washing dishes after a council meeting, his brow furrowed for once with people other than his beloved, who were not yet in from the cold.

One night after Solstice I came in earlier, forced in by the cold, even in the forge. I found Diarmuid in deep conversation with the handful of elders and tradesmen who made up our council, all o' them listening and nodding as he spoke with passion.

His urging to move the hiding place o' the preserves and community food basket this year had turned out to be well founded—once again the public food basket had been raided, and once again the prince had tried to sell us grain from somewhere else for more gold than we could afford. The amount o' waste the prince poured into the river had tripled, and were it not for the wells the community had dug—and guarded—upstream during the winter, we would have spent our cold winter months choosing between death from frostbite from walking miles for fresh water, or cholera.

With the aid o' the council, Diarmuid had helped to elect two representatives, one from the tradesmen in the village, one from the farmers without, who would bring concerns to the prince—whether he listened or not. Diarmuid had very carefully made sure he were not one o' the tradesmen nominated.

"What's the use o' us bringing our troubles ter 'im when he doona listen!" Fisher burst out as I walked in. Fisher had become Diarmuid's biggest supporter after Clancy had left—he were by no means a fan o' letting that tower shadow our lives anymore.

"What matters is tha' we keep a record," Diarmuid said grimly. "So if we ever fight an' ever win, we 'ave a list o' ways we tried ter avoid war. We need ter tell our young'uns violence is last refuge, no' first."

There were low grumbles from around the table, and I felt for them. But then, I had grown up without a proper da, and with a mum battered by grief and burdens beyond her ken. Whatever pride and righteousness had armed those farmers who went to ward off the prince in the first instance, it had not been a fair enough substitute for strategy and forethought.

I'd listen to Diarmuid if I were them—he were the smartest man I knew.

But he were also merely a man.

His eyes watched me hungrily that night as I came in and washed at the sink. It were not a washtub night, and since I'd not invited these men to our house, I had no qualms about removing my singed jumper and tunic, then running the pump over a cloth and washing my face, neck, and shoulders.

There were some restive movements behind me, and I realized the room had been quiet for far too long.

Diarmuid were staring at me, and it were his turn to speak.

I caught his eyes as they lingered on my pale arms, stringy with muscle, and my neck and chest, so rarely bared in the winter.

A few men coughed, amused.

"Were there summat else on the agenda, Diarmuid, or were ye gon' ter spend all night gazin' at young Teyth wi' stars in yer eyes?" Abel asked dryly.

I grinned at Abel, who winked back. He looked happy these days—Kerrigan were growing round with child, and she would be ready to birth near Beltane. It would grant us grace if something good happened in the spring.

Diarmuid shook himself and turned away from the council, blushing.

"Forgive me," he murmured. "Has been too long a day, an' Teyth's been working long hours."

It were my turn to flush, but Canda spoke up, her voice an alto counterpoint to all those bass lines of the men.

"We been seeing yer handiwork, Teyth. Is a thing o' beauty, aye?"

I grinned at her, pleased. Cairsten had been spending a night or two a week at her cot, and she baked us bread and sweets on her rest days. Diarmuid and I liked Canda—in particular, we liked that she didn't seem to want to possess Cairsten more than we were ready for. Our bachelors' household suited D and me, as selfish as that were.

"Thank ye," I mumbled shyly. "I see it spreading, like a tree o' life. Perhaps a gift ter the town, when 'tis done." I had been thinking hard on it as I worked. What? To labor so long on a thing and hide it deep inside the forge? Nay. Canda's words—and the words o' the townspeople who came to watch me work on it in the afternoons—set free the bird in my chest that wanted to see my creation fly.

"Tha'd be lovely," Canda murmured with admiration, and the rest o' the council murmured in agreement before Canda continued. "However, it be good ye come in from yer work on occasion. Methinks yer husband grows lonely."

She said it with an impish grin, all in play, but it pierced me like an arrow. I looked quickly to Diarmuid, who were making busy passing a parchment around for everyone's signature, and he looked away quickly.

He *were*. He *were* growing lonely. I tracked back the paths o' the past weeks in my mind, trying to think o' other times I'd come in early, and could not, not since the Solstice fires.

There'd been rest days, aye, but our work day—*every* work day—had come to grow long.

My mouth dropped slowly, and Diarmuid met my eyes.

The hurt there cut me bone deep. In the silence the council slipped away, out through the forge, Cairsten with them on Canda's heels.

Diarmuid and I were left alone.

He stacked his sheaf o' parchment automatically and took the few steps to the fireplace, where the kettle were boiling.

"Here," he said, picking up the kettle. "Let me heat ye some water. Ye missed bath day yesterday. If yer gon' ter do it, ye should do it right."

I stood, still stunned, and let him make a large pot o' warm water for me, complete with a small measure o' sweet-smelling soap.

"'Ere," he said quietly, and I put the cloth in his hand, having already stripped my shirt.

He tsked and turned me around so my back were to him, and I suppose it were easier to talk to me this way.

"Ye mustn't mind Canda, yeah-yeah? She were merely jesting ye—"

"She were right," I said bleakly. "I doona mean ter take ye fer granted, D. I forget, tha's all."

"I know," Diarmuid said softly, rubbing the cloth under my arms where I would have missed if I'd still had my shift on. "Yer driven with that'un, I fathom tha'. Is part o' ye I canna change."

"Would ye want ter?" I turned to him, grabbing his hand and meeting his eyes. He peered at me unhappily, and I girded myself for whatever his answer would be.

"Ter change ye?" He thought hard, which were one more reason to love him. "Nay," he said after a moment. "Nay. Not ter change ye. But ter...." Absently he moved the cloth across my chest. My body—dormant for what, a sennight? a fortnight? when were the last time I'd tumbled into bed with him?—awoke and grew heavy, languorous and aching, suddenly full o' his touch while craving more.

"Ter what?" I asked, pulling at the drawstring of my breeches and letting them drop ter my feet.

He smiled faintly, as though knowing I were trying to use my body to say good things for me when there were no other act o' goodness in my own record.

"Ter ease summat in yer heart," he said at last, his voice rough and crumbling. He bent and pulled down my smallclothes and continued to wash me, his movements slower, adult and blatant. He squeezed my cock as he moved it to wash my stones and behind. I spread my legs to give him better access, suddenly wanting him bare as I were. I didn't reach for his clothes, though. I realized his heart were bare enough now, in the kitchen, after his loneliness had been exposed in front o' his peers.

I stroked his hair as he squatted to wash my backside, the creases behind my knees, the insides o' my thighs. When my privates were clean, I loosed the leather band that held his queue. It fell forward, coarse and straight, and I pulled my fingers through it, the very sight making me harder and the feel o' it pulling the string taut within me that made my body scream in want.

"Ye ease summat in me heart," I rasped, tugging at his hair.

He stood slowly and I took the cloth from his hand, setting it on the counter and framing his face with my newly cleaned hands. I were naked in our kitchen, and he were fully clothed, but my shame fell away as did my anger and hurt, and suddenly I needed my husband with all the fierceness o' my soul.

"I am not enough," he whispered before my mouth claimed his, but I heard.

"Ye are," I said when I pulled back from the haven o' his mouth. "Ye are enough. Ye must be."

"Nay," he whispered, holding my face and lunging upward, taking my mouth with force and desperation. He kissed me hard, pushing me back against the counter, rubbing his callused hands over my shoulders, my chest, my waist—claiming, trying to *make* me his when he didn't seem to believe I already were.

I let him, and shoved my hands under his jumper and tunic, finding his nipples and pinching slightly, giving an edge to what I were saying, needing him to believe me, because even *I* didn't know it were a lie.

He gasped, and when he opened his mouth, I captured his lower lip gently with my teeth.

"Aye," I muttered, willing him to believe it. "Aye."

He pulled back and stripped his shirts off, then shoved his breeches and smallclothes off just as quickly. We were both still wearing stockings, since the floor were cold, but we still had the habit o' leaving our boots at the door before we came in.

"Nay!" he said, standing in front o' me with defiance and a tinge o' anger. "Nay! I'm not enow, Teyth. I can live with it, though it hurts me, but ye canna lie ter me, yeah-yeah?"

I stared at him hungrily, thinking o' all those fervent couplings in the dark and wondering what we'd missed by not lighting a candle, by not making noise or speaking our feelings while we were making love.

"Nay," I countered, needing him. "Nay." And I believed it. "Tis no lie, D—I need ye. I need ye more than breathing, I'd swear ter it."

"*Then take me!*" he snarled, his voice breaking and my heart with it.

Ah, *gods,* he'd been here for me, there for the taking this past winter, and I'd lost the thread o' that in my self-absorption. I picked up that thread now and used it to pull my lover back to me, to kiss him hard, relentlessly, until he were senseless with it.

We stumbled down the hall and I shoved him onto the bed, frantic with the need to be inside him.

He fumbled the balm into my hand, and my heart stilled for a beat. He were trusting me with his body—with his heart and soul—and I'd been careless already.

I took the balm reverently and reached between his buttocks, into his crease, fingering his entrance carefully, rubbing the balm with gentle little strokes around his rim. He sighed, relaxing, spreading his knees and planting his feet against the edge o' the bed.

The light from the oil lamp spilled down the hallway, and I didn't close the door. Look at him, so beautiful, giving himself to me. How could I have forgotten that? How could I let cold metal and empty fancy keep me from his side any longer than necessary?

I stroked the slick over my cock, letting it warm and grow slippery with the heat o' my skin, and then I leaned over and kissed him, slowly, powerfully, not wanting him to forget that I'd had his mouth, made it my place, even if my madness should call me away on another day.

He groaned and thrust up against me, his perfect cock grinding against my stomach. I positioned myself, still lost in the kiss, and then straightened up a little to shove myself inside.

Too rough, I thought in distress. Too rough! He were not used to receiving on his end, and I were too rough.

But augh! He felt so good. So good, wrapped around me, and I whimpered, needing to move.

His face tightened in harsh lines as he strained to take me all in, and then relaxed. He sighed and went lax, like that were where I belonged.

I were not gentle, but he didn't want me to be. He urged me on, filthy words falling from his mouth with abandon, every syllable whipping me like a horse to plunge and rear and scream. He wrapped his legs around my backside and drove me faster with his feet on my arse.

In that moment, that's all there were, our voices raised in desire, in anger, in hurt, and the slap o' our bodies against each other as we strove desperately to fill the empty places I'd left hollow for far too long.

He gave a cry first, his hand on his cock, and he spurted over his chest and stomach. It looked lovely, and I yearned to devour it, to take it inside me, but first... first... first....

His body clenched around mine and I cried out, filling him inside.

We shuddered, still breathing harshly, still sobbing, and while my breath still tore my chest, I bent and licked his stomach clean. My movements slowed as I did, became easy, playful, because his skin and come were my drug and I would savor it on my tongue.

I worked my way up to him, and those squirrel-bright eyes regarded me soberly.

I took his mouth again, letting him taste himself, and then I kissed him fully, with all my heart, until he were boneless against the bed.

Finally I collapsed at his side and closed my eyes, stroking his chest just to feel his heartbeat and know he were still there.

"I love ye, aye?"

He took a deep breath to answer. "Yeah-yeah."

"Yer enow, Diarmuid. 'Tis me tha's lacking. Aye?"

He turned his head. "N—"

I stopped the word with my hands. "Say it," I demanded, and it were the one smart thing I did. "Say it be not ye, but me. Aye?"

He closed his eyes in sorrow, but it were my spend running from his body, and I'd taken him as a man, not a child who needed shoring up from his own weakness. We, neither o' us, could deny which one o' our unit would do the breaking down.

"Yeah-yeah," he whispered, turning his head.

I grasped his chin and turned his face back to me. "I love ye, Diarmuid," I said soberly, praying he could give me the answer I needed.

"I love ye too, Teyth. Brokenness and all. Yeah-yeah?"

"Aye."

BROKEN HEARTS

IT WERE easy at first to remember how to be a good lover. I wrote a schedule in my mind and asked Diarmuid to help. If I were not in the house in time to bathe in warm water or eat warm food, he were to get me. And I insisted that I help with dinner twice a sennight.

It worked. As easy as that. My family were my priority, and I could make it so.

Some nights, Diarmuid were having council meetings, and he brought me bread and meat. I worked late those nights with his blessing. I had no voice to spend in council, but that did not mean I weren't working for my village.

The sculpture continued, a tree o' life, silver and gold twisted over a scaffold o' tin, one and a half times a tall man. Some of the metal were mine and Diarmuid's gift from the wood, aye, but some were gifted from the people who came to see it. I were given baubles and old jewelry, pins and rings, even the decorative bits o' old swords. Once the word spread that I were giving the work to the center o' the village to watch over the bonfires at the celebration, everybody wanted to add their piece. The stonemason were building a pedestal to the north o' the square, and women had planted flowers in beds around it. This art weren't just mine, it were *ours,* and I found that their love made it bigger, made it more beautiful, more subtly and elegantly twined.

Those months before Beltane were beautiful, the happiest o' my life. Cairsten spent time with Canda, aye, just enough for Diarmuid and I to be loud, to see each other in lamplight, to be completely alone.

That were good times.

So were meals around our table, the three—or sometimes four—o' us. Canda were pleasant company, and she and Cairsten spoke merrily of the other members of the village. There were affection in their every word, even when they were exasperated.

"Teller's late wi' payment again," Cairsten growled two nights before Beltane.

Canda scraped more greens onto his plate and sniffed, ladylike, which were funny because when she were working with the horses she swore as bad as Cairsten ever did, or worse. Not that Cairsten minded—he seemed pleasantly besotted with her lean brown person and did not seem to mind that she didn't tie her hair back or bother to blacken the streaks o' gray that twined with the corkscrew curls.

Because she didn't force her way into our home, but merely took the space we allowed her, we gave her more. She were at home with us, and at home leading Cairsten through the forge some nights and into her own cot behind the stable. We'd never been there—but then, it weren't meant for us.

"Teller's drunk in the tavern now," she said soberly. "He's not recovered since his son were pulled into service."

We all met eyes. Teller's son were a pretty lad, recently sixteen. The word o' mouth that the prince were coming didn't always reach the outlying farms, and that's where the lad were, helping a neighbor with planting in return for garden space, when the carriage had rolled by. We'd seen the lad, wearing livery, since, but he very carefully didn't look his father in the eye when he were running errands. Whether for shame—although we never shamed those who returned from the prince's service—or because he didn't wish to attract any attention to his family, we didn't know, but Teller had taken it hard. His wife had died bearing his daughter, and the two children were all he had left.

"'Ave ye talked ter Mecera?" Diarmuid asked. The girl were barely thirteen, but she did a good job talking to her da.

"I'll not be pressuring a slip o' a girl fer her da's silver," Cairsten muttered.

"Yeah-yeah, but she does his accounts," Diarmuid said practically. "She makes him work so they 'ave money, an' she'll know the pay is due. We're honest, she knows it—she'll be good fer the money."

"Aye?" Cairsten asked, looking bemused. "I forget, children grow fast here."

"Tha's not what ye said when I told ye I fancied Teyth," Diarmuid muttered, and that caught the whole table unaware.

"No?" I asked, surprised. The idea that Diarmuid might've gone to Cairsten before that night o' Beltane had never occurred to me.

"Nay," Diarmuid said, grimacing good-naturedly. "Now, I forget the words exactly, but 'ow did that go?"

Cairsten managed to look sheepish, hard for a giant man with a mane o' mostly black hair. "I doona remember," he obviously lied.

Canda burst into a peal o' laughter. "Oh, I do!" she crowed. "I remember it clear. He comes stomping into my stall surly as a bear, sayin', 'Young upstarts, falling in love with infants *when* they're infants—got no right, I'm telling ye, no right at all!'"

"Ye remember all tha', do ye, woman?" Cairsten asked, beleaguered.

"Oh, aye," she said, winking at us. "I remember tha' 'cause I had ter kiss ye ter shut ye up about it. Ye almost swallowed yer tongue, ye did!"

Cairsten's embarrassment turned fond. "Turned out ter be the best tantrum I ever threw!" he proclaimed, and we laughed some more.

'Twere a good moment—warmth and happiness seemed to seep into our little brick house, even to the cold metal of the forge, and we embraced Cairsten before he wandered down the corridor after Canda to "walk 'er home," as he said. Aye, he said he were only going for an hour, but o' course, he always seemed ter get lost in her bed before he came back, but they were so happy, who could blame him?

That night we cleaned up the last of the dishes, talking quietly about the night. Of course it came up.

"I doona know ye went ter Cairsten first," I said, leaning back against the counter. Diarmuid turned to me and smiled shyly. It always muddled me when he did that, twisted my stomach and my heart all together, made my blood throb in all my quarters.

"Yeah-yeah," he said, studying the cupboard behind my ear. "Ye were young, an' quiet about yer feelings. Ye were runnin' wi' yer mates, an' I dinna know, ken? Were it just me, wantin' ter think ye might've felt summat fer me, or would ye find Clancy or Kerrigan more appealing?"

I smiled, and that Beltane felt much further away than a mere four years. It felt lifetimes gone that I had been the half-clothed boy pulled from the puppy pile and told to go home.

"When I were a young'un," I said thoughtfully, "Kump dragged me ter town. 'E had business with the liquor sellers, but tha's no surprise. Anyway, he dragged me past the forge, an' ye an' Cairsten were workin'. Cairsten frightened me, ye ken, because he were so great an' brawny. But *ye*—ye were the prettiest man. I loved ye then, aye?"

Diarmuid's brown face washed harder with color. "Yeah," he whispered.

I smiled at him, suddenly so full o' love it were like the tree would grow itself, just from the magic running through my veins that came from looking at my beloved.

"Look a' me," I commanded gently. My Diarmuid, who would lead the council in closet rebellions without so much as a blush, looked at me coyly from under his brows, as embarrassed as a virgin.

"Yeah?"

"Yer my inspiration—the thing tha' makes me art. When it stands in the square, ye need ter know tha's me heart on display there, every tendril o' it trying harder to wrap around ye."

He ducked his chin against his shoulder. "Ach, Teyth—this be why ye dinna speak so much, yeah? When ye *do* speak, ye say bloody great things."

"Aye," I said softly, pulling the dishcloth from his hands and then pulling him into my arms.

That night I remember clearly. He took me that night, for all his bashfulness in the kitchen. He took such exquisite care o' me, it were like 'e were the artist and my body were a work o' living flame.

When the morning dawned, peeking through the window because we'd left the furs up, I were lying behind him, stroking his hair from his forehead as he slept. Today we'd be moving the sculpture to the village square, and I were fluttering inside. It were the people's art now, not just Diarmuid's and mine. Today they would see it, and ach! I wanted so badly for their approval.

"Yer worrying," D said in front o' me, and I groaned softly into his shoulder.

"Yer supposed ter be sleepin'. 'Tis a leisure day, aye?"

"Yeah-yeah." He grunted a little and thrust himself backward, so the bare skin o' my chest were cupping the bare skin o' his back, and I thought randomly that my whole body would be incomplete if our skin weren't breathing together like this.

"What if they doona like it?" I asked, for once volunteering something, only because it were riding me so hard.

"They will."

"Not everybody!" I had heard some people calling it "stringy" or "haunting" or "frightening." I wanted to go to each one of them and explain how the shape o' the thing were perfect for what I wanted, how each twining o' metal and branches were the twining o' two hearts, and o' metal and air, and o' gold and silver, and o' one and many. I wanted to *make* them see with my eyes, to see that it were beautiful, at the same time I disdained them for not seeing the same thing in it that I saw.

"Yeah-yeah, not everybody," he sighed, rolling over in my arms. It were a discussion we'd had before. His eyes were half-opened, and he hunted for words, threatening to fall asleep between each. "Were everybody ter find it pleasing, Teyth, 'twould no' be art, yeah? 'Twould be summat else. A horseshoe. People find horseshoes a pleasing shape— put 'em over their doorways. But yer piece, it be bigger'n a horseshoe. It means more. Not everybody be pleased with tha'. Ye canna help what people think to be beautiful, ye ken tha', yeah?"

"Aye," I mumbled. His words soothed me, as they had since winter, and I closed my eyes. When next we opened our eyes together, full sunshine were coming through our window and Cairsten were throwing the front door open, telling us to rise and shine.

WE'D ASKED a good many hale strong men to help us move the thing from the forge to Canda's wagon, and they appeared after breakfast, all o' them eager—excited, even—to get a glimpse of the thing in its entirety.

I'd covered it with a tarp, though, and prepared it for travel by shoring up parts o' it with scaffolding in various places. It were hard to see the shape o' the thing as we all grasped it by the wooden scaffolding on the bottom and lifted it to the cart.

But eventually the beast were loaded, and Canda hooked up her team and pulled the cart the three street lengths to the town square. The people o' the village—Kerrigan an' Abel, their family, Kaspar's parents, in fact *all* the people we knew and cared about—traveled in our wake. This were a holiday for them, and the glow in my chest were fierce because I'd made it come to be.

Hubris, that were. Diarmuid and Cairsten had made it come to be. The people who'd donated their fine metals—they'd made it come to be. But this were still my day.

We got it to the town square and were lifting it out of the cart when we heard it.

The rumble o' the gilt carriage through our streets.

There we were, about as vulnerable as we could be, a thing o' great value not yet established on its pedestal, and the prince were coming.

"Heave, boys!" Cairsten called, and we did not need the urging. I'm not sure what the others were thinking—but for me, if we could just get it on the stone pedestal, bolted and sure, there were nothing he could do to it, nothing he could do *about* it, that would change the shape o' the sculpture, or our world.

We'd just scraped it on top o' the stone, shoving for all we were worth to get it positioned, when the carriage came around the corner.

"Ye bolt it fast, boy," Cairsten murmured. "Me an' D'll cross tongues with this'un."

I pulled out my kit, with the solid iron bolts and the hammer and wrench, and started directing the people around me to do what I couldn't. Abel were the one who pried at the scaffolding, and Teller yanked at the tarp. Kerrigan handed her husband tools, for all she were waddling and past overdue, and Fisher took the lumber from Abel's hands and stacked it in the back o' the cart. We were so busy on our tasks, trying to make this thing *be,* that I didn't even notice it had been uncloaked and revealed for all that it were until I heard the gasp of the crowd about us.

For that moment, that one shining moment, I caught my breath, tools in my hands, and looked up.

It were glorious—silver and gold and bronze, all the metals we could gather, twisted and twined. The different colors didn't subtract, they added, and I'd used them like a painter uses his palette, painting my metal with different hues.

It stood against the blue sky like a real tree in that heartbeat, stretching for the heavens, beautiful in that effort to reach the sun.

I felt a slow smile start on my face, before the angry voices from the carriage reached me and I remembered my task.

Ach! I worked fast. Bolt, hammer, wrench—there were six places the tree would be secured to the stone, and I skipped every other one so that the thing could balance sooner. I would finish the job, I knew, but for now I wanted it standing so I could turn to see what my family were doing while I determined to give my gift.

"So this is where my tax money is going!" the prince sneered.

Cairsten's returning snarl took no one by surprise but the prince.

"Yer *taxes*?" he roared. "Tell me, people. Be anyone here in the square back on their *taxes*?"

Irritated shouts o' "Nay, not us! Nay, 'e bled us dry!" and "Nobbut left o' our grain after tha'un came through!"

"Well, if you can afford *this*—"

"The metal were a gift!" Diarmuid said, his composure as even as it ever had been, even when dealing with a man who carried armed guards at his back. "This were a work o' love for our village. This weren't taxed, and it weren't forced. Ye canna look on it an' be proud? We're supposed ter be yer people, Yer Highness"—oh, how that word must have stung his tongue!—"and ye canna be proud tha' we'd make this fer ourselves? I read yer treaty—we surrendered to ye so ye'd take care o' us, isn't that how it went? But we took care o' this ourselves. Dinna think it be reflecting well on ye, that this stands in yer village, yeah?"

Oh gods… gods o' wood and fire, gods o' air and light, my Diarmuid were pleading.

"I do not approve of it," the prince said. "Take it down."

Behind me I heard Abel, working furiously at where I had left off, hammering and bolting and wrenching. I thought to buy him time, is all.

"Nay," I said, moving away from the sculpture and into the prince's field o' vision. I filled the place between Diarmuid and Cairsten, although they were both closer to the prince than I. "We willna. 'Tis ours. Our village, our square. This marks it for us. Is yer need fer power so great ye'd take beauty from us as well?"

"You call this beauty?" he asked, puzzled. "It's… it's an abomination!"

I were stung, and what I said next were rash. "So're ye, raping our young'uns an' stealing our food. Are ye so scared o' us ye canna even allow us our gods?"

He gaped at me, as though he didn't know this. For me, it were the equivalent o' the one time I'd mouthed off to Kump, but what followed were a thousand times worse.

The prince wore at his side a short, slim sword. He stood staring at me in growing anger, fingering the ornate golden hilt. "Ye dare ter…." He swallowed the peasant words and stared at me, fulminating.

"I am your prince," he spoke again coolly. "I give you protection and safety, and the least you can return me is respect."

I opened my mouth, but Diarmuid turned toward me, mouthing, "Go!" at me with increasing panic.

I took one step, that were all. One step so I could pivot and turn my back on him, walk away from this proceeding and all I had invested in mounting my art for the world to see.

As I moved, the prince yanked his sword from its sheath without warning and hurled it at me.

I were stunned, standing still with shock—and would have died as I stood there, mouth gaping like a fool's, but that Cairsten saw it before I did.

Cairsten threw himself in front o' it, because I were his boy and he wouldn't have me hurt.

It were Cairsten who thudded into the late spring mud, the pommel o' the sword protruding from his chest, his great heart skewered in one negligent throw.

The sound that burst from Diarmuid's throat weren't human. I were standing a little to the side and behind him, and I were able to grab him about the waist as he rushed the prince, swinging him around so my back were to Cairsten's body as it gurgled in its own blood and its heart ceased to beat.

"*I'll kill 'im!*" Diarmuid shrieked, and my own heart almost died with our father's.

"Ye canna!" I pleaded. "Ach, beloved, he'll kill ye too!"

"*No!*"

Diarmuid fought, but he were fighting to get away from me, and my limbs were longer. I clung to him, sobbing, not wanting to look behind me.

I had to, though, when I heard that calm voice, amused, saying, "Well, I guess you can keep it there *now*."

I turned and looked over my shoulder. He crouched next to Cairsten, hand on the haft o' the sword lodged in the man's great chest.

"Ye'll meet yer death at our hands," I said, my voice clear for all that my world were ripped asunder. "Ye enjoy this moment now. Ye'll never have another one this sweet."

He yanked the sword out, and Cairsten's blood gushed into the mud below.

"Clear this garbage from the street," our monarch said, his voice bored, and Diarmuid went limp in my arms.

The prince turned around and left us, his village shocked silent at an act o' war for which there were no recourse, not even violence.

Diarmuid, Canda, and I fell to our knees and embraced the man we'd loved.

And wept.

THE CART were there. So were the tarp. We loaded Cairsten into the cart and drove him into the forest.

Canda stayed with the horses, and we promised her we'd look after him. We were both strong men, but bearing that great form on the tarp, limp with death, into the heart of the woods nearly killed us both. Our muscles were shaking and screaming with pain by the time we saw a clearing that looked near to holy enough to lay Cairsten to rest.

I hadn't looked at Diarmuid, hadn't barely seen his face as we'd made our way here. I could not look at my beloved as he grieved. The things in his own heart were so very nearly the things in mine, and I had no words, no comfort, no kindness even in mourning, not even for the man I loved. As we knelt in the loam, he reached to Cairsten's still face and closed those merry blue eyes.

"Take care o' him," he said out loud to the forest. "Ye hold his wife an' child. Take care o' him for us, let him see his family in ye." His voice broke, and he lowered his head to our father's chest and sobbed.

I draped myself over his back and joined him.

There were no words. The forest had him now, but he were the heart o' us from the very beginning. How were we to be men when the man who taught us the craft were gone?

The rush o' earth over his great body were subtle at first, as though the forest were respecting our grief. But it were also inexorable, and Cairsten sank into the ground, the familiar whorls o' the forest's patterns marking the ground beneath us.

This pattern weren't in silver or gold, though. It were in flowers. 'Twere Beltane, after all, and what sprang up as Cairsten's body disappeared were bright gold and purple flowers, flowing like the silver o' my tree.

Diarmuid let out a final cry then, and I wiped my eyes on my shoulder. He were not talking, were not sane, and for once I were the strong one.

I were the one who wrapped my arms around his shoulders and guided him to the cart, where Canda were sitting with her head on her knees, all o' her tears spent alone.

I helped D onto the buckboard and slid in next to him.

'Twere Canda who spoke into the silence. "'E seen ter?"

"Aye," I said.

"'Twere quick."

"The forest takes her own," Diarmuid murmured, surprising me.

Canda looked at both o' us. "What does she give in return?" she asked, the question so like Cairsten's that I could almost pretend he were waiting for us back in the forge.

"Beauty," I rasped. The word felt like poison. And so did the thought o' that wrought-metal tree, reaching for the sun like a beggar.

I wanted to make another one, another tree, but this one twisted like brambles and hate. This one would be gorgeous in destruction.

Beauty?

I didna ken the meaning of the word.

BEAUTY SLEEPS IN SILENCE

I REMEMBER so little o' our return to our home. There were food, as the village gave us some o' the feasting for Beltane, and we must have eaten. Must have spoken, must have bathed and slept and relieved ourselves. But every moment o' normalcy were shattered, destroyed by the realization that Cairsten would never tread across his own boards again.

There were so much to miss, and so much to love about the man we missed. Two days after Beltane, Canda came to us and told o' a wake, o' storytellings, o' celebrations, dancing, and life, all o' which had been at the Beltane fire under the tree I'd forged.

Diarmuid and I heard o' the celebration, and Diarmuid made the pretty noises.

"I'm glad he were so loved, Canda. Is... is good ter know he'll be missed."

"We... we did not mean to grieve without ye, Diarmuid. Is just... the thing tha' happened in the forest—tha' seemed so very private."

He nodded, swallowed. "Yeah-yeah," he said, voice naught but a rasp o' metal on metal. "Ye had a part o' him too. We ken tha'. We still ha' no words, yeah?"

"Ye need ter find 'em, D. Tha'un, he is silent too often."

"Yeah," Diarmuid said tersely. "Thank ye. Thank ye fer the food, fer the kindness." He paused, and in that pause I read the thing I had not yet thought of. "We... we *are* silent too long. In a week, yeah? In a week, or a month, would ye... would ye remind us tha' we ate together? Ye... ye lost 'im too."

I'd been slouched at the couch, letting their painful conversation wash over me, but her voice broke when she spoke next, and I had to look up.

"Aye," she whispered. "My son, 'e's asked me ter stay in the cots wi' his family this summer. When I return for the winter, I shall look ye up."

Diarmuid's voice cracked a little. "Ach, Canda, I'm so heapin' sor—"

"Nay. Just… nay. Not sorry. Not at fault. Not e'en a little. Me heart hurts, tha's all. An' is not so safe as 'twas, even with the treaty."

"Yeah," he muttered. "'Tis no treaty, not no more."

She reached out and wrapped a hand around his neck, leaning his forehead to hers like, I imagined, his true mother would. "Do. Nothing."

He gasped and gaped at her, and she shook her head.

"Nay. I willna take it back, Diarmuid. He lived fer ye, an' whether it hurts ye or no, he died fer ye. Do. Nothing. Nothing tha' will bring down the wrath o' tha' bastard in the tower. Not 'til yer grief's seen some air. Not 'til yer anger doona blind yer eyes. Wait. Wait 'til next Beltane, if ye must, but wait. Plot, plan, whatever ye may, but *do nothing.*"

Her voice broke again, and I knew the set o' D's shoulders. He were staring at her, weren't he? Glaring, as he thought how ter evade her promise.

"Please, Diarmuid. 'E loved ye an' Teyth. Plan ter live, aye? Not die fer him. Plan ter live!"

"N—"

"Do it, D!" I snarled, not moving. I couldn't bear to move, lest my body break apart, but I could snap, surly, and demand. A petulant child—how could I have thought I'd grown?

"Tey—"

"Fer me," I said, but not pleading. "Fer Canda, fer Cairsten. Enow wi' politics, fer a year. Please, D? I canna…."

I looked away. I could not bear it.

"Yeah," he muttered, grudging. "Fer ye two. Yeah-yeah."

He looked at Canda as they embraced good-bye, but he couldn't look at me. Not for the rest of the night.

I do not know if he looked at me the next morning, tried to search out my eyes, tried to find some forgiveness in me for either o' us. I do not even know if we ate. For all I know, I relieved myself by pissing in a corner.

All I remember o' that day three suns after laying Cairsten in the ground were that I restarted the cold forge that day. First I stoked it, hardwood upon hardwood, pumping it to beyond heat. Then I had tin, that most basic o' metals, and some copper to make alloys. I started with the tin, not caring that it were not precious, that it were more common than dirt.

I were not laboring for beauty here.

I heated the ingot and pounded, rolling the metal, extruding it, keeping it hot, and then began to twist it. The rhythm o' it—the heat o' the forge, the clang o' the hammer as each blow rang up my arm, the hiss o' the steam as I tempered the metal—were safe. If it did not give comfort, it coated my heart in the plating of honest work. There were no thinking or feeling, no grief or love in the forge. There were only the work, the next ingot, the next hammer blow, the next dash o' flux to make the metal stick.

The urge to make another sculpture consumed me.

That first day, I contained it. Diarmuid and I worked on things that had mounted during the week. Come closing time, Diarmuid disappeared into the house, probably expecting me to come in after an hour as I'd grown used to doing.

He did not understand that first day, that when we'd opened the forge, opened the oven, and stoked the coal, what we'd really done were open the gates o' hell so that I might walk right in.

He came out later, and I were still at work. He waited until I'd quenched the next branch and tapped me on the shoulder. I lifted my eye protection, but I did not look him in the eye.

"Nay," I said shortly.

"But Teyth, 'tis past lunch and on to dinner."

"Nay."

"But…." His voice quavered, and I looked up. His eyes were wide and shiny, and I could not bring myself to think on the silence of the house, the echo of his footsteps, and the painful choice o' measuring food for two instead o' food for three.

An armor plate fell from my heart with a clatter that startled me. Just that, a tiny chink in the armor, let the thought in. *If not for me and my cursed art….*

That quickly I cold riveted the plate, pulled my glasses back on, and turned to my work.

"Nay."

He stood there, helpless and tearful, and I turned to the frieze taking form on my anvil and poured the solder on to join the next bit.

He were gone when I were done.

I honestly don't remember the next time we spoke. Were there words when I came in? Did he try to touch me when I lay down to sleep?

If so, I felt naught.

My skin were as impervious as my heart.

The next day, and again.

The sixth day, I realized we were short on scrap metal to use for my project. I'd turned out the regular workload like an automaton, a clockwork man, precise but with no heart. Diarmuid lifted his glasses and said, "Closing time," and I nodded, then turned to the last ingots.

"We're running low," he said, sounding desperate to say anything.

"Aye."

"We—I can trade for more, but I dinna know if it be good fer ye to keep—"

"Do what ye must," I snapped. "There be ways ter get metal tha' don' involve trade."

"But Teyth! The miners come but a few times a year! Do ye want me ter—"

And like that, I felt something. "Ye will *not* spend any more o' this family's gold on my folly, Diarmuid! Ye hear? I ha' metal or I ha' none—tha' be *not* yer bother. 'Tis bad enow what I've done ter us, 'tis bad enow—"

"*Ye dinna do this!*"

I were so surprised I dropped my tongs. It were good the metal were cool enough to not set fire to the outside of the barrel.

"I did—it were my—"

"Cairsten *loved* wha' ye did wi' yer talent, ye ken tha', Teyth? He *rejoiced* in yer art. Ye dinna hear him, for yer eyes are ever inward, but I did. He loved me, Teyth, but he *celebrated* ye!"

"Tha's supposed ter make it better?" I cried, and then realized I *were* crying. No. Oh, no. I were not going ter do this. My chest ached with crying, my throat were closed with it. I were *fucking weary* o' hurt. "He died fer what? Fer a heap o' metal—"

"Fer a symbol o' *hope!*" Diarmuid burst out, and his voice held so much passion I wanted to shake him.

"Hope? A symbol o' *hope*? The only hope I have is that ye suffer no more fer my gross folly!"

"How's this not makin' me suffer?" he pleaded, and I couldn't look at him.

"Just... just pretend I'm nothin'," I muttered. "Silence. Is all I were ever meant ter be."

"No...," he whispered, and the word, his hurt, abraded me, chafed my skin and ripped it bloody.

"*Go!*" I screamed, throat raw. "*Just go! Go! Go! Leave me, damn ye, and I'll slit me own wrist on me folly and leave ye out o' it!*"

He wiped his hand over his eyes, and I were not that blind. There were dark circles there, and he had not slept any more than I had.

"Later," he mumbled. "When yer sane."

He turned then, disappeared, and left me to reheat the rod and hammer it some more. I used metal from the crucible to solder it to the piece, and looked around, realizing there were no more.

I could not go back into that house. Not without metal waiting for me the next day. There were only one place I could think o' that would give me what I needed.

It were late. Families were inside their homes, and even in late spring, there were fires to ward off the chill. The tidy row o' crafters' cottages and houses were filled with warm yellow light from every window. The sun had set a bit ago, but there were still gray in the sky, and it made it easier for me to weave and hide, to slide past the guards who spent more time looking at the town than on where any danger would come from. Nobody saw me slip past the gates, and nobody were out as I walked determinedly into the forest, the little knife I'd brought with me as a child tucked deep in my pocket.

I avoided the field, ripe with flowers, where Cairsten lay. Twice the forest brought me to the small glade where Diarmuid and I had made love.

Three times I walked away. I knew what it were trying to do.

Finally I found a knotted tree, grotesque and dark, and I crouched in the shadows o' its bole.

"Not gold," I whispered, the thought o' Diarmuid making my chest ache. "Not silver. Common. Plain. Ugly and weak at heart."

I pulled out my blade and held it to my arm. Not my wrist, no, because I could not finish my piece if I bled too much at one time. My arm, where there would be plenty. I didn't even flinch when I drew the knife, quick and clean, through my flesh.

It dripped steadily, and the earth knew what to do, even if the forest spirit were reluctant at first.

Copper and tin, equal measures, spilled out of the ground as the blood soaked in, and the tears I'd dammed up while shouting at Diarmuid broke loose. Oh, thank ye, gods, thank ye for not making me bleed him dry. My own soul I could crush under this weight, but not his. Not while I labored in the forge we'd loved as children, in the home that had saved us both.

The wound closed up eventually and I slid to the ground, weakened by blood loss, by hunger, by grief. I closed my eyes and slept there on the forest floor, waking up shortly before dawn, when I gathered my precious metal into my shift and staggered home under its weight.

The guards were sleeping as I slid by, but Diarmuid—Diarmuid were asleep at the table as I staggered in, dirty, bleeding, exhausted.

He blinked awake, gasping when he saw the wound on my arm. I kept my back turned to him as I stripped down and washed in the cold water from the pump, gasping at the shock o' it on my hurt.

"I'll get the bandages," he said after a sorrowful pause.

"Doona—"

"*Don't* tell me how ter care fer ye," he snarled, and I found I didn't have the wherewithal to fight him, not with dawn a few moments away.

His hands were cold and impersonal as they bound my arm, and perversely I wished for a touch, a bit o' tenderness. He weren't my brother, he were my husband, and for a year, a happy year, we'd shared the same bed and hopes and silly laughter. But now he were a stranger, and I had made him that way.

I didn't know how to fix it.

Didn't know if I wanted to.

Fixing it would be like breaking down a piece o' work and melting it in the crucible, hoping the metal had not grown too brittle to hold.

And it would hurt. The bitter purging o' it would leave me naked, arse up, like I were before Kump. A babe with no weapons, no armor, no recourse. I could not be that way again, not even in front of Diarmuid.

I couldna.

I wouldna.

His next words as he tied the bandage undid me.

"I still love ye, Teyth. Whatever yer demons, we're still wed. Are ye gone ter tell me all tha's gone now?"

I couldna do that either.

"Nay," I whispered, surprised at the word.

"Then I'll wait," he said, sounding more weary than happy. "Until I canna wait no more. Yeah-yeah?"

The silence in the kitchen boomed loudly with every heartbeat until I could not stand it.

"Aye," I said, and that word gave him permission to pull me to my feet and pour me into our bed.

I staggered out of bed a few hours later, but I worked. And then I stayed and gave myself to that gnawing, wanting drive, the desire to make something that would last beyond my next breath. The forest gave it to us, and we would honor it.

I would honor it.

I'm not sure if I said a word that day.

Or the next. Or the next. Or the one after that.

The days passed in a haze. The only certain thing etched into my brain were the sculpture growing in the back o' the forge. It were fighting me, in a way. I'd try—I'd try to make it vicious and ugly, but the spear I'd put at cross-purposes one day were actually in harmony the next. Finally, after I'd given up quarreling with my own creation and it grew in size, in beauty, I looked at it and despaired.

I'd wanted my monument to grief to be ugly, hideous and black like the thing in my chest, but it were not. It were beautiful and painful, gorgeous in its agony, heartrending and exquisite.

Looking at it purged me somehow, and on the days I did not hate myself for not being able to create true hatred, I hoped.

If it could still be beautiful, maybe… just maybe….

I dripped blood into the forest how many more times? Once? Twice? Again?

One night, near to Samhain, when the woods were too chill to be out without a jumper, Diarmuid followed me. Later I would realize that he'd begun to look for my pile o' ingots to deplete—it were how he knew I'd go running to the forest.

I were weak by this time, scrawny, living like a scarecrow in tattered clothes, my hair a nest for twigs and fleas, but my blood were as red as ever. The tree I watered with my pain were growing stronger, straighter—nourished by my pain, aye, I suppose, but also by the strength I did not know I had. Every smallest drop now yielded more and more, and Diarmuid walked over a wheelbarrow's worth o' nuggets littering the ground as he came in the dawn to squat by me.

I looked at him blearily. When had he gotten old?

"Ye smell," he said bluntly, and for the first time in ever I tried to remember the last time I had bathed. I couldn't.

"I'm sorry," I slurred, feeling wrung out and empty. "I.... Ye couldna let me rot here, watering the tree?"

Diarmuid looked behind me, grimacing. The bark were red, purple red, and the branches mayhap have been straighter, but they also had strange bends, like human limbs.

"The tree been watered enow," he said. Dry humor. He'd made me laugh as I were growing; it were still there. How could I still feel that it were there? He pulled in a breath, shuddering with it, and I watched abstractly as the tears hit the ground, turning to gold in fivefold the quantities. If we'd touched each other in months, I would have joked about what our spend would create.

"Gold," I rasped, struggling to reach for it, and for the first time he sounded angry, as were his right.

"Leave it! Leave it, Teyth. Ye've littered the ground wi' the fruits o' yer blood—I'll be damned if I let ye gather me tears along with it. Now come."

"But the—"

"We'll come tomorrow," he snapped. "I'll come with ye. We'll gather it in a wheelbarrow, but first, home. Bath. Bed."

"Ye dinna want ter rut wi' me," I muttered. Our beds had been split. I didn't know when. He'd shoved them apart to either side of the room again, and when I stumbled into our room, I fell face first on a cold mattress. Perhaps trying to touch me had broken his heart enough.

"Yer right," he acknowledged. His voice dropped, became singsong as he helped me take steps across the field o' sharpened nuggets where once earth and grass had been, and together we staggered out of the woods.

"No more rutting," I mourned. "Diarmuid willna touch me no more. Never good enow. Should ha' held on ter the touch when I could."

"I dinna say never," Diarmuid muttered. "'Til this madness passes, or I canna stand it no more."

"Ye should leave me," I said, feeling noble. His smack on the back o' my head did not hurt. Didn't even shock.

"Ye should come ter yer senses," he said tonelessly. Oh gods. I'd done it. He didn't care anymore. My heart wailed, and I wept as we stumbled home, leaving silver sprouting in our wake, side by side with the gold.

The tub were waiting for me, still warm. He stripped me down and bathed me as he never had when I were a child. Cloth all over—in my hair, between my legs, under my arms. 'Twere not a sensual thing, no, but it were… caring.

Even I had to admit it were caring.

When my voice rasped in the kitchen, I didn't know it were mine.

"It be nearly finished," I whispered as he knelt in front o' me, scrubbing my scarred and wounded arm with movements delicate and tender.

He stopped, and for the first time since Beltane, I saw him.

He'd aged, aye. His hair had strands o' silver, even at twenty-six. But his eyes were still brown and squirrel bright, almond shaped and sly. His mouth were still lean, and I could still see the lines in his cheeks from when he were wont to smile. And he'd stayed awake and dragged me out of the forest—when this night, with the near to full frosty moon and the frozen blades o' autumn grass in the fields, *this* night o' all o' them, could have been the night I rose from my body to walk the forest forever.

"Yeah-yeah?" he asked, tendrils o' hope growing from his voice, when I'd tried so hard to kill them all.

"Aye."

"What then?" He tried. He tried to keep his voice neutral, but he couldn't.

"I'll sleep for a week," I laughed weakly. Then I thought. "I'll… I'll make dinner. Eat lunch. Bathe in warm water, aye?"

"I'd like tha'," he whispered.

I didn't mean to give him hope, but I did anyway. His hair had loosed from its queue, and I reached out and pushed it back from his forehead. "Maybe I find a way to push the beds back together," I said.

He closed his eyes and nodded.

"Aye?" I were a bastard, I were, to promise what I could not deliver. But ach! I wanted. I wanted to, for him, so badly.

"Yeah-yeah," he whispered back.

That much hope must have hurt him, because he straightened and reached for the bath sheet. "Food," he said brusquely. "Then bed. Tomorrow be rest day. Our work be caught up. Ye… ye'll go work on yer piece, Teyth, but… sleep. Yeah-yeah? If I wake before ye, I'll even make ye eggs."

Ach! Once upon a time, he'd bought my soul with eggs, and those eggs were dearly paid for in his blood. I knew what it cost him to offer. I could not lie to him, not now, not when the hope ached in his voice.

"So close," I murmured, stepping out o' the tub and collapsing at the table to eat. Simple bread, simple cheese—and yet I had not eaten in… hours? Days? I could not remember. Kings had not feasted so well as I did on bread and cheese. "I canna rest, canna think, even, with it being so close to done."

I heard his pained grunt behind me as he set up the siphon to water the garden. Then, to my surprise, he moved to me back, wrapped his arms around my shoulders, and snugged his chin against the hollow o' my neck.

"I'll make eggs, then," he said softly. "I'll bring them out to ye. Ye canna finish if ye dinna eat, Teyth."

I swallowed. "Yer… yer so good ter me." How many times had I come out o' my waking dream in the forge to find bread and cheese on the stool behind me? "Why… I'm such a selfish fucker, D… why?"

He kissed my temple. "I dinna always know," he murmured. "Sometimes I do. Tonight, I know. Tonight, I see in ye such an amazing potential fer grace." He sighed. "But…." He straightened and moved away and resumed cleaning up after my bath. He did not need to finish the thought. He couldn't do this forever.

I finished the bread and cheese, and he set the plates in the sink, blew out the oil lamps, and pulled me to my single bed. I looked at it in despair, the distance between the beds mocking the closeness we'd once had. I were dressed in naught but a towel, and I hung that over the headboard and pulled a nightshirt from the drawer. I didn't remember dressing for bed in recent months. Mostly I'd just fallen in, clothed. But I were clean now, and that old remembered blessing o' being bathed and well fed were starting to awaken in me the things I'd forgotten about being human.

"Stay," I murmured, climbing in and grasping his hand. 'Twere the most selfish thing I'd ever asked.

"Let me put on a nightshirt," he murmured, ever fastidious.

He climbed into bed with me and made me turn over so I were facing the wall. Maybe it hurt too much to see my face, or maybe he just didn't want me to see his. I were too tired to measure the meaning, but I took the arm he'd placed around my waist and tucked his hand next to my chest.

I went to sleep willing myself to stay as well, at least for a plate o' eggs.

THE EGGS I had, and quiet smiles, and some human conversation with my husband, the man I professed to love.

The armor around my heart began to warm, and not to fall off or shatter, but to soften. Even while the forge seemed to whisper my name, seemed to chant at me, to scream like a passel o' insane children begging for the metal I'd left in the woods, begging for my heart and soul back in their clutches where I belonged, the part o' me at the table remembered—this were what art were for. To take moments like this and make them forever. To make what were human in us immortal.

I finished my last bite and willed myself to stay in my seat, not to go kiting off for the forest to gather my blood-begotten palette for my hard-edged art. Diarmuid were talking o' council matters and how he were trying hard to keep his promise to Canda, but the prince had not stopped his random—seemingly *mindless*—violation o' our personhood. It were important talk, but horrible, hurtful, and something inside me cringed at facing this pain again head on. Diarmuid—he were the brave one. I saved my anger and my pain for the metal taking shape in the forge.

But Diarmuid... his tenderness o' me the night before would not let me leave him. My concerns were not more than his—sane and fed, having slept well the night before, I knew that.

Still, something in my face must have shown. He reached across the table and took my hand.

"Ye try so hard fer me," he said, his look sad and patient. "If I doubted ye loved me, watching ye try, tha' takes it away. Go. Go ter yer work, yeah? It's rest day—I'll go into the forest and fetch yer nuggets."

A part o' my heart leapt at this, but a part o' me knew the depths o' my selfishness.

"But 'tis yer rest day too!"

He shook his head, and his eyes welled over. "Ye sat," he said, smiling through his mist. "Ye sat and ate my eggs. Ye listened. Sweet spirits, Teyth—if ye knew...." He shook himself. "'Twill be worth it, should I have so much o' you in a fortnight."

Finally. Finally, I could give him something. "Before then," I said, smiling for him. "Before then, I shall be free o' it."

He nodded then, not trusting my words. I could not blame him. But something in me seemed to have healed over these months o' work. We were not fixed, no—but no longer did the chasm between us seem deep and cold.

TWO WEEKS o' uneasy peace followed. I were still late in, but when Diarmuid came out with my dinner, I spared moments. I put down the work, spoke to him, made an effort, caught up on his day. Once, when my patience were about ready to break, I took a deep breath, stepped back, and, wonder of wonders, walked away.

I bathed in warm water that night, ate dinner with my husband, and sat on the couch, holding him while he read.

We slept in the same bed that night—chastely in our night shifts, aye, but I remembered what it felt like to have a man warm in my bed. As I held him, for the first time in months, I felt my manhood stir. In that moment, I were flooded with want for something other than my art. The blood rushed under my skin, amazing me with the heat, the intensity, and I savored it. Oh, yes. Human. I were remembering being human by degrees, climbing down from my perch as lightning rod for the gods.

The next morning I woke early, kissed Diarmuid on the cheek, and whispered, "I be finishing today. Maybe late. But 'twill be done."

He smiled sleepily and stretched, touching my face. "Yeah-yeah?"

"Aye."

THREE DAYS later, I'd not slept, not ate, and had been pissing in a jar in the corner. So close. *Gods,* so close. I'd pound one spire into place and see the need for another, and another. I worked furiously, *feverishly,* barking at any interruption, snarling at Diarmuid like a fevered animal.

I were almost done—'twere almost finished, almost done riding me, riding my dreams. Soon, soon I would eat regular meals, bathe in warm water. Gods, gods, I would hold my husband again.

Soon, soon… it were… just one more spire, one more addition, one more bend, one more weld, one more—

Augh!

I sliced my hand on a spire while standing on scaffolding to reach the very top. I looked in wonder as the blood welled up and dripped down the metal, following a labyrinthine path to the packed dirt below. When it hit the ground, it simply pooled in droplets, and I wavered dizzily. Why weren't metal sprouting in its wake?

And then I looked up at the sculpture—a crooked-branching, fluid tree o' life—harder, more bitter, but also richer in its darkness.

'Tis done, I thought. Followed by the truer thought, *I'm done. I've spent enow blood on this. There is no more to spend.*

I looked around blearily for Diarmuid, and he were not there.

I felt a shaft o' disappointment and wandered inside, trying to fathom the time. It were night, early evening, and by the shouts outside, I thought it must be Samhain. I pumped cold water on my cut and walked through the silent house to the cabinet in Cairsten's room that held the bandages.

It were there that I saw Diarmuid's clothes, half piled on the dresser as though he'd thrown them into Cairsten's room in a frenzy.

I stared at the mess, trying to make sense o' it. Then I walked into our bedroom and saw the two beds, separate. As they had been for months.

When had I promised him? Two days ago? Three days? A week?

He were a tidy man—he would not have left that mess for long. This must have happened....

What were that noise?

Samhain.

And I'd promised.

I'd promised, and it were Samhain, and he'd gone to the bonfire without me.

I felt an irrational stab o' rage. Without bothering to grab a jumper or coat, *barely* remembering to put my boots back on, I charged out into the Samhain night, dodging children running the village as I'd run it with my mates so long ago.

The village hadn't changed—that were my first thought.

For so long, I'd been wandering through a dream, my only forays into the outside world the ghostly nighttime visits to the forest. I'd not seen the town for people and warmth, just the coldness o' embers dead on the hearth.

It were lively, I realized, shivering and not bothering to care. There were people here, laughing, talking, gossiping. For all we feared the whim o' a tyrant, the fact were he sat in his castle more days than not. Most days we had friends, family, livelihoods to mind, unless... unless, like me, you buried yourself in the half-life o' a representation o' rage.

A half-life, while living with a whole man.

Oh gods.

Diarmuid had been grieving too.

He couldna ha' waited? One more day. Just one more day, to make everything just so.... Just one more.... I were just trying to.... Couldn't he see?

It were like the thing—the wretched, wretched *thing* that had been birthed from my mind on the floor o' the forge—were screaming to me.

I am bigger than you. I am bigger than him. *I am bigger than all the small lives that surround me. How dare you put your lover first, when I need you to* live!

And my heart, which had been locked in silence from the moment my da had died on a mist-covered farm field when I were but a child, suddenly wanted a say.

He's mine. Mine! *There is no other way, no other person. He canna—he canna leave me. I'll die first, I'll kill him and die o' the lack.* Diarmuid!

"Diarmuid!"

My voice carried sharply across the voices at the bonfire, and he looked up. He were standing in the light, talking to Fisher, Tanner, Canda, and....

Jad?

Jad, the boy who'd tried to kiss me, who were now looking at Diarmuid as though he were the man he'd neglected to see? His hand were on Diarmuid's arm—casual contact, perhaps, but that's not what I saw.

Wildfire swept my body, and my expression must've been something fierce, because in a moment Diarmuid were alone. He were alone and gazing at me with a sort o' hurt fury that, were I sane, I'd say I deserved.

I were not sane.

He strode around the bonfire, dodging children and dancing elders as he did, and grabbed my sleeve in a temper.

"Decided ter grace us wi' yer presence, did ye?" he snarled.

We were passing the close space between two shops, and I grasped his wrist and yanked hard, pulling him into the shadows where only he and I could exist.

"I doona expect ye ter go lookin' fer a new man quite so soon," I hissed, and he turned his face away.

"I dinna know why ye'd think I'd wait," he cried. "It were not like ye wanted me yerself!"

"Want ye? I want nothing *but* ye—"

He turned back, sparks spitting from those bright brown eyes. "*Dinna lie ter me!*" he yelled, loud enough to bring others running if they feared for his safety. More likely, they simply feared me.

"I not be lying!" I shouted back, and the hell of it were, I believed those words. "I not be lying! Who do ye think could pull me back from that sinkhole, aye? What do ye think drove me these last weeks!"

"What drove ye?" Diarmuid shouted, angry. "I dinna care what drove ye—selfishness, pain, the woods, it makes no difference! Why should I care what were ridin' ye—*it were not me*!" I'd never seen him angry, and I were already fractured into so many parts, it were no wonder that part o' me were fascinated. Such hectic color washed his cheeks I could see it even in the shadows. He pulled his lips back from his teeth in a snarl, and for once, the kindness, the reason that had set his shoulders even as a young man, had fallen away. Part o' me, the feral, savage part, were crowing in triumph. I'd done that. He could move his clothes—he could rut with half the village—but *I'd* done that. I were the only one he could become a base man, an animal for. The two o' us, we'd rut in the forest like wolves.

"*Yer* what drove me!" I bared my teeth. "Ye think I want ter sleep in separate beds, D? Ye think I *want* ter live in the house with a man like ye an' not take him? Yer *mine*, damn ye! Ye promised! I've nothing o' me own, not even me own blood, aye? *Yer* all I have, and ye *move out!*"

"Ye dinna even notice!" he shouted, voice cracking with hurt. "I told ye last night, Teyth—if ye dinna come ter bed last night, dinna bother, *ever!*"

"Do ye think I'm even *there* when I'm working?" I demanded. "Tha' werena Teyth yer husband—*that* were the thing that drives 'im when he's weak!"

"When yer weak? Ye've been *weak* these past months, laboring on tha' thing day an' night—"

"I were *grieving!*" I howled, and oh! it were unfair.

"*So were I!*" he screamed back. "An' not just fer Cairsten, the only father I've ever known, damn ye, but fer *Teyth,* me lover an' me friend an'—"

"An' the bastard who must work in metal!" I returned. "An' ye knew tha'. Ye knew tha' when ye took me. Ye saw it growing in me all those years ago. An' it's a fucker—a fucker wha' owns me—but when it lets go o' me soul, *who do ye think I turn to*? I'm *empty* without it, D, empty an' aching, screaming an' lonely, an' the only one who can fill that chasm, paint that abyss is *me husband,* me lover, the man I've wanted sin' I were small. Can ye not wait fer me?"

He were going to refuse. Who could blame him? What did I have for trade? My skinny, beleaguered body? My mind half gone?

But I could not let him go.

I plunged my head down, taking his mouth with the fierceness o' a summer storm. I expected resistance. I expected him to fight, to bite my lips, to knee me in my swollen groin, but what I got back....

He kissed me back—angry, biting, teeth clashing, tongue battling, the sweet fury o' angry desire sliding down my throat like liquor.

I took charge, forcing him back against the wall, shoving my wounded hand down his pants and grasping his manhood.

Stiff, it were, turgid and fat in my palm, and I squeezed as I kissed him, squeezed and stroked up, waiting for his groan before I slid down again, squeezing the base.

He pulled away from me, flaming mad, and snapped, "Ye dinna get ter kiss me, grab me cock, if ye dinna intend ter keep me, Teyth. Ye'd better plan ter keep me in yer bed, in yer heart."

"I do," I gasped, biting at his neck, along his jaw, suckling on his flesh, tasting, nipping, *marking* him, so that no insolent farmer's boy might ever put his hand on my Diarmuid again. "I'll keep ye, I'll mark ye, I'll *fuck* ye—ye hear? Mine! Yer mine! No one else can do fer me like ye!" I punctuated my words with that hard, merciless stroking, and he were bucking, dripping across my fist, the salt o' his spend burning my large wound and the many small cuts my vicious calling had inflicted, but I did not care. I dropped to my knees there in the freezing mud, pulled down his drawers, and fed his cock into my waiting mouth. I wanted—*starved* for it, swallowing the crown in the back o' my throat, wanting him to fill me.

He grunted, grabbed my hair and bucked, his own skin probably as starved as mine for touch, for sex, and his come were thick and salty, the come o' a man who'd not even touched himself in too long a time.

He groaned and yanked on my hair, dragging my head back while I swallowed.

"Yer not done," he rasped. "Yer not done. Ye say ye want me? Take me. *Take me,* damn ye. *Make me* yers. Dinna just say I'm yer husband, *touch me* like yer husband! No guilt, no fear. Yer too ashamed ter take me, yer too ashamed ter have me!"

I were not ashamed.

I surged to my feet and ravaged his mouth again, splitting my lip against his teeth and sucking on his tongue until he beat upon my chest. I let go and he fumbled at his belt for the balm, and for a minute, I resisted.

For a minute I were possessed o' tha' forest savagery, and I wanted him, but not like he wanted. Not rough and angry, but screaming—taken, truly taken, against his will—bent over, bloodied, broken, and mine.

I tore my mouth away and took the balm in my hand, opening it with shaking fingers.

"Stretch yerself," I commanded, taking in breaths o' air. There were darkness in all o' us, and I'd been open to it long, aye, but not long enough to be the animal in my dreams.

Diarmuid, heedless o' the darkness I held at bay, locked eyes with me and thrust his hand behind him. There were no dignity in his person—he were naked from the waist down, thrusting his fingers up his arse—and the darkness eased. Freely. He were doing this freely, just for me.

I wanted him like this. I grasped his shoulders and whirled him against the wall, then fumbled for the stays o' my trews. They fell around my ankles, and I were as naked as he were. He were still fingering himself, whether for preparation or for pleasure I didn't know.

"Ye done yet?" I whispered harshly. "I want ye. I want inside yer body, inside yer arse. I'll take ye, D—"

"Take me," he grunted, pulling his hand out and bracing it against the side o' the building.

"I'll take ye an' fuck ye an'—"

"*Take me!*" he cried.

"An' make ye mine!" I crowed, finding his entrance and shoving in.

He cried out, for my cock were not small, and I thrust forward hard—filling him, becoming the focus o' my cock, letting my heart, my body, my animal rule my actions, my emotions, and center me completely on my lover.

"Mine!" I panted, thrusting into him hard and long. "*Mine!*"

"Yers!" he gritted between his teeth. Right there, ah, gods! Right there, in his body, right over his gland.

"Aye?" I grunted, shoving into him again.

"Yeah-yeah," he moaned. His word. All him.

"*Aye?*"

"Yers, yeah. Say it, Teyth, I'm yers!"

"Mine, aye. Yer *mine!*"

A quick, brutally hard and fast fuck against the wall, aye, but it were passion, all passion and need.

His arse held me, sucked me inside him, and it were such a warm place, such a haven compared to the places in my own heart I'd been plumbing these last months. I shuddered, tingling with the shock o' heat to my skin in the cold night air.

"Come," I begged him, although his seed still coated my tongue. "Come, lemme hear it agin th' wall, D. I'm gonna fill ye, all o' ye. Ye willna be able ter see fer my seed risin' inside ye."

"Aurgh!"

That were it, that strangled cry, and he convulsed around my cock, tucked his mouth against his biceps and *screamed* as his gland were battered into orgasm. I buried my face against his throat, bit 'is neck hard enough to bruise, and filled him with all the warmth in my body.

The shudders o' climax shook us while we panted smoky breaths into the coming frost. I wrapped my arms around his shoulders and squeezed before I slid out o' his body.

"Thank ye," I said, as distinctly as I could manage. "Thank ye fer being mine."

"Yeah," he mumbled, and he sounded lost and broken. Of course he did. He must have thought he'd sold his soul to a man who could not love.

"I'm finished, D," I whispered in his ear. "I'll put it away. It will be no more. We'll work, side by side, like we did before it started. No more great project, no more undertaking. 'Twill—"

"Nay," he breathed, pulling away.

For a moment—for a moment I thought this were good-bye, and he must have known it, too, because he brought his hand to my gruffly bearded cheek and cupped it.

"Nay?" I quavered. I'd thought I'd known the taste o' heartbreak, but I'd been wrong.

"Nay, ye willna put yer art away forever," he murmured, kissing my cheek. "I want yer heart, Teyth—not much good wi' out yer soul, yeah-yeah?"

"Aye," I mumbled and crushed him to my chest. "Yer my soul, D—"

"Ye dinna need ter lie, Teyth," he said wearily. "Ye broke me, after all. Proved my independence were a sham, took me. Ye dinna need—"

"My soul," I insisted, ignoring the insidious call to my blood. What needed I with art when I had my heart and soul? He shook his head, perhaps too weary o' pain to argue, and leaned his head against my chest. Not silence, but quiet fell over us, and the still raucous celebration o' Samhain rang sprightly in the night without us.

We pulled our breeches up around our hips and made it to our house. Then D seized my hand and pulled me into Cairsten's room.

His clothes still lay haphazardly around it, and he shoved them away without qualm.

"But, D—"

"'Tis a grownup bed," he muttered. "And we're sleeping here like men."

We did, crawling in naked and exhausted for the moment. D let me clutch him to my heart.

We awoke sometime in the night and made languorous, slow love. Diarmuid stretched me, filled me with slick, and then filled me with himself and slid inside me so gently, it were only the stretch that let me know he were there.

It were enough. I chased my climax on unsteady legs, finally having to grab myself while he moved or I never would have found it.

By the end he were heaving, fucking me sharply, some o' the anger finding itself even in the wee hours o' the morning.

I did not mind. It seemed he were not the only one who took the anger as a sign o' wanting. It had been long, so long, since either one o' us had felt needed. The harshness in the midst o' the sweet made it real.

CRACKED MIRROR

THE NEXT morning, I stumbled out o' bed early to relieve myself. When I were done, hurrying naked from the outhouse in the frost o' new winter, the old habit o' going to the forge almost overtook me again.

I thought of the piece and realized I needed to do something to get it out o' my mind.

I were still naked—and freezing—when Diarmuid walked into the back corner of the forge, betrayal written all over his face.

Not that I blamed him.

"What're ye—"

"Putting a tarp on it," I said shortly. "I doona want it lookin' at us when we're workin'."

"Wait."

Just that word, and I were a slave to it.

I were standing on the scaffolding, folds o' canvas in my arms, and I turned to gaze down on him. He looked small below me. Diminished somehow, but also far away. My teeth chattered in the sudden chill, and I yearned to be on the ground next to him, where we were equals.

"Wait?" I asked, uncertain.

"Let me see," he asked simply.

I couldn't look at it. Couldn't. "Aye," I rasped, turning toward him. Diarmuid, I could look at. Fitfully, I clutched the tarp and studied him—and his reaction. He'd had the sense to throw a nightshirt on, and my first thought were that I'd not been the only one not eating. The second thought were that he were making an effort to see the thing like it hadn't cost us months o' our lives.

My teeth chattered harder and I wrapped the tarp around my shoulders, suddenly mindful o' my nudity and my body as I'd not been the night before. I'd bathed recently, but I were skinny. My hands and forearms were a mess o' scars and wounds, new and old, and my beard were growing in wispy and unattractive, as I forgot to shave. I were pretty sure Diarmuid could count my ribs, and the mole on my back probably stood out like sin on snow.

I needn't have worried whether he saw my body or not. Diarmuid weren't looking at me, naked in front o' my creation. He were looking at the *thing,* the thing we both loved and hated, admired and reviled.

His frown o' concentration reassured me. He were *looking* at it, thinking about it. To him, it weren't just twisted metal—every spire, every whorl, every twist, angle, and line had meaning. He were assessing, recognizing the human things in the contrivance o' elements.

"Yer metalwork's improved," he said, his voice the detached tone he used when he were teaching me letters. "Smoother, the joins better hidden."

I preened in the simple compliment. Months we'd gone and not spoken to each other—this were like water on a dying man's tongue.

"It's sad," he murmured then. "The lines, the twisting—they're slower, an' sharper. There's anger here. Dinna get me wrong, Teyth, the other one had spirit an' a goodly amount o' fury, but *this* un'—if this were yer heart when ye were creating it, perhaps this be wha' happens when ye keep yer words in silence."

I shuddered, keeping my eyes on him, waiting for disgust as he searched the metal tree for my innermost heart.

He turned to me and smiled—a sad smile, but not repulsed or disgusted, and my eyes burned. Still good.

"'Tis beautiful," he said softly. "The village willna like it as much as the first—is too painful ter look at, somehow. But it be a thing o' beauty, beloved. I… I know it shames ye. These last months… they were naught ter be proud of, not on my end as well. But… dinna doubt this part o' yer soul. There still be grace here, yeah-yeah?"

"Aye," I choked out, suddenly busying myself with the tarp. It weren't doing any good to sop up the tears—it might as well be useful.

"Nay," Diarmuid begged. "Dinna. Please? Please, dinna cover it?"

"D—"

Now his voice broke. "It be the only part o' ye I have, these last months. I dinna want ter miss it."

"Aye." It were all I could say. I dropped the tarp where I stood and clambered down from the scaffolding, feeling awkward and foolish.

But when I got to the ground and were picking my way around the curls o' discarded metal I'd not yet cleaned up, Diarmuid greeted me with an embrace, wrapping his body around my chilled shoulders and rubbing his hands up and down over my back.

I shuddered and buried my nose in his neck, tearful the more for these old remembered intimacies made new.

"Wha's the matter, hey?" he asked gently, peering into my face.

"I'm so glad ye like the piece," I said.

He nodded, as though that made sense, but we both knew it were more. We both knew it were all in the lyrical twists o' tin and copper looming behind me in the forge.

He steered me into the kitchen and wrapped me in a blanket while he started cooking. I asked about clothes and he turned to look at me.

"No. Eat today. Sleep. Bathe." He grinned quickly over his shoulder as he pulled eggs from the cold box. "Let me do summat wi' tha' wild animal on yer face, yeah?"

I grimaced as I rubbed my beard. "Aye."

"Good. Clothes tonight, when we go into the woods."

I blinked slowly. "What will we do in the woods tonight?"

His smile were just as slow. "Remember when we made love in the woods, Teyth? An' it were holy an' good?"

I closed my eyes and skipped beyond the horror o' spilling my own blood on the ground, back to when magic were sacred. "Aye," I whispered, eyes still closed.

I opened them when I felt a puff o' his breath on my face. "Then we'll go let the forest know there be more o' us than anger an' sadness." He kissed my forehead and turned back to the stove. "I liked not the look o' tha' tree."

I remembered it—red bark, limbs shaped like human limbs. I could see why.

"Aye," I agreed. He were melting butter in a pan, planning to fry eggs and a slice o' ham in it. I realized my mouth were watering and me stomach roaring. "So," I said breathlessly, "could ye add another slice o' ham ter that plate, ter give me strength fer the comin' day?"

His grin were a meal in itself.

IN ALL, we had such a scant handful o' perfect days together. This day after a tumultuous Samhain, with the iron gray sky and halfhearted smattering o' snow—this day were one o' em.

We ate at the table, talking o' the things we'd done since we'd last eaten there. He spoke o' council meetings, and o' how hard it were to hold his tongue, and how the prince had committed no atrocities in a scant month.

"'E's frightening, how 'e comes out and suddenly destroys lives," Diarmuid said soberly, and I nodded.

"I… I ha' no words, no way to speak against 'im," I apologized, and he cocked his head thoughtfully in response.

"Yer piece—did ye see it last night in the square?"

My mouth twisted. "I had eyes fer one thing last night, D— weren't the bloody art."

His appreciative smile snuck up on him, like he were trying to be serious but I'd said something that pleased him beyond reason. He were still smirking when he finally managed to speak.

"People love tha' piece," he said at last. "They leave flowers there fer their own loved ones who were taken. Some in the battle, ye ken? Some just… taken. Canda, she left flowers fer Cairsten last night, fer his whole family, fer yers, even." Diarmuid gestured with his chin. "Tha' thing in the forge—we should put it up. Maybe across from t'other. It be angrier, sharper. Perhaps we'll be getting offerings o' knives."

I took a forkful o' eggs and one o' toast, chewing thoughtfully.

"Aye," I said, my voice soft. "Ye and yer council, ye can do tha', if ye wish. Me? I have no…." I shrugged, uncomfortable. "I ken summat about meself in tha' piece. Things I doona like."

We were sitting at corners, Diarmuid to my left, and he pressed his leg up against mine. "Yeah," he said softly.

"It's… ye could take it, an' I'd never look on it no more, an' tha' would be fine wi' me," I said at last, squirming where I sat.

Now he leaned against me, touching the line o' our arms together.

"Yeah," he murmured again. "Tha's why we must keep it near, Teyth. Ye canna stay so silent when ye see yer heart spilt day on day, yeah-yeah?"

Painful. True. "Aye," I agreed reluctantly. I took another bite o' eggs, and so did he. We finished breakfast in the best kind o' silence.

THAT NIGHT, after bathing and sleeping, eating and talking, we spirited out o' the village like ghosts. I had no knife on my person, and my wound had closed up. We were going in innocence, to make some amends.

The forest were familiar to me now—the home o' an elder relative, a kindly auntie, a mother's friend. None o' these I'd had, mind ye, but I'd seen Abel and Kerrigan the night before, watching anxiously as Kerrigan's da held their daughter. The candlemaker's would be a good place to be a child, and that babe would know what it felt to have generations o' which to not be ashamed.

For Diarmuid and me, the forest were that, and I found both o' us touching the boles o' favored trees as we passed. I'd had no idea I even cared for one o'er the other, but I did. Some had scars from missing limbs that marked them, and some were a different breed.

I loved the ones with the bark that fell like puzzle pieces, and that smelled like vanilla.

I followed D to the first place, the place o' Cairsten's field.

There were no snow there this night.

The wildflowers were as ripe and as lush as they'd ever been. But in the light o' the nearly full moon we could see that some o' them, the ones forming divots o' dark against what we knew to be purple and gold, would be crimson in sunlight, like blood, with black stems.

Diarmuid and I shared a look. "So that were what it did wi' me blood," I said admiringly. Not all o' it had been the great, frightening tree.

He were none too impressed. "What think ye the forest would ha' made o' yer tears?" he asked sharply, and a winter wind washed over the summer meadow.

There were nowhere I could look—not Diarmuid's grim expression, not Cairsten's meadow, not even the vast night sky that witnessed our little dramas.

"I doona ken," I said apologetically. "I—until I spilt the blood, D, I had no tears ter shed."

Diarmuid clasped my hand and twined our fingers, then spoke to the meadow.

"We miss ye, ye great bloody bear o' a man. May yer family be keepin' ye peace—tha' be the only comfort we have."

A ripple crossed the forest glade, and in that wind I could hear him, swearing at us in the forge, being patient with me over my letters. I could hear him say the words Diarmuid told me o', that I'd never heard myself.

Our Teyth, he doona say much, but look a' the things his heart says.

Oh, aye. He'd been proud o' me.

Together, Diarmuid and I clutched hands and wept. As we turned to go, a bundle o' flowers laid itself down by Diarmuid's feet—just that simple, scythed by an act o' will.

Diarmuid stopped and took them. "We'll leave 'em under yer tree in the square."

Then he took my hand and we walked, losing ourselves in the twists and turns o' the place. About the time I were tired and wanted to walk the crisp snow back to our home, we stumbled into another summer meadow.

Like Cairsten's glade, there were no reason for it—just were.

Small, a clearing with soft grass, every blade and every shadow illuminated by the moon. Diarmuid made a soft grunt and unfolded the blanket he'd brought tucked under his arm.

"Ye knew this'd be here?" I asked in disbelief. He'd made me carry a basket with a bottle o' wine and a loaf o' bread.

"Nary this, so much," he replied with a smile, folding his legs on the blanket and looking up at me in the moonlight. "But... ye came ter the forest and bled, and the forest gave ye yer heart's desire. This place, it loves us. Every year the townspeople hunt here, an' every year it gives them the last meat o' autumn. The women come ter find berries, an' we eat o' summer during the coldest months. And ye an' me—we've seen it do marvels." He shrugged, a simple gesture o' faith that I'd carry in my heart for eternity. "It were an easy bet ter make."

I set the basket down in front o' him and sat myself adjacent. Closing my eyes and putting my face to the moonlight, I heard the music o' nearby water and smelled the edge o' snow around our enchanted summer. I felt thin, transparent, almost as I did when I were working, as though the gods were breathing through me and the world, all o' it—the earth, the wood, the air, the water, fire, and iron in my blood—were sacred.

"Ye ever felt like... like lightning?" I asked, eyes still closed. "Like ye existed fer the gods ter breathe life into the world around ye?"

"Yeah-yeah," Diarmuid answered softly. His hand on my arm raised the fine hairs there, and I shivered. Now Diarmuid were sacred too.

"Aye?"

"Yeah. When ye touch me with yer heart, Teyth—I feel like I can touch heaven."

My eyes snapped open, and my skin tingled. "Is tha' why we're here?" I smiled. "Are we touching heaven?"

"Yeah," he breathed, and heaven were his mouth on mine.

Something about making love in the open air, under a great harvest moon—something changes ye. Makes ye strong.

Maybe it were the resolve to never let my lover slip away from me again, and maybe it were the knowledge that he still wanted me, for all the flawed work I were.

But I do not remember base things, human things—hands and mouths on cocks, sphincters stretched, pinched skin, hard suckling, marks o' teeth and nails—although judging from our appearance as we soldiered home through the snow, those were things that lost us in the physical glory o' climax.

I remember instead the brightness o' his eyes, and the warmth o' his mouth. The heat o' his spend on my body, the way he squeezed his eyes tight when I were inside him.

The soft sounds he made when we were coupled, and the bright cry o' triumph when he came.

My lover were my lightning rod to the gods in that meadow. We were greater than human, greater than art.

We were immortal.

When we were done, we drank some wine and spilled some more on the ground for the gods, and split the loaf the same way. And then, near the dawn, as the frigid wind o' dying enchantment blew through us, we dressed and clasped hands and went home.

We slept long into the next morning, and neglected the forge for one more perfect day.

THE DAY after that, we were up early, starting the forge like we had for the best parts o' my life. We stoked the fire, stacked the metal, prepared the projects while it were burning hot.

We'd not been in town the day before—we'd existed in a bubble o' our home and the afterglow from our time in the forest—and that, perhaps, were our undoing.

We found out later that Canda had been by twice to tell us that the prince were coming out to make sure the Samhain bonfire were cleaned up and covered with earth. He liked not the pagan festivals o' our village, and this year he were making them as short as he could.

Like Diarmuid had been saying—he were capricious, and that were the frightening part o' him. Diarmuid and I had just found our stable foundation. How were we to keep to our feet when the lightning struck beneath them?

I were in the back, pulling up the last ingots o' tin and copper from my stores for the piece, when the clatter of the carriage boomed through the forge like thunder.

All this time, all this fear—and he rolled up to our home like a summer storm.

By the time I peered around my bloody great folly, a footman were lowering a stepladder so that he might descend.

He had not changed appreciably since the first time I'd ever seen him, nearly ten years before. His fur coat were cut different, his hair swept back into a queue tied by a gold ribbon, but there were only a few more lines on his face than before, and his eyes seemed unclouded by any pain.

Well, they'd been easier years for him than for us, hadn't they?

"You," he said peremptorily to Diarmuid. "You—you were responsible for that monstrosity in the square, weren't you?"

Diarmuid put out a restraining arm to me, but on this score, the prince and I were of one mind.

"Yeah-yeah," he said levelly. "Tha' were us."

"Oh, yes. There used to be three of you, didn't there?"

Diarmuid's face were etched like the flashes o' metal I'd had in my mind when I saw him in moonlight. Cold and alien, the face o' a god.

"There were. Have ye come ter rob the town o' its two remaining blacksmiths? I be warning ye, 'tis late ter go sending ter another town fer an apprentice. Yer kingdom be falling apart fer want o' a forge."

The prince arched one eyebrow at him and glanced at me dismissively. "Don't be modest. I think you've more than proved these last months that this town will work very well with only one smith, haven't you? I mean, even *I* know *this* one has spent all his time playing in metal like a child plays with blocks."

I froze, and Diarmuid's expression altered subtly, became molten. "Yer tower," he said, his voice neutral. "Ye like it?"

The prince looked behind him, startled. The tower loomed as it always did, gray and polished granite, his giant stone phallus, raping the sky above our heads.

"It's... functional," he said with a twist o' lean lips.

"His 'playing' will be remembered long after yer tower. Ye think ye rule from there? Ye'll make a name fer yerself? Tha' sculpture in the square is a memorial ter kindness. Children make drawings o' it—they hang it in every home in the village. I watched no fewer than eight smiths drawn here by tha' thing's fame. They sketched, they went home, they copied." Diarmuid gestured to the back wall, where we were wont to put plans. I'd not looked there for too long, and at his gesture I walked over warily, picking up the sheaf o' parchments from under a stray tin ingot set on top to keep them down.

"Yeah-yeah," Diarmuid continued fiercely. "Smiths, telling us o' their triumphs, o' their own trees. Sketches from three kingdoms o'er. Ye think yer tower will last?" He shrugged, met my stunned gaze with a righteous triumph. "Yer tower is dust."

The prince's blow to the back o' his knees stunned us both. Diarmuid grunted and dropped to the floor, and I stepped in front o' him. I'd not even realized I'd grabbed the iron bar until I swung it out, knocking the prince's sword from his hand.

There were a moment o' shock, and I locked eyes with the monster that had plagued our dreams.

I snarled and lowered my head, prepared to fight to the death to defend Diarmuid, and for the first time, he saw me.

"You?" he asked, more dismissive than afraid. If I looked over his shoulders, I'd see six guardsmen, swords in hand, prepared to end my paltry life as I stood. Behind them, a crowd o' villagers gathered to see the show.

"Ye doona touch 'im."

"Haven't you lost enough?" he asked, as though he weren't responsible for those losses.

"Ye doona touch 'im!" I responded stubbornly. I would not parley with this man. I would not explain.

"I'll touch whomever—"

"We're wed," I snapped. "We're wed, and he's not of age."

Diarmuid stood and placed a heavy hand on my shoulder. "He changed tha' rule, Teyth," he said softly.

"I did," the prince said, smiling. "Are you ready to go, now that you've pointed that out?"

Diarmuid shook his head. "Why dinna ye skewer me here?" he asked pleasantly, like he were not talking about the annihilation o' the sun.

The prince grunted and leaned in, speaking just loudly enough for the three o' us to hear.

"Because we have an audience," he snarled. "And don't think I've not been aware of your movements, young blacksmith. I need to stop you. Dead, you're a cause for rebellion. Broken? You're a reason for them not to fight." That settled between us all, and it sat heavy. Then he smiled at Diarmuid—a horrible, corrosive smile o' lust and power and things I did not understand. "And I want you," he said deliberately, like he hadn't wanted Diarmuid since he'd first stood up to him with Kaspar, "but it must be alive."

I looked at Diarmuid and realized he weren't frightened. "He'll kill ye," I said, horrified.

"Yeah-yeah," Diarmuid answered, as though it were inevitable.

"*Nay!*" I screamed, startling the two o' them from the huddle.

"Teyth—" Diarmuid murmured, voice more than gentle.

"Nay." I turned toward the prince, who were smiling as though we were entertainment. "Me. Ye want a blacksmith? Take me. Not Diarmuid."

"What makes you think I can't take both?"

I grinned unpleasantly. "D said it. A blacksmith, 'e's the heart o' the village. Without D, there be no wagon wheels, there be no horse tack, there be no hinges. We fill twenty orders from yer steward every week. Ye *need* us. But ye doona need me at the forge—ye need Diarmuid."

"No," Diarmuid whispered, looking at me in horror. "Teyth, ye promised not ter leave me—"

"And I *lied!*" Oh gods. I had. "I lied, D. Cairsten died, and I left ye. I doona mean ter, but I did. I canna let ye be taken—not by this'un. Not by such a one. The town needs ye, and I need ter know yer alive!"

"I canna...." For once, Diarmuid were at a lost. "I canna... not without ye, Teyth—"

"O' course ye can," I wept, unashamed, even in front o' such a one as the prince who disdained us all. "I.... Ye canna be taken. He wants ter break ye, D. I've done this sort o' breaking—I'll be fine. Ye—"

"*No!*" Diarmuid cried. He whirled to the prince. "Ye've wanted me fer years—we both know it. Dinna listen—"

The prince looked at me and nodded. I felt the grip of the guardsmen on either side o' me, and the blow in my kidney that they used to immobilize me while they rapidly bound my wrists.

"*No!*" Diarmuid were shrieking now, falling to his knees in the street. I could not let him do that. I had to give him hope somehow.

"D!" I cried as they were shoving me in the wagon, hands behind my back. "D, come fer me when he's done, aye? Come fer me!"

"Yeah-yeah," Diarmuid muttered brokenly. The carriage had but one window, and as the prince climbed in, the last thing I saw o' him were Canda, one o' the onlookers from the street, wrapping her arms around him as he wept in the dust o' our home.

The carriage started to move, close and dark, appointments in indigo and velvet, and I fell awkwardly to my arse, facing the back.

The prince were laughing at his own joke, and I smiled at him sourly.

"What?" he asked, still elegant. "You think I did that out of kindness?"

"Nay," I said, knowing this weren't a victory. "Ye did it because ye think losing me will break him."

The prince tilted his head, suddenly looking at me as though I existed. "Yes. Yes, that's why I took you. Why do you think it won't?"

I laughed softly and leaned back against the cushions. "Ye think yer the only one who's cruel?" I asked, hating myself and thinking longingly o' the time that I'd lost and, it looked like, would not get back. "He's been married ter me fer a year and a half. Yer naught. I'm the crucible, aye? I tempered 'im. If he can survive me, he can survive whatever ye put me through." I smiled bitterly, but it were a smile. "He's bigger'n ye. He's bigger'n this village. He walks, and the earth trembles beneath his feet."

The prince's inelegant snort were pure peasant. "He says the same about you and your... whatever."

Oh, my trees. Aye. They had roots in the bedrock o' this village too.

"Ye have a lot o' books?" I asked as the carriage rolled under the archway to the castle proper.

"Yes—how did you know?"

"Because if I had nothing but leisure, I'd have lots and lots o' books. I'll bet ye've got books upon books and ye never read 'em, because ye think ye got the world figured out."

"I read as many as I can," he sniffed with dignity, as though I'd somehow offended him.

"Them words, them pictures in the books—how long ago ye think they were written?"

"I have no idea," the prince said, and it were as though, to him, I'd grown a soul.

"Long time ago, I reckon," I said. My arms were growing numb and sore at the shoulders, and I knew, distantly, that there would be a time I longed for a discomfort so petty. "An' we still read 'em, and teach 'em ter our children. Ye think ye'll live longer'n them books?"

"My tower—"

I shrugged and watched as the portcullis closed behind the carriage. Here we were, in the courtyard o' the castle, a place from whence so few returned. It shouldha been shrouded in mystery, yet I felt no excitement, no curiosity. I had been sheltered in the arms of the forest spirit, who blessed my lover and my union. I had channeled the will of the gods as they'd breathed life into cold metal, making it molten, making it spirit. Perhaps I were simply jaded to the ways o' human power, but this great edifice o' stone and vanity held no magic for me.

"Yer tower?" I repeated, musing.

"Yes."

"Will fall," I said, closing my eyes. "I lived wi' this monstrosity most days o' my life. Ye came, ye built it, ye cast a shadow o'er the village, but ye know what?"

"What?"

"I have big patches o' me heart untainted by this bare stone. But there's no part o' me—none—tha's not colored by the first word I read in a book. Do what ye may. Diarmuid kens I love him. Is more'n I deserve."

I were taken by guardsmen and dragged through the courtyard and into the tower itself. There were people I knew there—tending the horses and carriage on the outside, cleaning the floors on the inn. The farmer's boy who were taken not the year before ran by, dressed in crimson and gold livery, looking over his shoulder at me with big eyes. I nodded to him, knowing that a word would be out o' character for me.

"Bathe him," the prince called to the guards. "Take him to the workroom. I have matters to attend to."

I were bathed in a great porcelain tub full o' hot and fragrant water. I'd bathed the day before, but I minded not the guards scrubbing my privates, marking me with this man's smell. I wanted none o' Diarmuid on my person when he touched me.

They toweled me dry when they were done, and shaved me—all o' me—under me arms and me groin and even between the cheeks o' me arse—and combed the hair on me head, which were about all I had left. But they did not dress me.

Instead, they latched a leather collar around my neck like a dog, and snapped a leash to it before binding my hands.

I were not impressed.

My lover had found me filthy, flea ridden, whoring my blood for my fevered vision. He'd taken me home, bathed me, fed me, and loved me still.

What need I fear the prince's humiliation? Had I not inflicted enough on myself?

The worst were yet to come, I knew. I saved my spleen for the pain.

They took me up several flights o' stairs, each flight wrapping around the core o' the tower and looking down upon the center contained by the flight. It were dizzying—how many floors were there? Five? Six? Twelve? My brother had only plummeted four or five. Odd, how ye know how great a shadow a thing casts, without thinking on how great the thing itself.

In the end, the guards took me to a vast, airy room. It were not a torture chamber, as I'd first imagined, nor even a dungeon, since we'd journeyed up. It were dominated by a bed—one with a mattress, clean white sheets, and what looked to be clean straw ticking. But no covers. Next to it were a table with... well, I could not fathom. Some were cock shaped, so I assumed they were for sex, and some were small clamps, and again, I would imagine for sex. But there were also shackles for both hands and feet—some metal, some leather—and implements that, in this context, I could only imagine were for pain. I remembered Diarmuid forging some o' these items, and the two o' us looking at them curiously and studying the spec pages to be sure we were doing them right.

Looking around, I imagined that we were.

I'd known. Girls and boys, he took them to his tower to ruin them. O' course, in our village, there were no ruining, were there? A boy or girl came from the tower, supposedly in disgrace, an' it mattered not. Clancy had been welcomed, both in our town and by her new husband.

O' course, what happened in their own heads were not always controllable by the town. Self-loathing followed Kerrigan's sister's lover to the end o' his days—which happened at his own violent hand.

I looked around the room with new eyes.

The prince buried his bodies on the western side o' the village, but we saw the new graves, the new markers. There were not so many graves as all that. The prince didn't torture people to death—he simply "broke" them.

It were reassuring.

A stone window arched behind the bed, with a crossbow hanging on a hook next to it. The guards had latched my leash to a hook on the floor, and I took a few steps toward the window and looked out.

Our village were there.

From this angle, I couldn't see directly down, no, but I could see out. About half the square were revealed from my position, including, gleaming dully in the winter sun, the Beltane tree.

A detached part o' my heart acknowledged that it were indeed beautiful, and hopeful, and all o' the things Diarmuid claimed it to be.

Another part reveled—oh, how that tree must have galled the spoiled, angry man who liked to "play" with people's lives in this room. Were that what the crossbow were for? Were it to fancy us all dead?

Beyond the tree were the village gates and the path that led out to the farm cots, the neighboring kingdoms, and the vast forest.

It were then that I realized something odd.

The angle o' the window were such that the forest were cut off. If I stuck my head out the window, I might see how far it stretched, but from here, I had an impression o' just a small patch o' trees.

Were it possible the prince did not know how vast were the unseen kingdom right next to his?

The thought filled me with courage the like I had not anticipated, and it gave me the most amazing blessing.

My heart, my soul, my mind became like that forest cave, the one where Diarmuid and I had made love and quelled my grief. Secret. Filled with the barest o' things to sustain life. Whatever I said, whatever I did in this room after that, there were that place, that forest place, that his Highness could not touch. It made nothing hurt the less, made my blood no less red, but it were something.

It were everything.

After an hour o' standing barefoot on the stone floor, I gave it up and sat cross-legged, resting my chin on my chest and sleeping fitfully. The leash were run through a ring on a pole in the middle o' the room so I could not lie down, and I were almost amused.

Annoying, painful, but… petty.

O' course, it might not be petty after days, but if he were doing this himself, he probably had no self-control for things like sitting or standing for long periods o' time.

I hardly stirred when he entered the room.

"Stand up!" he commanded, sounding startled.

I turned my head and looked at him. "What'll ye do? Beat me? Rape me? Strip me naked and shave me bal—"

He had a knuckle bar across his hand, and he struck me.

That were how I lost three o' my teeth.

When the explosion o' pain had subsided, I pushed up to my knees and looked at him, spitting my teeth out as he watched.

"Usually," he snarled, "I give my subjects three questions. Make them worth my time."

I sat back on my haunches, only mildly surprised. Child's games, all. I had no interest in any gift from him, but there were some things I wanted to say.

"Aye," I said, pulling my lip up. Drool and blood were trickling from my mouth, but I'd spent my pain for that blow. He'd offered me something. I were taking it. "One. Wha'd ye say ter my little brother ter make him jump?"

His mouth parted slightly, and he almost looked dear, like a puzzled kitten. Then he seemed to recall himself. His eyes narrowed, and he chuckled to himself like it were a particularly good joke.

"I told him that if his heart were pure enough, he could fly."

I closed my eyes against that. Aubrey'd had the purest heart I'd ever known. 'Twere a particularly cruel lie, one designed to destroy.

"That were brilliant," I said, but not in admiration. "I'm sure yer cock got hard when his brains splattered across the yard."

Of all things, he looked outraged. "That's *vile!*" he spat.

I were not too bound to shrug. "If ye can think o' a reason fer me ter think better o' ye, by all means tell me, but tha's not one o' me questions."

He gaped at me, and I were stunned a bit myself. Silence. Weren't that my name? Apparently there were bright, whetted words honing themselves in that silence.

"I wanted to hurt *you,*" he said, almost like he were surprised the words were coming out. "Because if I hurt *you,* I'd hurt *him.*"

I nodded. "Aye. Aye, ye did. Tha' feel good, did it—nay. Doona answer tha'."

His look were stricken, as though no—it hadn't felt good at all. But I didn't want to use all my questions for a thing I fathomed in my own slow brain.

"Well, what *are* your questions?" he demanded, and he sounded shaken.

Poor, poor man.

"Right, then." Blood thundered in my ears, and my mouth were swelling. Soon it'd be a misery, and I'd be lost in a haze o' pain. "Second question. What be yer name?"

His mouth dropped slowly open, and his face... well, I were the one who were s'posed to be naked.

"I'm… I'm John Fredrick Francis, King of Ironwood. How could you not *know* that?"

I laughed. Oh, aye, my mouth hurt, my body hurt—my heart hurt most of all.

"Ye and yer tower. We didna even name our village. Fer all its grandness, aye, this place is naught but a lump o' dust. We lived an' died in the shadow o' it, but we did it wi'out ye. There were life—"

He hit me again, broad force, and those were the last words I said for a while.

A FURY o' beating—that I remember. Somewhere in there he grew hard, and he shoved his cock where them things fit.

Silence were no longer my name.

I screamed, gibbered, begged—I were, in the end, only human. When ye've pissed and shit blood long enow, there be no dignity left to save, and your only recourse is to scream through a raw throat.

I do not remember what had been done to me when I started to laugh helplessly, in such agony I were hysterical and crazed. He resorted to throwing iced water on my body, washing away the blood and the shit, the vomit and piss until it were just me, naked on a stone floor, shivering and shaking, rocked by that savage laughter.

"*What?*" he shrieked, spittle flying from his mouth. He'd been rutting with a battered meat suit—he had blood from his chin to his cock. In my degradation, I were cleaner than he were.

"Is jus'," I giggled, "jus'… ye never… answered tha' las' question!"

He shoved a hose in my mouth until my lungs burned and my vision went black, and I remembered no more.

CONFUSED IMAGES then. More pain, o' course. My stones an' cock feeling swollen, as though something inside were ruptured. Being left to freeze on the stone floor.

But then….

The farmer's boy? A lass I'd seen grow up? Children from our village, now grown and stuck inside this awful place. One on either side, telling me to shh, quiet now, he never looked in the trash heap when we disappeared, and now he'd think I were dead.

Ah.

No bodies.

The trash heap—it made fuzzy sense, aye?

I lay there in the winter night, covered with a soiled blanket, conscious o' the snow drifting down from the black sky.

THE NEXT morning I heard the shouts first—men, looking for me.

"D, he's 'ere!"

D?

A gentle hand brushed my face, and I opened one eye to a slit.

He were there—face drawn and pale, eyes bright. He bent over me and kissed my temple, weeping.

"There ye are," he whispered. "Yeah?"

I couldn't speak—I were not even sure how many teeth I had left.

But I could pull my lips up, just a wee bit.

I were Silence once more, but for Diarmuid, I could say, "Aye."

BROKEN

I DO not remember much of the months between Samhain and Solstice. I am aware there were weeks during which I did not know if I'd live or die.

Diarmuid, Canda, Clancy and her new man, her family, even Kerrigan, Abel, and their toddling little girl—all o' them spent time by my bed. They fed me soup, changed my sheets, helped me use the bedpan.

I would have been embarrassed, but if I were not humiliated by my enemy, I refused to be humiliated by my friends.

Some night, perhaps two weeks after I'd been fished out of the trash heap and carried home in Diarmuid's arms, I remember tossing with fever, throwing up blood, and sobbing on Diarmuid's thigh as he wiped my mouth yet one more time. I were only missing four teeth, from the side o' my mouth, but it were still hard to talk.

"Ye should ha' lef' me," I slurred, remembering that tranquil white snow, the infinity o' sky beyond. "Ye should ha' le' me die!"

He'd been stoic, kind, a comfort and a warmth around me, but that thoughtless utterance—that were what broke him.

He wept over me, broken sobs, thanking the gods, the forest, the sun and the moon that I were still alive to draw breath.

"I couldna live still," he choked. "I couldna live, not without ye. Yer not the only one, beloved. Yer not the only one what lost too much ter live."

I found courage then, strength to stroke his hand, to take one more breath, to force my eyes open in the morning, waiting for one more fresh wave o' hell an' pain.

He worked in the day, training Coyle, a lad from a nearby farm. I could hear him instructing the lad patiently, with none of the swearing Cairsten subjected us to.

I missed Cairsten more for the swearing, truth be known. Diarmuid's patience, when he had me to come home to, that were such a terrible cost.

But he would come in, and speak to whoever had been my companion during the day. Then he would sit at the foot o' the couch, under an oil lamp, and read to me.

Every book I'd loved as a child, he read. It were little known to me at the time, but when I were lost in my creation, he'd buy books and lay them on the table in an effort to entice me to stay. He read me those, as well.

I watched Kerrigan and Abel's little girl run around our rug, and heard the boy from the forge come in and play with her, and that drama made me happy. I played a fancy in my head in which they grew up and courted, and that were as fine as a book when Diarmuid weren't there to read.

I improved.

Eventually I could speak and make myself understood. The surgeon came and took the plasters off my arm, my shoulder, my ribs, my thigh, and for a while my days were spent lying down and stretching the muscles that had slept dormant while the bones healed.

Then I sat up and fed myself.

The day I walked to the outhouse were a particular triumph.

I couldn't be Silence when surrounded by friends and family who had only my well-being at heart.

I learned to sing nonsense for the baby, and remembered the joys o' telling stories with my friends.

And best and most precious, I learned to talk to my beloved in a way we'd never spoken when I were whole and sound. We talked o' books, o' histories, o' politics, o' cities and cottages, o' paintings and sculptures and art.

We talked o' us and what our world would look like in five years, if it were as we willed. What would it look like in ten? In twenty? As we grew old and in our dotage? He talked o' finding a baby among the cottages, one who needed feeding or care, and o' bringing the babe into our home.

I thought he'd be a wonderful father, but I confessed to being jealous at the thought.

He laughed and said we would talk about it again.

I'd always known the heart o' my beloved, the stout courage, the gentle integrity, but in our talking, I learned to love the all o' him.

And that included the part that needed to see a village that would allow our future.

By Solstice I could move cautiously around the house. We still needed help with lunch and dinner, but I could make breakfast for us and the young towheaded, brown-eyed Coyle. The boy stayed with Canda, and I think that gave her healing too. Two days after the Solstice celebrations, while I dozed on the couch with a book, Diarmuid met with the council for the first time since Samhain.

"We agree!" Fisher shouted after some heated debate. "Even if Teyth weren't the worst case we've seen, one were too many. But we fought this fight before, Diarmuid, remember? Remember that battle? Because there are them who grew up fatherless after that misty day in October, and those men who died were doughty, fearless, and fighting for their families!"

Diarmuid nodded. "Yeah," he said grimly. "Yeah, they died. Because they met armored men in battle. They were undertrained and underweaponed, for all their hearts were in the right place. But by discarding one o' our own on the trash pile, he's shown us a way to fettle 'im sure."

"Explain what ye mean," Canda said, her own voice grim. "Because Beltane is coming like a charging stag. We've put Teyth's second tree up, and I'd do it again—I'd make my own, if the gods had willed me his gift—but it be an act o' war, and we need more than anger in our hearts."

Diarmuid grunted assent, and I wondered idly when they'd put my tree up. I could see them, the sweet and the bitter o' my heart, up in our square, the elegant twistings o' the tree with hope versus the grim angles o' the tree without.

They'd be beautiful, I realized, and I almost missed what they said next.

"The boy who led us to the trash heap—his mum sends him a basket o' bread every week. She walks up to the gate and is allowed to hand it to him, so we know the message will be there. He's been smuggling victims ter the trash heap fer the past year—'twere how we knew ter look fer Teyth."

Oh. Oh gods. Diarmuid had known about the trash heap when I'd only just come to myself. How would I know? Diarmuid—he'd been saving our village while I'd been entrenched in my fancy. Helplessness overwhelmed me. Who were I, to take his time and own his heart?

But then, Canda had declared my art an act o' war. One she wished she could make. Perhaps it took us both, Diarmuid and I, to change the pieces in the puzzle o' our world.

"He sneaks one o' us in—someone who knows metal and can break the chain on the portcullis," Diarmuid said grimly. "'Tis easily done—and if it be done toward the morning, while the guards in front o' the village sleep, before the shift change, we'll catch them in the wee hours. In the morning, they'll realize it's broken and send guards out the east side o' the tower. They'll have ter swing south to come in through the gate, yeah-yeah?"

They all nodded with him.

"We'll be there, blocking the entrance. We've archers training from the cots who will be inside the gates. There will first be sally after sally o' arrows, which will either take them out from the front or drive them back. I helped forge the portcullis—it will take them a week to break it down or fix the chain themselves. He will be sieged outside o' his own village. In the meantime I have a friend, one village over—ye all remember Kaspar?"

They all made assenting sounds, and a few o' them glanced nervously at me. I did not fear Kaspar, but I did fear, more and more, this plan.

"We siege him, for a week—less. Kaspar's wife's family is part o' the ruling family. They will send soldiers here, and they have a prince—a young one, idealistic, hopefully sane. If we let him take over the tower, we have a treaty already agreed upon, one that will let him tax us reasonably and tha' forbids the suffering o' our young people. One tha' holds 'im accountable for…." His voice shook, and he looked at me boldly, his eyes bleak. "Accountable," he repeated. "Fer the damage tha' he do."

All the council looked at me, and all o' them nodded.

It seemed they agreed, and though I had much I wanted to say to my husband, I would not gainsay him, not when he had the hearts o' our elders in his palm.

They refined the plan and dispersed, promising to keep their efforts quiet and to think upon yeah or nay.

Diarmuid finished cleaning up after them and then came and sat quietly on the couch with me. I stretched out my arm with ginger ease, and he laid his head on my chest with equal delicacy.

Just that, only that, and I were happy.

"Ye dinna approve," he said after settling in.

"'Tis dangerous," I replied. "Not tha' I doona approve o' ridding us o' him, but ye plan ter hold 'im off." I closed my eyes and saw, for a minute, half o' the village spread out before me from a turret window. "He can see ye, D—he can see ye as ye scurry. I could see this place, and it gave me heart, but he'll…."

Diarmuid nodded. "Yeah," he said softly. "I can see—we'll need another plan. But is coming, yeah-yeah? Ye see tha' it be summat we must do."

"Aye," I muttered, disconsolate. I tightened my arms, weak as they still were, about his shoulders, and closed my eyes in pleasure at the intimacy.

In our hearts, we were peasants—we would not think on tomorrow.

BY THE time Solstice passed, I could take short walks into the forge and even to the marketplace, provided there were a neighboring tent with a friend who could let me rest before I turned back.

I used a cane, because so much o' my body had been broken that I couldn't move well without it. 'Twere a painful lesson in humility and mortality, that. I would walk about the village square and see the works o' art I'd conceived in my hale-bodied best, and even through my pain, I saw the depth a boy lacks that a man has. Should I go back to the forge again, I thought, I could conceive of such beautiful, well-balanced pieces—pieces with depth and fire, o' life and death and pain, and even harder, *joy*. And I would not do it at the expense o' my lover or my friends. I could create much better beauty when those things were in balance in my life—I would never forget that, I *knew* in my heart.

And as I went about my snow-covered crawls of the village I loved, I also saw *it* through grown-up eyes. I saw the stone walls that were taller than any man. They needed to be repaired every spring, and boys would run around the outside o' the walls with ladders and buckets o' mortar. I'd been too busy in the forge to do my job with the walls, and I thought now o' laughing voices and shouted games.

I saw how easy it were to forget the forest, and the farmers, and the other villages existed beyond those walls. This village, it were the center. There were no other thing. There were the mud-and-stone track beneath my feet and the great blue. There were the shadow of the tower and the glory o' the sun. The gardens that would grow from the water beneath. Earth, air, water, and fire—but no wood. No spirit.

During those mad, whirling months when I'd been so invested in my work, I had been all about the spirit.

Hobbling painfully around the small track, cramped by any measurement, I were aware that there must be both in a life. Know your village, and know the world beyond.

It were such a small realization, yet it felt profound. All o' that mad chasing for a thing, a thing to make pieces o' my soul last forever, and it were that balance that would give it the peace to do just that.

Perhaps making that realization made me clairvoyant. Perhaps it simply put me on that plane, where I could see spirit and the physical all in one.

Perhaps it were stinking peasant's luck.

But as I limped around my village and thought deep thoughts engendered by pain and experience, a chill coursed my spine. My eyes were drawn upward to the great tower, and even from the distance, my eyes searched out the window o' that terrible, terrible room.

A figure stood there, looking down.

I knew the thin white face, the pale silver hair. But even if I hadn't, I would have recognized the implement in his hand.

He sighted down the barrel of the crossbow, directly at me.

Abruptly, I remembered that third question, the one I'd never asked. *Do ye fantasize about picking us off? Like so many chickens in a coop?*

Apparently he only went for the wounded cockerels. My blood shouted in my ears about how he couldn't kill me—Diarmuid would try to scale that tower wall with his fingernails and teeth to bathe in that monster's blood.

I continued to gaze upward, tempted to hide in the cart that were being hauled slowly in front of me, pulled by a reluctant donkey. There would be no protection there, I thought bitterly, and I looked about as slowly as I could.

I were walking by two houses at the time, lined up like most houses on our row and separated only by a strip, perhaps two men wide, o' bare earth. I stepped into this gap and leaned up against the wall, and after a moment a shaft flew with almost casual aim, piercing the donkey's skull and sending him crashing to the ground.

There were great hue and cry then, and I stayed, heart thundering, between the houses until Diarmuid came to see what were happening. He found me, standing on shaking legs, still out o' sight.

A great crowd had gathered in the gathering twilight, and Diarmuid asked quietly for the crowd to escort us home while we traveled in its midst.

'Twere a great and brave thing to do, but the self-crowned King o' Ironwood seemed content with his killing for the day and we made it inside, where I allowed myself to be subjected to a hot bath and lots and lots o' tea.

"Why?" Diarmuid asked, when I were at the point where I could speak. He were pouring another kettle into the tub, and I welcomed the hot water as it swirled through that which were cooling. "What were his purpose?"

"Cruelty an' boredom," I responded easily, fanning my fingers through the water to make it mix. "Did ye think better o' him?"

Diarmuid sighed and set the kettle on the hot pad on the table. He pulled up a chair by the tub and leaned his weight on his elbows, pinching the bridge o' his nose. "Why would he come here, all those years ago, bring an army at his back and proclaim himself king, if all he had to offer were cruelty an' boredom?"

It were not an idle question, but I had an answer only my own.

"I think there's some who see not the outside and in o' things, beloved," I said at last. He looked tired and worried, and I yearned for the days when I'd been able to give him comfort with my young and hale body.

He looked at me and nodded for me to go on, so I suppose breaking my silence were the thing that would comfort him the most.

"He wants ter rule because he thinks it makes him important. He passes down mindlessness because he thinks it makes him a ruler. He knows not what it is ter make a living with his hands. He thinks a living is what other people do ter serve him. An arrow shaft and a dead jackass mean as much ter him as a pin and a dead bug ter ye. He doona understand that ye doona kill the bug because ye can—ye let the bug live because the bug too has its place."

I looked at Diarmuid, trying to see if he understood, and Diarmuid were nodding, so I had hopes.

"Ye've gotten very wise in the interim, beloved," he said after a moment.

I smiled, the compliment meaning more to me than he could know. "I've had a good teacher and too much time ter think," I responded truthfully. "All time ter reflect, no time ter do."

Diarmuid grinned at me, suddenly the boy who'd first shown me books and hoped I'd like them too.

"Do what?" he asked playfully, but since he were running a hand down my bare chest, I had to assume he had a suggestion o' what we were to do.

I were so grateful I almost wept.

"Be touched like tha'," I said roughly, tilting my head back. Diarmuid stood, which disappointed me until he stripped off his jumper and knelt in front o' the tub.

His bare chest, even winter pale and worry thin, were still a thing o' beauty.

I reached out my hand, still damp and warm from the bath, and smoothed a bit o' suds across it, running my thumb in circles around his dark brown nipple.

"I like ter do tha' too," I told him, feeling shy as I never had been. Ruined. I were ruined now—bones at odd angles, ribs that would never lie straight, too thin from healing, whiter'n snow in most places, discolored permanently in others.

"I been waitin'," he confessed, breathless. He leaned over the tub and kissed me, the humid haven o' his mouth as comfortable as the wet heat o' the bath itself. The terrible relief o' basic human desire flooded my veins, and my flesh swelled, stretching my skin, making it taut and sensitive.

"I want," I reassured him. Ach, gods, how could I not want? He hummed and reached into the water, finding my cock half-erect. At his touch it hardened completely, and I arched my hips, letting the air kiss the head while he stroked the shaft. Oh, oh yes. Diarmuid's hands on my body again. How could I be so blessed?

"How ye feelin'?" he asked, and it were not a lover's question but a caregiver's. The bath were good, but I'd been sitting awhile. Often, I'd need help out and help walking afterward when I'd been in this long.

"Ye want ter finish this in the bed, aye?" I asked, biting my lip in hope.

His smile were slow, careful, as though he were afraid o' getting hurt but had to speak anyway.

"Yeah-yeah," he answered.

He stripped entirely and helped me out o' the tub, then dried us both off. He helped me walk back to the bedroom, and together we nestled under the covers to escape the chill o' a house in the winter.

His hands on my skin were a wee bit cold, and when he circled his fist around my cock I let out a breathless little gasp—and then grasped his in return.

He kissed me—long, soft, sweet—and together we bucked in each other's hands while the kiss went on, and on.

My peak came suddenly, my body denied pleasure for too long in all the pain to last. My cock tingled, and I moaned in surprise as my free hand beat feebly against his brawny arm. Oh, oh gods! So quickly! My want, it were bigger than just this one climax—longer, hours longer, taller, *more*—that were my one thought as I spilled slickly into his fist. More.

But as the thick wet coated his fingers and continued to torment my cock head, I heard a low, tearing groan echo from the pit o' his stomach.

"Not yet!" he cried and came, jerking, and our seed coated the space between our stomachs as we lay on our sides and trembled.

I laughed and sobbed into the hollow o' his neck. "Not fair," I said when we both had our breath back. "I wanted tha' for so long!"

"Oh, me too," he panted. "We must do tha' again, yeah?"

"Oh, aye, D—we *must*!"

We laughed quietly and he helped me put my nightshirt on so I could eat a quick dinner o' leftover stew in front o' the fire.

We sat on the couch after dinner and I leaned against his chest, both o' us under a thick wool blanket that were a Solstice gift from Clancy and her husband. She'd worked it while she'd helped keep me company during my recovery, and we'd spoken so dryly and playfully o' being former spouses that her husband, plain as Cairsten said but sweet as any flower, had laughed in understanding. I think if he'd had any doubts as to his wife's ability to love him after me, they'd been put paid in those quiet moments o' hope and knitting.

Diarmuid and I spoke o' them as we sat, and we spoke o' Kerrigan and Abel and their little girl. We spoke in yearning tones o' Cairsten and the rough, uncouth things he'd say about a dead jackass in the road, all the while helping the poor farmer who'd lost half his earthly wealth with one arrow loosed in pique.

We did not speak o' death, mine or his, or how if we went through with the plan come Beltane, neither one o' us were likely to live to see another winter.

You cannot live to spill spend on your lover's skin if you die every day you take in breath.

A MOON cycle. Two.

Spring threatened, but we were left with the end o' winter, suffering cool mists in the early black o' morning. By the river it would be too foggy to see, and in the town the mists rose from the muddied ground where the snow were still present in patches.

One night Coyle came running from Canda's place, breathless and worried. The boy who worked inside the castle had gotten word to his mum that the prince would be on his way out the gates late the next morning to collect taxes.

He'd see the trees, as metal-gray as the sky, but with touches o' color and heart flowing like blood under the surface.

Diarmuid nodded and told the boy to sleep on the couch that night. The next morning we'd be sending him on his way to Kaspar's village, a parchment tucked under his belt.

'Twere a dangerous duty, but we were sending him with Clancy and Kerrigan and Kerrigan's little girl. Aye, it were good to have cover, and quicker to have a cart and a story o' going to visit relatives, but

Abel had exchanged long glances with Clancy's husband when this part o' the plan had been hammered.

They wanted their mates clear o' the trouble, and that were all there were to it.

If I could have stood the journey on the cart, I'm pretty sure Diarmuid would have sent me too.

The truth were, I'd fallen ill once or twice since Solstice. Not enough to worry Diarmuid entirely, but enough to pull my recovery from the brink o' health.

Where we'd originally planned for me to journey around the back o' the trash heap and through the back ways o' the tower to cut the chains o' the portcullis, now we'd taught Clancy's da, Fisher, the tricks o' the great metal cutters and given him the task.

I'd fought bitterly at first, through a hacking cough that only proved Diarmuid were right about my health.

"Where will I be, beloved?" I asked, feeling helpless and useless.

He grimaced at me and held out his hand. "Next to me, confronting the guards," he said softly.

I'd smiled then as I never had, not even as a child. "Ye'd let me do tha'?" I asked. Oh, aye, I knew it could mean death, but a death at Diarmuid's side were all I asked.

"Yeah-yeah," Diarmuid said, his tone making light o' his nonchalant words. "I have more fear fer what he'll do ter ye without me than I do with me by yer side."

I nodded my head, thinking the opposite were true. That I would probably live a long, bitter life if I hid here in the only home I'd ever loved, but far preferable were facing the same fate as my beloved by his side.

THE PRINCE came. We were all standing in the square, our allotment o' taxes in our hands. Diarmuid and I paid in tin and copper, and gave the extra to those who'd had a particularly rough winter o' it. No one in our village would go hungry to pay the tithe to a man who gave us naught but fear in return.

I stood by Diarmuid as the assessor came by. The thin, unpleasant man who showed his disdain for us by not looking us in the eyes held his hand out for our bag o' valuables. When the larger than usual bag o' metals were plopped into his palm, it nearly broke his wrist.

We ignored him, instead keeping our eyes on the prince, who tried to avoid our direct stares.

It were hard for him. Wherever he turned, the townspeople were staring at him, the heat o' nearly fifteen years o' anger in their eyes.

"Is there a difficulty?" he asked after a moment, and nobody spoke. "I am your *prince*!" he yelled into that deadened silence.

"Aye, what's yer name?" someone shouted out.

It weren't me, but I'd told o' my three questions and how it had pricked him hard that we did not care who he were.

"I am Prince John—"

We jeered.

"John Fre—"

Our jeers grew louder, more brazen. He'd only brought three guards with him on this trip—apparently he thought we were cowed after my abduction.

Must a man work earth or craft with his own hands to know what another man will do to not give it up?

We kept up the noise, obnoxious, disrespectful. He'd climbed to the top o' the carriage to deliver the taxing decree. Now, as he shouted us down, the horses startled, sending him falling to his arse.

The laughter must have galled him no end, and I could stir myself for nothing resembling pity.

I'd stood naked before this man before he'd beaten me into the stone. Let him be naked before us, even for a moment. Aye, vengeance can be a petty thing as well as a great and terrible one, but truth were I needed to see him humbled, human, before I saw him felled.

Otherwise, it would not be real.

He stood then, eyes no longer cold and detached. Aye, we'd poked a dragon with a stick, and we each knew it.

"These *things* in my square are an abomination!" he snarled, and we quieted to hear him. "They will be removed tomorrow, if I have to use sulfur and saltpeter and detonate half of Ironwood!"

His cry were greeted with cold silence and the same glares that had greeted him when he first stood before us.

"We dinna ken tha' name!" Diarmuid shouted, pulling his lips back from his teeth. "Perhaps ye might not have so much trouble if ye were in the right village!"

More laughter then, and the prince waved his hand rather desperately. The clatter o' armed soldiers rattled through the village, and although the castle weren't in our line o' sight, we knew that soldiers were issuing through the portcullis.

By the time they arrived, the square were empty o' everyone save the council o' elders, including Diarmuid and myself. Folks had given us their taxes and fled, but it were no difficulty. We stayed, waiting for the guards to flood the square, and then Diarmuid addressed the little tax man with a voice flat and plain, while looking the prince in the eye.

"This bag is Krebs, the tailor, yeah-yeah?"

"Yes," the tax man said, making a notation and taking the small bag o' coins for his basket.

"Tha's eight coppers, one silver. Write it down."

"I *said* yes!" the man said testily, but Diarmuid weren't speaking to him.

"And this is for the three farmers in the northwest corner, by the wall." He continued staring at the prince, affecting no emotion, no expression.

"Yes," the tax man said, looking nervously from the prince to Diarmuid.

"Tha's three coppers, two silver. Write it down."

"Yes," the man said, suddenly remembering that with this master, it were best to be invisible.

Diarmuid didn't break eye contact, and he stood for all in the village. When his handful o' tithes were gone, we handed him the ones that had been left with us. Diarmuid recited the name o' every farmer, every craftsman, every villager, along with their taxed amount, and the prince were trapped. He had all o' his guardsmen out there—he couldn't send them away, or he'd lose face. He couldn't go back without them, because the people he were afraid of were still out in the village.

And he were forced to listen to the recitation o' the people, every name, that Diarmuid knew. And not one o' those people knew the prince.

By the time we were done, my knees were wobbling, and it were hard to breathe from standing so long.

And the prince's face were red—from anger or mortification, it were hard to tell. He looked at Diarmuid nakedly, longingly. It were clear to all that the man the prince had yearned for since he were just a boy defending his young lover had just shown why for all his finery and claim to the great tower, the prince were not—had never been— worthy.

When we were done, we turned away as a group, walking around the gathered troops and not looking back.

"I'll destroy them!" the prince called. "I shall come back tomorrow and rip them down from the bolts, melt them into soup, and cast *garbage* from the molten slag!"

Diarmuid turned to him, and I tugged at his hand. 'Twere not worth it, not to defend me.

"Those sculptures," Diarmuid said, a beatific expression crossing his face, "they will survive us all."

He turned with my tugging then, and together we walked back to the line o' tradesmen's homes, each to their own home except Canda, who would stay with us this night.

We'd asked—we were her boys tonight, as Cairsten were not there.

Quiet dinner, quiet evening. Diarmuid read to us from his favorite book, the story o' the king with the knights who all stood for justice. It were a fairy tale, but comforting—gave us a shape, as it were, to shoot for.

We embraced Canda, bid her good night, and retired to Cairsten's room, which still held his trappings. We'd never made it ours with more than our clothes.

Diarmuid slid into bed, nightshirted against the cold, and held out his arm so that I might rest against his chest.

"I miss him still," he confessed roughly, having read my mind, probably, thinking about Cairsten.

"I miss them all," I whispered. Then, "Except Kump—the forest can keep tha' fucker. Oh, an' Kaspar, which be mean, but, well, aye. I were jealous o' him, even back then."

Diarmuid chuckled as he were supposed to, and kissed the hair on my temple. "Tha's very grown up o' ye ter admit," he said softly.

I grinned up at him, not minding my hair or my teeth or the irreparable twistings o' my body. "Well, I am near ter twenty-one," I said gravely.

It should have been tragic, but we laughed softly into each other's necks for quite some time before falling fast asleep.

CASTLES FALLING

DEEP INTO the night, at the flux o' morning, there were a solid knock on our door—three hard taps—and we were set into motion.

The three o' us arose, drank hurried coffee, and ate cold bread, all the while peering out into the fallow garden.

A low, close mist hung over all things. It were this night or never. The girls and Coyle had left at first light yesterday. Two days to get there, two days to gather, two days to return. Before that time we wanted our town in our own hands, to give to another ruler like a gift. The prince would send his troops out to destroy the art—our symbol o' hope—today. It were our job to stop him.

It were time to go greet the army that lived in our backyard.

Diarmuid had spent the winter forging swords and light armor for all those taking part. It were no army, but threescore villagers standing behind the closed gates while Diarmuid and I stood in front to parlay.

The captain o' the guards stood halfway between the forest and our home. He were one o' the men who had helped drag me away from home; I had never known him as more than a helmet. His men were arrayed behind him as the sun lurched over the village walls to the side o' the tower, casting thin, late-winter light in the eyes o' the men facing their own village walls with surprise.

These men took wives from our village, spent their rest days walking the market place, eating at the baker's or the pie maker's. They gave orders to the tailors and took their children to play with the children o' the villagers and farmers, and now they were told to come slaughter us.

I did not envy them, but I did not pity them either.

There came a time when you decided that what were right weren't what you were told.

"What be the meaning o' this?" the captain asked, puzzled. He advanced his horse a few paces as he shouted, but I placed a hand on Diarmuid's sleeve. We were in the shadow o' the wall right now—I had not forgotten the crossbow and the window. The prince were not here, so where were he?

"Ye dinna need ter be involved," Diarmuid said politely. "Ye stand fast, it be a siege. There be another prince or mayor or whatever, comin' ter takeover. Ye may work for him if ye might."

The captain's eyes darted left and right to his men. Then he cantered completely forward, stopping where the sun met shadow.

"What be one from the other?" he asked, pleading. "This'un— 'e's not so bad, eh? Ye let us through, let us take the art down—what be the harm?"

Diarmuid's face were set in grim, angry lines. "The art is ours," he said flatly. "An' he's only not so bad because he never shites in his own pot, does 'e? 'E shites in *ours,* because 'e's not close enow ter smell. We're tired o' the shite, sir. We want ter see if someone else might not shite quite so much tha' we're dyin' from the stench."

The captain grunted, as though he took that hit personally. "He... I mean, I'm sorry about yer man here." He nodded at me. "About yer da. But—"

"But what?" Diarmuid asked, not backing down. "Does there need ter be an excuse there? Does there need ter be forgiveness? He's not a child, that'un. He's a grown man, an' he's treating us like toys." Diarmuid looked at me, remorse in every breath. "An' he's breaking us."

The captain looked at me and took a deep breath, sighing, then looked to the men uneasily sitting their steeds sixty paces behind him.

"Ye have a ruler coming?" he asked, unsure.

"I've got no will ter rule," Diarmuid stated. "I run the council— 'tis as big a pair o' trousers as I've ever wanted."

"'Cause I've read the books too," the captain said, scanning behind us as though the wall had turned to something else. "A bad ruler, aye. Ye don't want that. But ye know what's worse?"

"Instability," Diarmuid answered sagely, and I were lost then. I'd heard D say it before, but until the man in the tower had personally set out to pollute my life, I'd had no use for politics, mostly.

"Aye. Ye don't want a vacuum at the helm. Ye sure?"

Diarmuid had asked Kaspar, and Kaspar had promised. Even I would take that man's word. "Yeah-yeah, I am," Diarmuid responded, and the man nodded gravely. Perhaps he had children, and he feared for them. Perhaps he had a wife who'd needed to be rescued from the trash heap. Whatever it were, he looked to his left and his right and shook his head, backing his horse up.

"Stand down!" he called, and the officers sitting their horses at attention sheathed their swords and dropped their shields.

"I'll wait fer me orders," the captain said, nodding. "'E'll need ter deliver 'em in person."

He backed up one more pace and turned his horse around—

And then fell off the horse and to the ground in a clatter o' armor.

We all stood, stunned, looking at him as he writhed, not killed immediately from the arrow in the back. The horse danced frantically above him, and Diarmuid and I looked at each other in shock.

"I'll get the horse," Diarmuid said, swearing, because that were D. This man had helped us and needed our help in return. Likely it were he'd been wounded for us, for telling his men to stand down. Diarmuid ran forward, ducking to make himself a smaller target, and I turned, dreamlike, to look across the village to the far-away window in the tower.

I could see him, the figure there, hands busy with the crossbow. He were winding, winding, winding....

I looked out to Diarmuid, who'd untangled the guardsman from his tack and were calming the man down. He looked up at the troops and called, "He needs help! Somebody, can ye not help yer captain?"

I did not see their reaction to that. Diarmuid stood, his back *to our enemy*, so focused on doing good as he always were, that he were not looking to see where the next blow would come.

I couldn't change it in him. I would not if I could. It were the thing, the thing I'd always loved about him, that doing good were his calling, part o' his soul, and he loved me with the same soul. I hobbled as fast as I could, my cane swinging, my feet stumbling on hummocks o' grass.

"Come away, beloved," I pleaded as he crouched by the dying man. "Come away. Diarmuid—come away!"

It took time to reload a crossbow, time—the prince weren't done firing, just cranking back the bow, sighting down the barrel....

Time.

Diarmuid glanced up at me as I drew near, and I could tell by the sudden panic that he had known the risk to himself—but now here I were, out o' the shadow o' the village wall, and random violence had us in its sights.

He looked back down at the captain, and I pushed my body as I did not think it could be pushed, lining myself up with his back just as he stood.

I heard the twang o' the arrow in my mind and wrapped my arms around him as it hit, piercing me through the heart, then him, both o' us falling to the ground in a gush o' blood.

I didn't feel our bodies hit the ground.

Diarmuid and I, we were together, our blood seeping into the earth and our minds and hearts twining around each other, like the two trees, hurt and anger joining together to grow into summat healed and strong.

I felt him pulse and pulsed in return, and together our hearts beat in the ears o' the forest spirit, joined by our blood in the same earth.

And we grew.

Our blood whorled, stretched, became runes in the earth, became branches, became twined metal, and we raced together across the ground to the wall o' the village. I heard Diarmuid laugh as he suddenly understood the beat o' my heart to beauty, and I laughed in return as I saw his need to do good. Together we were wood and metal, a shifting frieze o' living silver, o' glistening roots, growing, stretching, o'er taking the walls o' the village, spreading like ivy but faster, faster'n thought, faster'n the sun, faster'n the breaths o' the soldiers who looked on.

And Diarmuid and I, holding hands in our hearts, continued to grow. We circled our village, leaving a scant opening at the gate and an archway so they could get out, but taking that wall as our skeleton and the protection o' our people as our flesh. We clung to the stones with our roots and took strides with each tendril o' metal merged with wood.

Around the village to the tower, and there we were o' one mind. We gave a mighty roar, and the people o' the tower began to scamper out o' the far gate that the guards had come through, and Diarmuid and I, unhampered by bodies, dug our fingers into the stone.

Our root fingers grew and swelled, and we continued to extend around the outside o' the tower from either side while our fingers pried at the tiny chinks that attached it to the stone wall o' the village.

We roared, we screamed, we heaved as men will do when pushing a great weight—and it hurt us, scraped our bark-and-metal skin, cracked our curling shoots o' metal wood—and still we ripped with a thousand fingers, bleeding ichor, and pushed with the weight o' a thousand trees shoving their roots through parched earth.

There were a cracking, louder than our shrieks, and a shout from within. We continued to grow, to tear, to push, and we overran the sides o' the tower, pushing shoots and leaves into the window from whence came the arrow that killed us.

The prince were in there, slavering, screaming, hacking at our boughs with a sword, and Diarmuid laughed loudest as we twined round his flesh and squeezed. His bones cracked under our vines, and his flesh bulged and burst. He couldna die screaming for the gurgle o' his own blood as we crushed his ribcage and grew shoots from his heart.

He drew his last breath as the tower detached from the village wall and toppled, crashing outwards in a tumble o' stone and hubris.

The falling tower ripped out our vines—the angriest, the most filled with hatred and vengeance—and the parts o' Diarmuid and me that met to make the wall perfect and sound were the parts o' gentleness and brilliance, the parts that cared for others and wanted to create beauty.

'Twere the best o' us that surrounded our people, and the best o' us that shot up in a long arch protecting the pathway between forest and village, joining them together under a tunnel o' interlaced limbs.

And when that part o' us had done its duty, it were only Diarmuid and I, naked and laughing through the forest in the summer, falling to the meadow grass in perfect bare bodies to make love under the sun.

THEY NEVER found our bodies, Diarmuid's and mine—but then, proof o' our death and life were all about the people, so no one doubted.

The tree I'd blooded—the one with purple bark and queer, bent limbs—that were our home. We would wander, alone sometimes but mostly together, through the forest, sometimes quiet and sometimes talking and sometimes making love—in the shade or the sun, by the water, in the air.

We traveled the twined metal-wood wall and screened the visitors to our town, making sure we liked those who passed through.

We were there when Kaspar came, riding a horse at the front o' an army, a kind leader at his side. We watched as he wept when he heard the story o' the thicket that had sprung around the town, and Diarmuid rustled a breeze through his hair in memory.

Clancy and Kerrigan did the same, but Kerrigan's daughter reached her hand up to take the flower I offered, one o' bright gold like her da's hair. The women looked in wonder, for there were no flowers on the thicket, and Clancy held the girl to her chest and wept.

"Thank ye, Teyth," she murmured. "It'll keep us safe."

Kerrigan wept too—in fact, the whole town watered our roots with tears and gratitude and, more importantly in the end, kindness and memory.

Coyle took over the forge with help from Canda and Fisher, and the heart o' our village beat strong for many, many years. Our trees— and they *were* our trees, for Diarmuid's fierce love o' them mattered as much as my work—stood in the square as long as the village existed, but we visited less and less.

More often than not as the years passed, we journeyed through the wood. We frightened boars into the paths o' hunters, and tended the patches o' roots and tubers and berries the women found in the fall. One winter, we stumbled upon a family blue and cold for having become lost in the woods, and 'twere Diarmuid and I who took the girl child by the hand and walked her barefoot down the path arched o'er with interlaced limbs and delivered her to the single watchman on duty. She lived long there, but when her time were up, she brought her new family to meet her old family in the heart o' the twilight wood.

One day, we found a group o' men from the next village had pinned a girl against a tree and were savaging her. The minute her blood hit the ground, we knew what it were to kill—to kill again— and I wondered if the girl saw Diarmuid and Teyth from her hidden cave, or if she saw the forest spirit o' twined metal and branches. It mattered not—she escaped, and the brutal men watered our roots with blood.

We never saw Diarmuid's family, and he thought perhaps they weren't the nicest o' people, but it marred not his spirit. We saw

Cairsten too. Sometimes the three o' us went roaring through the woods, knocking down leaves during storms and forging twisted limbs out o' trees what fought the wind too fiercely. He boomed love and laughter over our clearing and looked askance at the tree o' blood I'd grown out o' grief for him.

"I'd sooner ye watered an anvil with yer tears, boys!" he thundered, and then he visited the village with us, standing in the enchanted shade o' the branches just long enough to see the tree I'd forged with my sweat as well.

He loved it, his love gleaming off the oft-polished metal like sunshine when it were a gunmetal sky day. He visited it oft when we were in other places, bringing his wife and son with him.

Some days, I could see Aubrey and my mum in the distance. Aubrey would frolic, chasing butterflies, and receive hugs from Mum, who looked young and worry free, sitting hand in hand with a man I could only assume were my da. Some days she would raise a hand tentatively and I would wave back, but we never spoke in death who never spoke in life.

In fact, the forest were thick with spirits traveling in and out of the ways o' time, and Diarmuid and I were only two.

More often than naught, that were how we preferred to be.

Twined around each other's hearts, metal and wood, the cold and the warm, the life and the death o' us. We would sit on the hillside in the shade o' the forest and clasp hands, listening as the limbs o' our hedge would rattle and hum as we did.

Rain, sun, spring, summer—all were naught, running from year to year to year. Canda and Fisher joined us in the forest, then Clancy, then Kerrigan, then Abel. Mostly they stayed with their loved ones. Time passed, and the village emptied, and the walls crumbled. Our twined wood-metal vine o'er took the ground, then surrounded the forest, keeping out the progress o' man and keeping in the old ways, the old heart, the old worships and loves.

Years passed, decades, centuries. The purple o' our tree faded to dusty rose, and the bent limbs straightened, curved gracefully, fed as much by our spirits as it had been on my blood. It became a good place, a sacred place, and children left flowers before its base every spring even after the village had crumbled to dust.

Diarmuid and I sat on the hill in the forest shade and watched as men came to unearth the past that we had lived.

The forge had lasted, and the implements, and the anvils, but only fragments o' the cloth and the pottery, which pained me. The books were treasured, their pictures revered, and Diarmuid turned to me, his almond-shaped brown eyes bright and kind in the sun shining through them.

"Look," he whispered avidly, as excited as we got in this time and place. "Look, Teyth, do ye see?"

I kissed his knuckles, his past warmth still infusing our touch, my lips still hungry for the taste o' flesh that had crumbled to dust long ago.

"I see," I replied, and together we rustled our hedge and the trees.

Below us, excavators were busy around the ruins o' the town square.

"Look!" I heard one o' them exclaim. "Look, there's two of them!"

"Trees of life!" the other one said, getting excited. "Look—we've seen that design all over—three different excavations, and there's been something like that. It must have been regional!"

"Yes, but what about this other?" said the first man doubtfully. "It's not... it's not life, is it?"

A woman accompanied them, and she stomped up in a sturdy, no-nonsense way that reminded me o' Clancy.

"Well, for every life there must be death," she said philosophically, eyeing my work with appreciation. "This artist—he was a master."

Diarmuid breathed softly against my shoulder, and I rolled my eyes.

"A master, yeah-yeah?"

"Oh, aye," I muttered, but I were pleased.

"Why haven't we seen more than one of these?" said the second excavator, regarding the work with a critic's eye.

"You know—the tree of life, that gets all the publicity, right? But the tree of death—"

"Silence," said the first one. He were a young lad, thin like me, with dark hair and bright blue eyes. He said the word while scanning the hillside above him, as though he heard the call o' something near to his heart.

Diarmuid and I waved cheerfully, and then, as his eyes widened, we disappeared.

There were a meadow in the forest, and we were always in the mood to make love.

AMY LANE is a mother of four and a compulsive knitter who writes because she can't silence the voices in her head. She adores cats, Chi-who-whats, knitting socks, and hawt menz, and she dislikes moths, cat boxes, and knuckle-headed macspazzmatrons. She is rarely found cooking, cleaning, or doing domestic chores, but she has been known to knit up an emergency hat/blanket/pair of socks for any occasion whatsoever, or sometimes for no reason at all. She writes in the shower, while at the gym, while taxiing children to soccer/dance/gymnastics/band oh my! and has learned from necessity to type like the wind. She lives in a spider-infested, crumbling house in a shoddy suburb and counts on her beloved Mate to keep her tethered to reality—which he does, while keeping her cell phone charged as a bonus. She's been married for twenty-plus years and still believes in Twu Wuv, with a capital Twu and a capital Wuv, and she doesn't see any reason at all for that to change.

Website: www.greenshill.com
Blog: www.writerslane.blogspot.com
E-mail: amylane@greenshill.com
Facebook: www.facebook.com/amy.lane.167
Twitter: @amymaclane

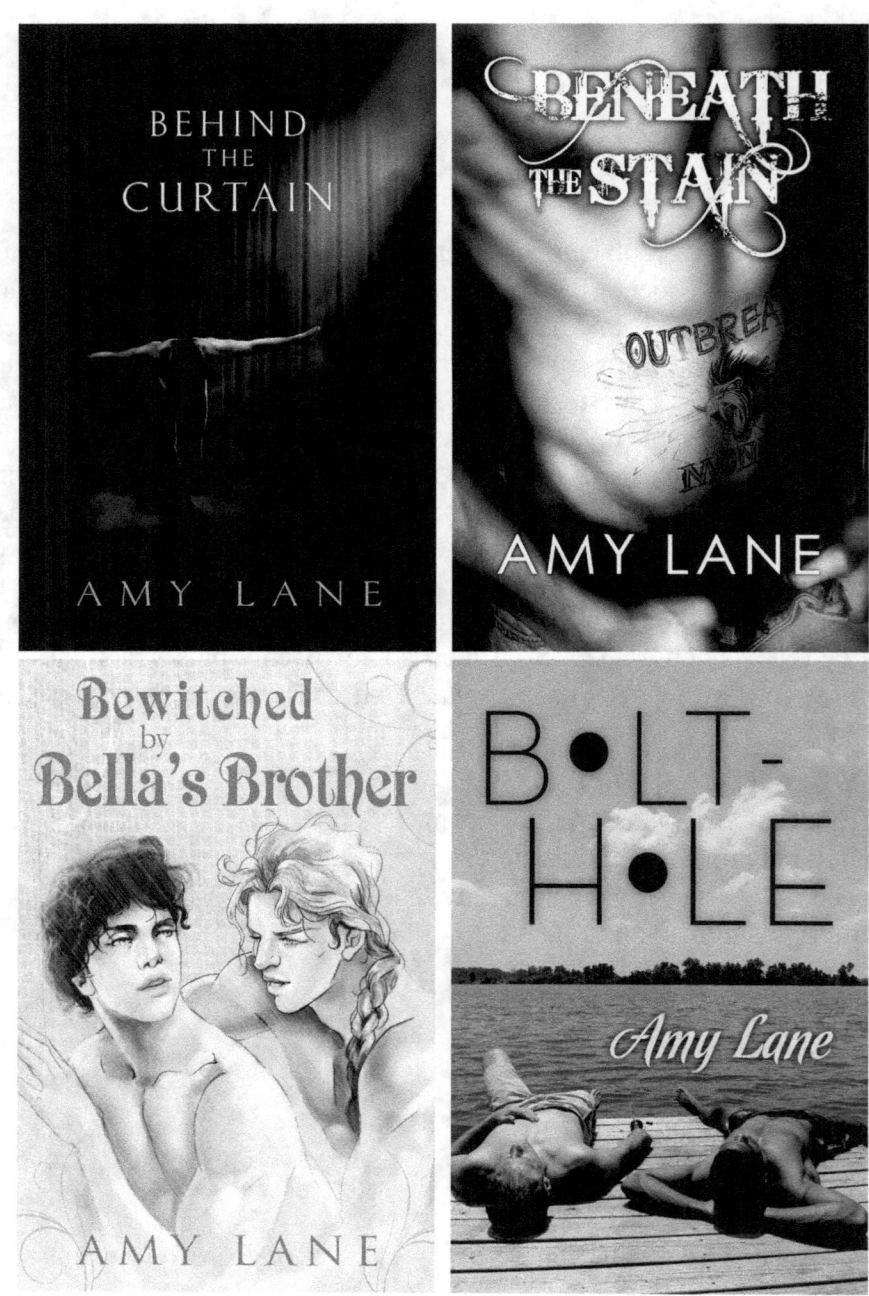

http://www.dreamspinnerpress.com

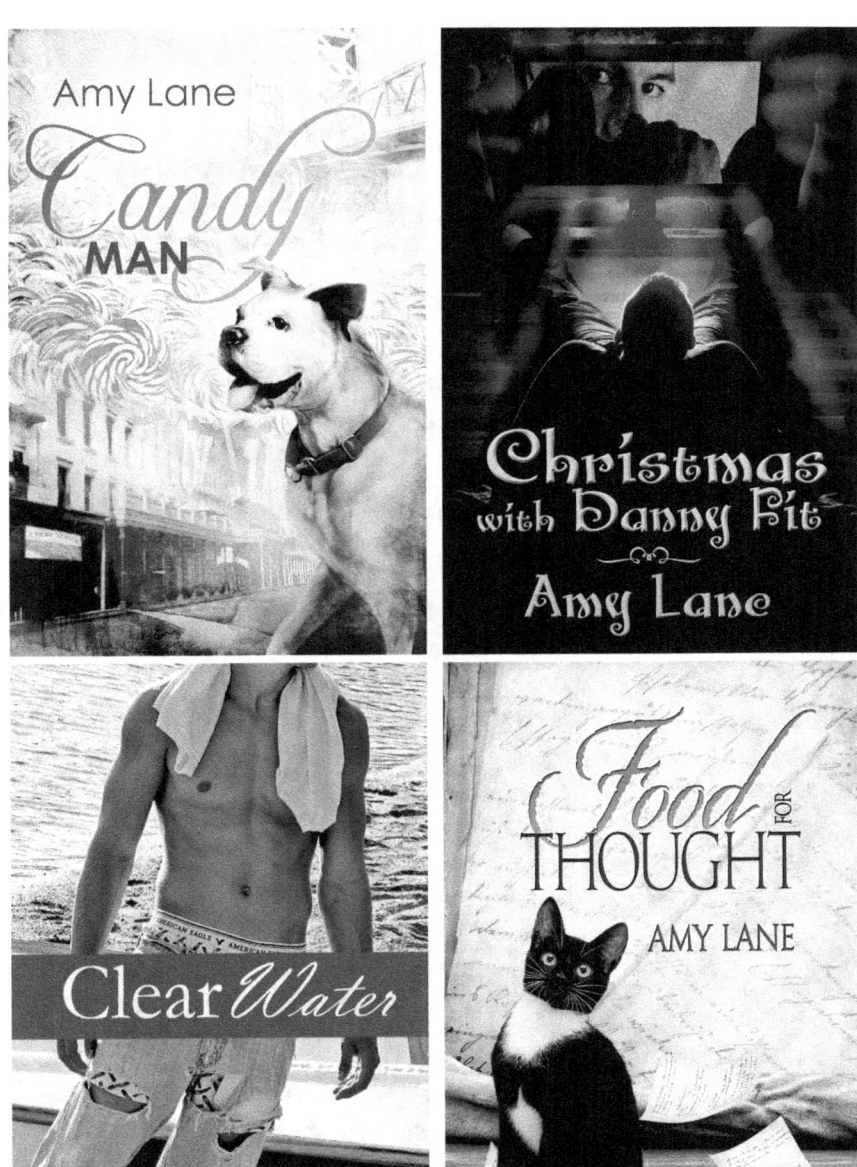

http://www.dreamspinnerpress.com

GAMBLING MEN:
THE NOVEL
Amy Lane

AMY LANE
GOING UP!

Dreamspinner Press
Fairy Tales

HAMMER
&
AIR
Amy Lane

If I Must

AMY LANE

http://www.dreamspinnerpress.com

http://www.dreamspinnerpress.com

Puppy, Car,
and Snow

AMY LANE

RACING
FOR THE SUN

AMY LANE

Shiny!

AMY LANE

Sidecar

Amy
Lane

http://www.dreamspinnerpress.com

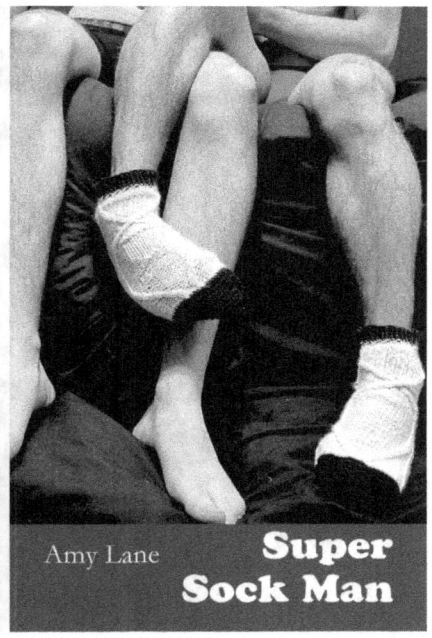

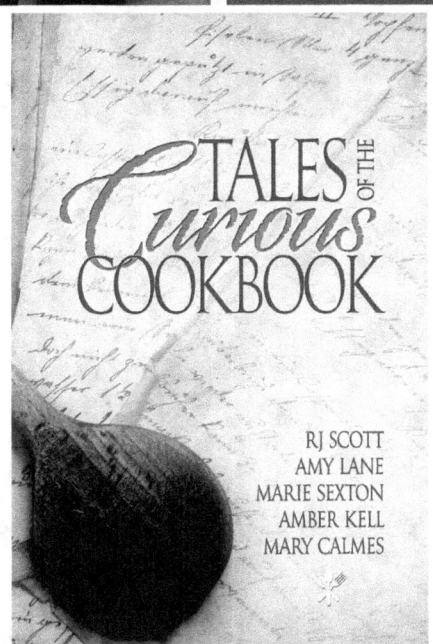

http://www.dreamspinnerpress.com

http://www.dreamspinnerpress.com

http://www.dreamspinnerpress.com

FOR

MORE

OF THE

BEST

GAY

ROMANCE

Dreamspinner
PRESS
dreamspinnerpress.com

www.ingramcontent.com/pod-product-compliance
Lightning Source LLC
Chambersburg PA
CBHW070122260626
47160CB00004B/1580